A superstar in urban lit, *Essence* bestselling author Danielle Santiago concludes her gripping Harlem trilogy with a sizzling, streetwise novel about an all-female drug cartel.

Twenty-year-old Arnessa didn't grow up on the streets. But when her mentally ill mother abandons her and her older brother is murdered, Arnessa has no choice but to hustle just to keep herself and her little sister alive.

Kisa "Kane" Montega and Kennedy took a break from the game. They'd built a drug empire in Harlem and were living comfortably off its rewards. Kisa now has a wonderful marriage, two beautiful children, and lives in a stunning home on the outskirts of Charlotte. Her cousin Kennedy has spent two years away from the volatile music industry, focusing on her children and building a solid foundation with her rap star fiancé, Chaz. But in spite of their successes, both Kisa and Kennedy are gravitating back to their old ways. They miss Harlem, the money, and the game all together.

After a chance meeting, Kane and Kennedy recruit Arnessa as a partner in their cartel. They teach her the ropes and reestablish their control in Harlem. Yet, the bigger their empire grows, the more haters they have to contend with—and the more each one of them stands to lose.

Sexy, suspenseful, and unflinching, Danielle Santiago's *Allure of the Game* gives fans exactly what they've been hoping for—a deeply satisfying conclusion to an unforgettable trilogy, packed with insight into the mean streets she knows so well.

## Also by Danielle Santiago

*Grindin'*
*Little Ghetto Girl*

Anthologies (contributor)

*Cream*
*Fantasy*

# *Allure of the Game*

## A NOVEL

## DANIELLE SANTIAGO

**ATRIA** PAPERBACK

NEW YORK   LONDON   TORONTO   SYDNEY

**ATRIA** PAPERBACK

A Division of Simon & Schuster, Inc.
1230 Avenue of the Americas
New York, NY 10020

First Atria Paperback edition May 2011

**ATRIA** PAPERBACK and colophon are trademarks of Simon & Schuster, Inc.

For information about special discounts for bulk purchases, please contact Simon & Schuster Special Sales at 1-866-506-1949 or business@simonandschuster.com.

The Simon & Schuster Speakers Bureau can bring authors to your live event. For more information or to book an event, contact the Simon & Schuster Speakers Bureau at 1-866-248-3049 or visit our website at www.simonspeakers.com.

Designed by Kyle Kabel

Manufactured in the United States of America

10  9  8  7  6  5  4  3  2  1

Library of Congress Cataloging-in-Publication Data

Santiago, Danielle.
  Allure of the game : a novel / by Danielle Santiago. — 1st Atria paperback ed.
     p. cm.
  1. African American women—Fiction. 2.  Women drug dealers—Fiction.
3.  Harlem (New York, N.Y.)—Fiction.  I. Title
  PS3619.A574A79 2011
  813'.6—dc22                                    2011011883

ISBN 978-0-7432-7762-4
ISBN 978-1-4165-7952-6 (ebook)

This book is dedicated to the newest edition to my family,
Madison Carter Cofield.

And to

Charlotte's finest James "Bro Waheed" Hood—RIP—you are
truly and forever missed.

We all hustlers, in love with the same thang.

—Sean "Jay-Z" Carter, "Allure"

*Chapter 1*

At 6:00 AM Arnessa slowly rolled out of bed, not completely rested. The thought of the monthly bills was enough motivation to get her rolling. The old wooden floor creaked under her feet as she walked toward the bathroom, still half asleep. Through the door, Arnessa could hear the shower. The sound of the running water only made her bladder throb. She burst into the bathroom even though she knew her little sister, Cenise, hated it when her privacy was invaded. Immediately, Cenise yelled over the shower curtain, "Can't you wait till I'm finished? Damn!"

Arnessa was too excessively focused on using the toilet to respond. It felt so good to let the urine out; she could feel her bladder contracting as it emptied. "No, I cannot wait my turn," she snapped as she flushed the toilet, which caused the shower water to turn cold.

Cenise shrieked from the instant chill on her skin, "Nessa, I'ma fuck you up when I get outta here."

"Yeah, whateva. Watch your mouth, little girl."

Back in her bedroom, Arnessa pressed play on the CD player that sat on her dresser. Jay-Z's *In My Lifetime* Vol. 1 pumped through the speakers. She bopped her head and rapped along with the lyrics as she went through the pockets of the beige Woolrich parker she'd worn the night before. She pulled out a wad of cash that totaled a little over $4,000. Sitting on the edge of the bed, Arnessa counted and separated the bills. She put $1,300 to the side and divided the remaining three Gs into $1,000 stacks. Arnessa folded each one and wrapped them in baby blue rubber bands.

Reaching into the back of her closet, Arnessa pulled out a Timberland box filled to the brim with one-thousand-dollar stacks all fastened with the same baby blue rubber bands. She closed the box, placed it back in the closet, and pulled out another Timberland box that was half full with stacks of money also fastened with rubber bands. She tossed the three new stacks into that box and put it back in its place.

Scanning the closet, Arnessa tried to figure out which of her many sweatsuits she would put on. Some that she'd never worn still had tags hanging from the sleeves, and others were in plastic bags fresh from the cleaner's. She grabbed a big black plastic shopping bag with MONY's emblazoned in gold across the front. From the floor, she pulled out a beige Lady Enyce suit and threw it across the bed. Arnessa opened the top dresser drawer, took out a cream thermal set and a lace bra-and-panty set from Victoria's

Secret. One would never guess that under Arnessa's boyish attire were the softest and frilliest underwear. She loved girly things, but she always felt the need to hide them, given her line of work.

After a quick shower, Arnessa rubbed lotion over her entire body. She sprayed her favorite fragrance, Happy, behind her knees, on the back of her neck, and behind each ear. Arnessa slipped on her thermals and put on her jogging pants, then exited her room, trying to catch Cenise before she left for school. "Yo, Neesie," Arnessa called out.

"I'm in the kitchen," Cenise responded as she stood over the counter eating a bowl of Farina.

"Here's the money for your tuition," Arnessa said, laying a stack of thirteen one-hundred-dollar bills next to Cenise's bowl. "As you know, a G is for the school, and three hundred is your pocket money for the week. And a week is seven days, not five. So make it last."

"Don't I always."

"If you did, I wouldn't be telling you now."

Rolling her eyes, Cenise continued eating.

Arnessa opened the refrigerator, "I'm leaving for Baltimore in a little while. I'll be back late tonight. If you want to have company, Nomie is the only person allowed in here while I'm gone."

"Why is Nomie the only one of my friends that can come over?"

"'Cause I said so. Now stop questioning me."

"You know, you're not my mother."

"I'm the closet thing you got!" Arnessa snapped, slamming the refrigerator door closed, "You little ungrateful bitch, and if you want your mother, go find her crazy ass and see if she wants you! If she even gave half a fuck about us, she would be here." Arnessa got in her sister's face. Looking into Cenise's eyes was like looking into her own. The slanted shape of them was the only sign that they were sisters.

Rebellion flickered in Cenise, but she held it in while Arnessa continued to rip into her with her words. "I'm out here throwing bricks at the penitentiary so you can have nice shit and go to the best schools, and all you know how to do is get fresh at the mouth. I should have let BCW take you when they came three years ago!" Completely pissed, Arnessa retreated to her bedroom.

Cenise just stood there, unable to move, trying hard to fight off the oncoming tears. Slowly, she moved her feet, grabbed her book bag, and left for school, crying all the way.

Arnessa refused to cry as she dug into a bag in the bottom of her closet. It seemed like the more she did for Cenise, the less Cenise appreciated her. She pulled out six neatly wrapped eight balls of crack and stuffed them into the inside pockets of her coat. Arnessa threw the coat back across the bed and went back into the kitchen. Opening the freezer, she pulled out a box of frozen broccoli. She opened the box and poured out what looked like six little fat carrot pieces. The little pieces were actually heroin balloons. They were wrapped in an orange plastic coating that made them undetectable to X-ray machines. Arnessa stacked them together, then wrapped them in duct tape, creating a penis-like shape.

Walking into the bathroom, Arnessa reached into her pocket and pulled out a Durex condom. She ripped open the wrapper with her teeth, slid the condom over the balloons, and tied a neat little knot at the end of the rubber. After lubricating the condom with K-Y Jelly, Arnessa pulled her pants down and squatted. Slowly, she pushed the package into her vaginal opening. Her inner walls were unusually tight due to her sexual inactivity. Boofing heroin was not one of Arnessa's hustles; as a matter of fact, she hated it. Even with the lubricant, the hardness of the package made the ordeal slightly painful. *I'ma fuck Tash fat ass up for this one.*

Tasha was Arnessa's favorite boofer and technically her only. The girl could put almost three hundred grams at one time in her oversized vagina, which was always wide open because she'd been the biggest broke whore uptown. She and Arnessa had met through a mutual friend two years earlier. At the time Tasha had been eighteen, with four kids, four different deadbeat baby daddies, and no viable income. Initially, Arnessa thought Tasha was the slut of all sluts.

As the two spent more time around each other, Arnessa began to understand that Tasha was a victim of her environment. Arnessa loved Tasha's realness and the fact that no matter what anyone thought of her, Tasha was always herself. About six months after they were introduced, Arnessa and Tasha had forged a bulletproof bond. Helping Tasha the only way she knew how, Arnessa gave her a job bagging up. A year and a half later, when Arnessa started selling heroin to a few dudes out in Baltimore and D.C., Tasha went from bagger to professional boofer.

It didn't matter how tight they were at the moment, Tasha was at the top of Arnessa's shit list. Small beads of sweat began forming on Arnessa's nose as she continued to struggle with the dope. Her phone conversation with Tasha the previous night replayed in her head. "Why in the

fuck would you make an abortion appointment for tomorrow when you know Wednesday is a B-more day?" Arnessa
asked angrily.

"That's the first available appointment that they had."

"Can't you go on Thursday?"

"No."

"And why not?"

"'Cause Thursday will be the first day of my second tri-
mester, and you know they don't do abortions past three
months no more."

Becoming more irritated than she already was, Arnessa
said, "Let me ask you this, if you knew all along that you
were not having the baby, what sense did it make to wait all
the way till the third month."

"Nessa, you know in the beginning that nigga was saying he wanted me to have it. I didn't even decide to have
one until he started tripping two weeks ago."

"How about from now on you use condoms so you
won't find yourself back up on the chopping block again?
Isn't this like your eighth abortion anyway? You better stop
using that shit as birth control before they be taking your
ass out that clinic in a body bag," Arnessa said unapolo-
getically before slamming the phone closed.

"There it is," Arnessa said aloud, her thoughts returning
to the present as she finally got the dope situated comfortably inside of her. Arnessa adjusted her clothes and exited
the restroom.

Brisk, cold air smacked Arnessa in the face as she
stepped out onto the stoop of her building. At 8:00 AM,
Harlem was already alive and running. Parents were walking their kids to school; good citizens were going to work;
construction workers hammered away; and fiends were

searching for their next hit. Arnessa walked down to the corner bodega where Super Dave was waiting for her.

At six feet five, Super Dave's lanky body towered over Arnessa's five-foot-four frame. Twelve years earlier Dave had been a living legend. He had been the king of the Rucker. Dave had a crossover that would smash Allen Iverson's famous cross. To see him take off from the baseline and slam the ball into the basket was a thing of beauty. Dave was such a great player that he was encouraged by many to enter the NBA draft straight out of high school. Instead of going pro, he opted to attend the University of North Carolina at Chapel Hill, one of the hundreds of colleges that had been recruiting him.

After completing his freshmen year, Dave returned to New York for summer break. As usual he wowed the crowds in the park who'd come to see him play. One night after a game, Dave's closest friend introduced him to a high that he would never be able to shake. The high was Southeast Asian heroin, the most potent type of heroin. That fall when Dave returned to school, he was unable to get the monkey off his back. After failing to pass several NCAA-issued drug tests and flunking all of his classes, Dave lost his scholarship. He returned to Harlem, no longer a legend of Holcombe Rucker Park, now just a legendary fiend.

He was one of few dope addicts whom Arnessa employed to move crack in certain areas where young block boys would be too obvious. Arnessa approached Dave, who was waiting on the corner, and quickly embraced him, slipping him the six eight balls. "That was six that I just gave you. Give two to Monica and two to Robin."

"Wh-wh-why that's all we gettin? I need to make my rent money."

"Yeah *right*, Dave, cut it out. Your girl get section eight man. I'm going out of town. When y'all finish, hit Tash so she can get that money."

Dave nodded his head, "Okay."

"Yo, Dave, I'm serious. Get that money to Tash. Don't play wit' me, or it's going to be problems. I'm being nice letting y'all eat while I'm away."

With that, Arnessa walked on down the block where she spotted her homeboy Ugie and a few dudes fully enthralled in a game of c-lo. "You niggas got problems." Arnessa said, laughing as she stopped behind the circle of gamblers.

"Yo, what up, Nessa?" the guys said almost in unison.

"It's too early in the morning for dice."

"It's neva too early to take nigga's money," Ugie said, turning to face her. He put his closed fist by her mouth. "Now blow on these dice, and give daddy some good luck."

"Nigga, please," Arnessa replied, playfully pushing his hand away then suddenly jerking her head in the direction of the screeching tires on the navy van that was coming toward her. *What the fuck?* Before the van came to a complete stop, three men—one black, one Puerto Rican, and one white—jumped out with their guns drawn. All three had their badges hanging around their necks. *Fuckin' TNT early in the fucking morning, damn,* Arnessa thought. She felt like kicking herself.

"You good, law-abiding citizens know the drill," the white cop said with an evil smile plastered across his face. "Hands on your heads. You too, sweet thing," he said to Arnessa.

She did as she was told. The Puerto Rican cop began patting her down. "Aren't you supposed to call a female officer to search me?"

"'Aren't you supposed to call a female officer to search

me?'" he mimicked. "Don't worry, I won't touch you inappropriately." He cuffed her wrists behind her back then slowly ran his hand across her butt. Arnessa turned and glared at him. He winked his eye and smirked.

"Fuck you," she spat.

The officer laughed as he threw her in the van along with all the guys. Ugie looked over at her, "Why you looking stressed? Ain't nobody dirty. They just gonna hit us with a gambling charge. We'll all get bail and be out in a few hours . . . unless you got warrants."

"I'm straight," she lied.

"Binds, Arnessa," the short brown-skinned female officer yelled.

Arnessa quickly jumped up as the officer unlocked the door. "Yes."

"You can go."

Arnessa quickly exited the cell. What she thought was going to be a few hours in jail had turned into twelve. She quickly collected her property and left the building. Outside in the extremely cold evening air, Tasha waited for her friend while taking long slow drags from her Newport. Her long brown shearling was no match for the icy winds that were blowing, but she had to have a smoke in order to keep her nerves intact. Tasha took her last drag, flicked the butt onto the sidewalk, and turned to walk back in the building when she saw Arnessa coming out. "Yo, Nessa," she yelled out. "Over here."

"You slow as hell, b. What da fuck took you so long? They almost put me on a bus to the island."

"Couldn't you at least have said thanks before you start spazzin'?"

"*Hell* no! If they would've caught me with this shit inside of me, I would've been done."

"Look, don't start with your mouth. And I paid your bail over three hours ago."

"You used some of that money from Dave?"

"Nah, he never called, and Rhonda said he never came through with their work. I did collect money from everybody else, though."

Arnessa rolled her eyes, "I knew he was gon' play me. Did you call B-more and let them know the deal?"

"Yeah, I told him I'll make the trip tomorrow."

"That's what's up. Let's get a cab. My day is a wrap now. I just want to lay down."

"What about Dave?"

"I'll deal with him when I see him."

# Chapter 2

On one of the coldest nights of the winter, Kisa "Kane" Montega was dressed in her pink silk pajamas and a full-length mahogany mink coat. She sat quietly in a chair by her tarp-covered swimming pool drinking Rémy from a whiskey glass. *Why am I not happy?* she thought to herself while looking at the lavish home where she resided with her husband, Sincere, and two children. There was something about the fifty-five-hundred-square-foot, six-bedroom house with all the works that just didn't feel like home. Home was the twenty-eight-hundred-square-foot town house she'd sold back in Fort Lee, New Jersey. Home was actually the fast-paced rhythm of Harlem, USA.

Harlem, the very place she'd been robbed and beaten while pregnant. New York City, the place where her child had been kidnapped and she had been shot. Yet it still held millions of wonderful memories. The place shaped her style and formed her attitude. Kisa hated leaving Harlem behind, but it was a move that she couldn't avoid. All the chaos that preceded her relocation to Charlotte was too much to deal with while she was pregnant with her son. The police suspected her involvement in her sister's homicide but were never able to prove it.

Shea's death had been another unavoidable event in Kisa's past. No one had hated Kisa more than Shea. Her hate for Kisa was born out of pure unadulterated jealousy. Unable to control her envy, Shea set Kisa up to be robbed while Kisa had been pregnant with her first child, her daughter Kai. A year and a half later, Shea had Kai kidnapped and held for ransom. At that point, Shea had signed her own death certificate.

Kisa sat in the back of her modern brick home longing for the city where she'd almost lost it all. She took one last sip from her glass and stood up but fell right back into the chair. *I must've drank a little too much,* she laughed to herself. Once again, she stood, this time slowly, and walked across the backyard with the tail of her coat dragging over the frozen blades of grass behind her.

Sincere watched his wife from the kitchen window as she approached the house. He walked over and opened the back door. "Baby, what are you doing up?" Kisa asked, slightly startled.

"Christen woke me up when he couldn't find you."

"Is he okay?"

"Yeah, he's good. Just wanted some juice. He's back upstairs in the bed already. What's up with you, though?"

Kisa turned her back to him and reset the house alarm, "I'm good, sweetie. Come on, let's go back to bed. The couple walked through the family room into their huge sunken master bedroom. Sincere helped his wife remove her coat and laid it over the loveseat across from their bed. Kisa climbed into the middle of the king-sized bed and slid beneath the covers. Sincere got behind her and spooned her body, wrapping his arms around her. "Kane," he whispered.

"Yes, baby?"

"Turn around."

Kisa turned over on her side to face her husband.

"I love you."

"And I love you, Sincere."

"Then tell me what's bothering you."

"I told you, it's really nothing."

"It's really nothing? Come on, Kisa, this is me. I know everything about you. Vodka is your party drink. When you want to relax, you have a glass of wine. The only time you drink Rémy is when you're depressed or when something's bothering you. So spit it out, sweetheart."

Kisa smiled at her husband's knowledge of her. "Okay, I know this may sound a little crazy, but I really miss New York."

"How you miss it? We're there at least twice a month."

"I miss living there—as soon as I arrive, it's business. By time I get everything at the spa in order, it's time for us to get back on the plane; I never have any time to enjoy myself. I'm going to end up selling the spa just like the salon. To tell the truth, I really miss Harlem. I want to move back."

"I really miss the City too, I've been thinking about moving back."

Kisa propped up, "You have?"

"Yeah, but I didn't think you'd want to go back. Not to mention your parents are so happy to have the kids here."

"Christen and Kai are another reason I want to go back. I want them to grow up somewhere with a lot of cultural diversity."

"Quit playing, girl, Charlotte got diversity. You just miss Eisani."

Kisa did miss Eisani very much. The pair were as close as two could possibly be. They were first cousins by blood relation, but by definition they were sisters. Kisa and Eisani were often mistaken for twins. Both girls had light skin, with bodacious figures that boasted tiny waistlines and wide hips. They even shared the same warm brown eyes and wore their hair in a similar long layered cut. Kisa's hair was the color of cinnamon while Eisani's was light brown with platinum and blond streaks. Ever since they were eighteen the two had been completely inseparable, and if you crossed one, knowingly or unknowingly, you crossed the other.

Eisani had lain low in Charlotte for a while with Kisa until the Shea scandal blew over. That didn't last long, though, because Harlem was the only home for her. She didn't give two fucks about the accusations that she and Kisa had played a role in Shea's death. Honestly, she had nothing to do with Shea's death, nor had she been present when it went down. Eisani was simply guilty by her association with Kisa.

Playfully, Kisa hit Sincere with a pillow. "I'm serious, Sin."

"Admit it, though, you really miss Eisani too."

"True."

"That's all you had to say. I hate that Butta's been home for a month and I've only seen him once."

"I thought he was coming down to visit for a while."

"Man, Butta trying to get that paper right now." Sincere smiled, thinking of his brother.

"So it's official, we're moving back?" Kisa asked, a sly smile on her face.

"We can move back, but what about the spa you have here, and the store?"

"The store is basically my mother's anyway, and Ashley does a great job running the spa. Besides, the New York spa makes triple what the one here does."

"Aight, baby girl, when you wanna do this?"

"I want to wait till after Kennedy's wedding, so like four or five months."

"That's straight."

"Sincere, do you think it's okay for us to go back?"

"Kisa, it doesn't matter where we're at, we can never be too relaxed. But you let me worry about things like that. While you concentrate on taking care of this." He looked down at his swollen dick.

"I always take care that." Kisa climbed atop of him, running her hands across his chest as she leaned forward and began kissing his neck. Sincere unbuttoned her pajama top, exposing her voluptuous breasts and hard nipples. He cupped each one, massaging them gently. Kisa let her top fall onto the bed leaving her nude from the waist up. Sincere pull her pants down as far as he could with her straddling him. She rolled off onto her side, allowing him to pull them all the way off. After assisting him in removing his own pants, she climbed back on, and just as he was about to enter her, their bedroom door swung open.

"Daddy, I had a nightmare," their seven-year-old daughter Kai whined, rubbing her eyes.

Sincere's dick went limp immediately. Kisa scrambled to cover their bodies with the comforter, "Kai, you know you're supposed to knock when the door is closed!" Kisa fussed.

Totally ignoring Kisa, Kai asked, "Daddy, can I stay in here, I'm scared."

"Go lay on the couch for a few minutes. Mommy and Daddy need to finish talking. Close the door behind you."

"Okay, Daddy."

"I'ma hurt that lil' fresh-ass girl one day, trying to act like she didn't hear me talking to her." Kisa rolled her eyes while quickly throwing her pajamas back on.

"Stop being jealous 'cause she's a daddy's girl." Sincere grinned.

Kisa cut her eyes at him, "And you need to correct her when she does that shit."

"Kane, didn't my mom say she just going through a phase."

"Phase, my ass . . . and it's like she got damn radar that goes off every time we 'bout to fuck. She always coming in here with her shoulder pads on ready to block."

# Chapter 3

Heads turned as they always did as Kennedy entered Maggiano's Italian restaurant. At five feet eight and well toned, she was strikingly beautiful. Her blond extensions hung to the middle of her back, totally complementing her light-brown skin. Quite a few men drooled as her dark beige mini–sweater dress hugged her body, accentuated by her camel-colored wedge-heeled boots. They looked on lustfully as she made her way up the stairs to the second level where Kisa was seated. "Hey, cuz, what it do?" Kennedy greeted Kisa with a hug before taking her seat.

"Ain't nothin', mama, just waiting on your slow butt so I can order. I should've known you were out in the mall shopping," Kisa told her, looking at the Neiman Marcus bags that Kennedy placed on the chair next to her.

"I sure was, but don't act like you wasn't either, 'cause when I went in Bob Ellis, the saleslady told me that you had just left out of there." Kennedy laughed, picking up her menu, "So, what's going on? What's the big news?"

"We're moving back to New York," Kisa answered.

Kennedy looked up from her menu, "When?"

"After your wedding."

Kisa's news caught Kennedy off guard. She'd thought Kisa was going to tell her that she was pregnant or something. Kennedy would've been happy to hear anything except that Kisa was leaving her. They'd grown really close over the last two years. Much like Kisa, Kennedy left New York amid controversy after more than a few traumatic experiences.

When she was eighteen, Kennedy's boyfriend had been killed execution style while she lay in bed next to him. When she was twenty-one, her cousin Nina, whom she was extremely close to, had died in Kennedy's arms after receiving a severe beating from her abusive boyfriend, Cream. By twenty-two, Kennedy had met her now fiancé, Chaz, a bona fide hip-hop star. After rapping on one of his songs, Kennedy got a chance to become a rap star herself.

Living out her dreams in the treacherous music industry hadn't proved easy for her, though. An old relationship between her and a rapper named Hassan sparked a beef between Chaz and Hassan that played out in the media. Added to that, Kennedy had gotten her face sliced open during a fight with Ria, the insane mother of Chaz's children. Not to mention that she had also been arrested by federal agents at her own album release party. But nothing could compare to the near-fatal stabbing of Chaz or the loss of the twin babies who died in her womb because of a brutal beating she'd sustained.

Kennedy suffered a massive breakdown soon after the loss of the twins. Leaving Chaz and the music behind, she moved to Charlotte, where, under the careful eye of her beloved grandmother, Big Ma, Kennedy was able to heal completely. A year later Chaz had moved to Charlotte, and the pair had rekindled their relationship. Now at twenty-five, all of the demons that had long haunted Kennedy were behind her. She was also on the verge of publishing her first novel based on her experiences.

Kisa sensed that her news bothered Kennedy. "Are you disappointed that I'm going back?"

"No, cuzin, not at all. I mean, I'm happy for you . . . it just seems like the people I'm closest to outside of Chaz will all be living six hundred miles away."

"Do you ever think about moving back?" Kisa inquired.

"All the time. *You* know how much I love Harlem. Shit, I'm Harlem made, born, and bred." She smiled charmingly, then her smile faded. "I can tell Chaz really misses New York, although he's there a few times a month. I know he hates being so far away from his daughters, his mother, and his sister."

"Has he ever asked you to move back?"

"No, he would never, with all the shit that happened. I haven't told Chaz, but writing the book was like therapy. It made me realize I want to record another CD. I would definitely move back up top for that."

"That's what's up." Kisa exclaimed, truly happy that Kennedy was even considering doing music again. She'd witnessed firsthand the shell that Kennedy had become after her breakdown. Seeing her cousin come back to life made Kisa's heart swell.

"There's something else I haven't shared with Chaz," Kennedy confessed.

"And what is that?"

"Brian has been calling me."

"Jordan's daddy?" Kisa quizzed.

"Yes." Kennedy rolled her eyes, disgusted just by the mention of her son's father's name. To Kennedy, he was a bum-ass loser. When he'd found out she was pregnant, he'd cursed her out as if she were a common stranger on the street. Kennedy took his reaction in stride, although it had been painful, and she was deeply hurt. She shed a few tears for a day or two, then never looked back. Until Chaz had come along, she had been mother and father to Jordan.

"What the fuck did that sorry bastard want? And how the fuck did he get your number?" Kisa questioned, her lips twisted to the side. To Kisa, there wasn't anything worse than a man who didn't claim or take care of his children.

"His mom called my mom and got my number, like two or three weeks ago. The first time he called he was talking 'bout how he ready to meet Jordan. Before I hung up on him, I told him, 'My son is almost five years old, you've never bothered to meet him; besides that, he has a father, so don't call no *fuckin'* more.' Yo, Kane, I was so heated."

"I bet you were."

"Well, I ended up talking to him after he kept calling and calling."

"What's his story?" Kisa asked, taking a bite of her Caesar salad.

"Oh girl, I had to get the violins out for his tale. First he told me how he never knew his own father, and the whole time he was locked up he felt so bad about the way he did me and his child."

"Not knowing his father was all the more reason he should've been there for Jordan from day one," Kisa added.

"Exactly, then I told him if you thought about the bullshit you did so much, how come you just calling and you been home for two years."

"What did he say?"

"Some shit about he had to get back on his feet so when he met his son he'd be correct."

"So you gon' let Jordan meet him?"

Kennedy bit a piece of olive oil–dipped bread and chewed while she thought about her answer. "Yeah, I'ma let 'em meet. I'd be wrong if I kept Jordan from ever knowing his real father. I don't want to be the reason he *never* meets him. That would be spiteful. One thing I try not to do is hold grudges. Life's too short for that."

*Chapter 4*

A day after her release Arnessa entered a small dimly lit bar on Eighth Avenue. From inside it was hard to tell that the sun was shining brightly on the other side of the windowless door.

Like quite a few establishments uptown, it was often referred to as a coke-head bar. Arnessa scanned the room for her mentor, Black Rap. She spotted him seated at the bar. Rap and Arnessa's older brother, Deon, had been best friends. Together, the two of them had made plenty of money slanging yayo, right up until the day Deon had been murdered. Witnessing his best friend's brutal murder was enough to make Rap leave the game behind.

Against Rap's advice, Arnessa picked up where Deon left

off. Prior to his death, Deon had been the financial back-bone of a single-mother home. Unlike Rap, Deon spent more than he saved. He'd also chosen to stash his money in the home of three not-so-trustworthy females. The day that he died, those females had kept the cash as their own. His main girl, Chanel, was the only one of three who had given Deon's family any of his money. Nevertheless, she surely didn't deserve a medal, because all Chanel had given his mother, Maria, was thirty thousand out of the one hundred ninety-seven thousand dollars that he'd kept at her house.

In the months after Deon's death, Maria grieved harder than when he'd initially been murdered. Grief and severe depression took over her life. The loss of her oldest child, her only son, was too much for her to bear. Even her daughters became nothing to her but a constant reminder of her sweet Deon. Maria barely said anything to Arnessa or Cenise, which was horrible for fourteen-year-old Cenise. All she wanted was some attention from her mother, especially since she hadn't come to terms with losing her brother.

So one day during the spring of Arnessa's senior year in high school, Arnessa came home to find Maria gone. She knew her mother wasn't coming back when she checked Maria's bedroom. All of Maria's clothes, jewelry, and toiletries were missing. She didn't care, since Maria had long stopped being a mother to them anyhow.

At an early age Arnessa had been taught by Deon to be strong, even when facing fear or danger. With that train of thought, Arnessa made the decision to do what she needed to do in order to take care of herself and Cenise. So Arnessa put her college dreams on hold and entered the game feet-first.

\*     \*     \*

"What up, Rap?" Arnessa took a seat next to him at the bar.

"Ain't shit, ain't shit." He smiled. Rap was such a real good-looking dude. He had the prettiest dark skin, and at five feet ten inches he had a lovable stocky frame. Arnessa always jokingly called him Gerald Levert. He and his wife, Jess, were always there when Arnessa or Cenise needed them. "I heard TNT grabbed your little ass yesterday morning."

"Luckily, I'd just unloaded some work before they grabbed me. So they was only able to hit me wit' a bullshit gambling charge."

"Don't look at the charge. Look at the bigger picture."

"What bigger picture, Rap?"

"Nessa, you already know your name is ringing bells in the streets. You on the police's radar, and before yesterday they didn't have your prints, your mug shot, or your name in the system. Now they got it all. Even if the charge don't stick, you in the system now."

"How I'm on they radar like that? I keep it simple and low—no jewels, no cars."

"Come on, Nessa, in the last two years you've taken over a lot of territory with Eugie and his wild-ass boys behind you. You got niggas noticing you that *you* don't even know about. They see you, a *chick*, getting money the way you are. A lot of niggas is not feeling that shit. That's all it takes for one of them faggots to run to the jakes and drop a dime on you."

Arnessa spun around, leaning her back against the bar, "I also lost my muscle for a while . . . maybe forever!"

"How?"

"Man, they kept Eugie. He got an attempted murder charge out in Hampton, Virginia."

"Where is Cee and Nick?"

"On the run from the same charge." Signs of defeat were beginning to surface on her face. "It's only a matter of time before Suef start aiming at my blocks again, now that I don't have no real fire power behind me." Just the mentions of Suef's name could fuck up Arnessa's day. To her, he was a low-life derelict who'd made a come-up when the leader of his crew got knocked and sentenced to life. Now he was running through Harlem, ruthlessly taking over blocks on some get down or lay down *shit*. He'd tried coming at Arnessa's territory, but it wasn't going down that easy with Eugie and his trigger-happy finger backing her up.

Rap took a shot of Hennessy and looked over at her. "You making good paper moving that boy to them dudes out in B-more?"

"The money down there is love."

"Why don't you just give up them blocks, get that B-more paper then?"

Staring at the ceiling, Arnessa contemplated Rap's advice. At the moment she felt down, but she wasn't out. Since she was a little girl she'd had a defiant streak that was hard to suppress. "Nah, Rap, I can't just relinquish my shit to that fuck boy like that. Nah, my dude, I'm not going out like that."

"You just like your brother, yo," Rap commented while rubbing his chin with finger, a sure sign that he was cooking up an idea in his mind. "I think I might have a solution to your problem."

"And that is?"

"My peoples just came home a minute ago; he a real good dude too. I'll send him around your way later."

"That's what's up." Arnessa hopped off the stool, giving Rap a pound. "I'm out, yo."

Rap stared at her usual attire as she headed for the door. "When you gonna start dressing like a lady?"

"When these niggas get off my dick and let me act like one."

Super Dave's body shook and shivered as he crept through blocks in search of a hit. All of the crack that Arnessa had given him was long gone—he'd sold it that same day. Over the course of two days he'd used the profits to shoot up as much heroin as he could. Dave knew that Arnessa was out and more than likely looking for him, but at the moment he didn't care, 'cause his need for a hit outweighed his fear. Little did Dave know he'd already been spotted.

*Look at his silly ass,* Arnessa thought while watching Dave from a short distance. She knew that he was in search of a hit; she could even tell by looking at him his body was aching. Arnessa turned to one of her two workers. "TJ, you got any boy on you?"

"Yeah." He nodded.

"Go over there to Super Dave and act like you wanna serve him, take him around the corner between the buildings where Bizzy be at. Marty, you come with me, but hang back in case he try to run."

Thirsty for a hit of the almighty heroin, Dave fell into the trap without a second thought. He watched TJ's hand lustfully as he sorted through the tiny folded cellophane bags. Arnessa crept up on him, holding a metal pipe. With extreme force she slammed it into the side of his knee, and his body crumpled to the ground.

"Where da fuck is my paper?" Arnessa demanded as she continued to attack his body with the pipe. Dave curled into a fetal position. It was a terrible shame to see what the long-term use of heroin had reduced the one-time athletic star to. His body was ravaged, leaving him weak and unable to fight off a woman who was less than half his height. Dave simply cried out in pain, "I got robbed."

"Do I look stupid, Dave," she yelled, striking his shoulder. "I told you not to play me!" Arnessa stomped him in the side with her boot. She made sure that she was brutal in her attack. Since Eugie was gone, she wanted to send a firm message to her workers so they'd think twice before crossing her.

"Ay, ma, cut that shit out," an unfamiliar male voice said from behind, capturing everyone's attention. Arnessa stopped wielding the pipe and turned around.

"Don't worry 'bout what she doing." Marty pulled up his shirt, displaying the gun tucked in the waistband of his pants. "Keep it moving, b."

The guy saw the gun and nearly laughed in Marty's face. "Cover that starter pistol up, lil' dude. Aren't you Arnessa?" he asked, focusing in on her.

Showing her annoyance, she replied. "And who are you?"

"I'm Butta, Rap's people."

"Oh yeah," she said, remembering her conversation with Rap a day earlier. "Give me a minute."

"Nah, ma, I don't got a minute," he told her, moving in closer. "And why you beating up on Dave like that? Don't you know this man is a legend?"

"I could give a fuck about his legend status! This nigga is a legendary fiend that decided to play me for my paper."

"How much he owe you?"

"Nine hundred and forty dollars," Arnessa hissed.

Butta pulled out a wad of one-hundred-dollar bills,

counted off twenty. "Here, this is double what he owe. You let him go."

Arnessa looked at his hand like it was covered with herpes. "I don't want your money. Yo, that ain't the point anyway."

"I think you've made your point," Butta said, looking down at Dave's battered body. He bent down and put the money in Dave's pocket.

Arnessa frowned. "What you are giving him that for?"

"Why you worried about it?" Butta stood up. "You didn't want it, now walk wit' me."

Arnessa obliged him, handing the pipe to TJ as she turned to walk away with Butta. Secretly, she checked Butta out as they walked. Butta's skin was the color of a freshly baked oatmeal cookie; he was a dark-skinned Dominican with green eyes. After years of wearing long braids, he now kept his hair in an immaculately cut Caesar. Though he wasn't flashy, Arnessa could tell he was caked up; he just had freshness about him. She knew his watch was expensive, though it had no diamonds.

"So," he began to speak, "Rap tells me you're having a lil' trouble."

"Yeah, and it seems like it going from little to big with each passing day." Arnessa said.

"Holla at me," he told her.

"I'm quite sure Rap told you that my muscle is gone and this dude Suef has been trying to get at my blocks for a minute. Now wit' my peoples gone, I don't stand a chance against this nigga."

"So you need muscle . . . I can provide that."

Arnessa stopped walking. "That's not all I need."

"What else?"

"Suef is a real greasy, slick-ass nigga. Somehow he done got to my connect too. Now my connect is refusing to serve me."

Butta shook his head. "I think I can help you with that."

Knowing nothing came for free, Arnessa asked, "So what do I have to do to get this help?"

"I wanna move some work on your blocks."

"Really, what you saying is you want me on your team."

"If that's how you wanna put it, let your workers move some product for me. I'll give you muscle and a good ticket on the highest-quality coke . . . fair exchange . . ."

"No robberies," she said, completing his sentence. "What kind of price can you do on, boy?"

"I can give you a great price, but I thought coke was your thing."

"It is, but I got a good lil' thing out in B-more."

"That's what it is then." He reached to shake her hand. "I'll meet you outside your crib tomorrow morning at seven."

"Aight," Arnessa replied, shaking his hand as a black Avalanche with dark tints pulled up to the curb. As he got into the truck, Arnessa told him, "You didn't ask me where I live."

Butta smiled devilishly. "That's 'cause I already know."

# Chapter 5

How in the hell did this hood rat low-level hustlin' bitch get connected with Butta?" Suef demanded angrily as he paced the barbershop floor, veins bulging on either side of his head. Trenton and Abdul sat in barber chairs opposite each other, listening as the number one man in their operation ranted. He faced yet another roadblock just when he was about to take over Arnessa's territory, which he'd been trying to gain for months. Playing dirty, Suef had a few corrupt cops pick up Eugie, her muscle, knowing the dude had warrants in Virginia. Next he stepped to Arnessa's main coke connect, promising to buy triple what she bought if the connect would no longer supply her.

Despite his underhanded tricks, Arnessa was still standing. Not only was she still standing, her profits were skyrocketing, thanks to her backing from Butta. That really infuriated Suef. Not only did he not get Arnessa's blocks, he was now losing business to the low prices she was offering. "I was trying to be polite, seeing that this is a bitch and all, but this ho is really starting to annoy me."

"How you wanna handle this?" Trenton asked, perching his chubby body forward, seemingly always ready for whatever, when in reality he was the type who liked to beat on women but couldn't go one round with a man. He was all bark. The only time he had any bite was when he had a gun or his boys backing him.

"I'm ready to catch that bitch and put the pistol on her. Shit, that's the problem, we should have went at her hard from the door," Suef stressed.

"I got a better idea," Trenton remarked. "Put the pistol on that pretty little sister of hers. Send that bitch a message, live and direct."

An evil grin appeared on Suef's face. "Bitches get all emotional when you bring family into it. Gettin' at her sister will make her back all the way down. Why didn't I think of that shit? Trent, you's a smart-ass nigga."

Trenton looked at his watch. "It's almost three, and I know where to find her right now."

Going to Loly's Dominican salon on Eighth Avenue for a fresh doobie had become a weekly ritual for Arnessa and her little sister, Cenise, years earlier. Before her abrupt disappearance from their lives, Maria had always stressed the importance of hair and skin care to her daughters. Although Arnessa had strong tomboy ways, she took great

care of her hair, even bringing her own expensive products to the salon. Both she and Cenise had thick jet-black
hair that hung below the middle of their backs. In pub-
lic, Arnessa never wore her hair loose. She usually kept it
wrapped up, with hair pins fastening it, or in a bun pinned
at her nape.

*Where is Cenise?* Arnessa wondered, sitting under the
dryer with a head full of large gray rollers. Cenise, being
very prissy, almost always beat her sister to the salon. Pulling out her Nextel, she tried to reach Cenise on her walkie-
talkie. After several unsuccessful attempts, she dialed her
number, only to get her voicemail. *She probably went to the
nail salon. That's the only time that girl don't answer that
phone.* Arnessa picked up the latest issue of *Don Diva* from
the chair next to her. Unable to focus, she flipped through
it aimlessly and put it right back down.

A little over two months had passed since Arnessa had
linked up with Butta, who she soon found out had king-pin
status. Now she was making money hand over fist. With
the good grade of cocaine Butta was giving her at a low
price, she was selling it faster than she could re-up. Instead
of twice a week, she was now sending dope to Baltimore
Monday through Friday, also thanks to Butta's better-
priced top-quality heroin. She even had to hire a second
transporter. With spring ushering warmer temperatures
into the city, business was only getting better.

Making such large sums of money made Arnessa nervous. She knew that this was the type of money that at-
tracted professional stickup kids. Not the little amateurs
from up the block. Arnessa was pulling in so much money
that she no longer stashed it inside Timberland boxes in her
closet. All of her funds were now hidden inside furniture

in storage units throughout the city—one in Brooklyn, one in Queens, and two in the Bronx. Once her hair had been blown bone straight and wrapped and pinned, Arnessa left the shop. She hopped in her brand-new black Dodge Magnum, her first car, her biggest purchase ever. She'd bought it only after Butta advised her to. "You gotta get a car," he'd told her, unable to fathom why she didn't already own one and how she'd made it thus far without one. In the short time that she'd known him, Arnessa had learned a lot from Butta. Whenever he was around, she watched and listened intently, absorbing any knowledge or skill he put out.

Arnessa entered her apartment and immediately observed Cenise's book bag and purse lying in the middle of the hall. Cenise's bedroom door was cracked. Arnessa pushed it open and saw her little sister balled up in the middle of the bed, still wearing her Catholic school uniform. "Neesie, why didn't you meet me at the shop?"

Cenise didn't answer.

Arnessa walked over to the bed and touched Cenise to wake her. Cenise's body was trembling. The girl turned to face Arnessa, her hair disheveled, her eyes bloodshot, and her bottom lip split.

Arnessa was floored by her appearance, "Cenise what happened to you?"

Cenise stared at her blankly.

"Cenise, tell me what happened to you!" Arnessa said, nearly screaming.

Feeling ashamed, Cenise lowered her eyes. In a tone slightly above a whisper, she began speaking, "I was walking from school on my way to the shop. I was on 144th when this guy came out of nowhere and pointed a gun at my stomach. He slapped me so hard I couldn't feel-feel my-my mouth."

Arnessa's heart dropped.

Tears rolled down Cenise's face. "Then he stuck his hand up my skirt. Nessa, he put his fingers inside of me!" Cenise sobbed.

Vomit tickled the bottom of Arnessa's throat. She swallowed hard to keep it down. She tried hard not to cry, but the tears flowed uncontrollably. Arnessa grabbed Cenise, hugging her tightly, and they cried together. "That's all he did, right?" Arnessa asked, holding out hope that he hadn't raped her.

Cenise nodded "But . . ."

"But what?" Arnessa pulled back and looked at her.

"He told me to tell you—"

"Tell me what?"

"Suef said to give up the blocks or he would be back to see me again."

Burning anger replaced the hurt that Arnessa had initially felt. This wasn't a random act, this was a message. The worst part about it, they'd used the only person whom she loved to deliver it. On the inside, Arnessa was raging, she had to take deep breaths to keep from exploding in front of Cenise. Calmly, she told her, "Baby girl, it's going to be okay. I want you to take a shower. I'm going to take care of this." She hugged Cenise one more time and left the room.

*I can't believe this muthafuckin' coward drug my baby sister into this.* Arnessa's hand shook nervously as she dialed Butta's number.

It rang a few times before he answered, "What up?"

"Can you come by crib?"

Arnessa's voice didn't sound right to him, "Is everything aight?"

Unable to mask it, she answered, "Nah."

Not wanting to walk into any type of trap, he questioned her a little further. "What's going on?"

"Ole boy from the East Side sent some nigga at my little sister."

"Say no more. I'm on my way."

Fifteen minutes later Butta arrived with his boys Shawn and Mannie. They all stood in the kitchen listening to Arnessa as she repeated what Cenise had told her.

"You think your sister would recognize him if she saw him?" Shawn asked.

"I'll ask her." Arnessa walked out of the room.

Shawn, an average-looking dark-skinned dude, stood about five feet nine. For the most part he was pleasant looking, proving the old adage that looks can be deceiving, because he was a straight murderer. "Suef and them niggas still be at that fake barbershop every day. Let's ride by, see if she see the dude. I know it's one of them faggots, if not Suef himself, that stepped to her."

"Yeah." Mannie nodded in agreement. Like Butta he too was Dominican, although he was often mistaken for Puerto Rican, with his fair skin and black wavy hair that he kept in two long braids that hung below his shoulders. "Them dick-head niggas still be down at that barbershop, the one on the East Side."

Arnessa came back into the kitchen. "She said she'd know 'im if she saw him."

Butta pulled Arnessa out into the hallway. "Pack whatever you need for you and your sister. Give your bags and car keys to Mannie."

"Where're we going?"

"I got somewhere for you to go. Shit is about to go down. Y'all can't stay here. I'm quite sure Suef knows where you live."

"Butta, I don't think they'd run up in here, and if they do I got burners."

*She is so damn hardheaded.* "Yo, we about to handle this shit on your behalf. The next time Suef or his boys come at you, it's going to be more than gun pointing and fondling lil' Cenise. The next time it's going to be kidnapping, rape, and murder." For some reason he wanted to protect her, maybe because she had an innocence about her, or her naïveté about how serious the game really was. On the low, he really liked her, but he thought she acted too much like a dude.

Reluctantly, Arnessa agreed. Quickly gathering clothing and toiletries for herself and Cenise, she gave everything to Mannie, who left in her car.

She and Cenise left in Shawn's silver Navigator with him and Butta. The dark tints on his truck concealed their identities as Shawn drove slowly by the barbershop where Suef and his crew hung. When Cenise saw Trenton standing out front chatting on his cell, she lowered her eyes, too afraid to look up.

"Is that the dude?" Arnessa asked. "Don't be scared, he can't do nothing else to you."

Still afraid to look at his face again, she nodded. "Yeah, that's him."

Butta looked over at Shawn. "Go to my crib, scoop Mannie, then we'll come and deal with him."

Butta's house was amazing, to say the least. Arnessa hadn't even known such houses existed in New York. Hidden behind tall trees, the three-story brick home sat atop a hill on a winding road in the posh Riverdale section. Arnessa's Magnum was already parked in the driveway when they arrived. Mannie came out of the house and got in the front passenger seat of Shawn's truck.

"Y'all stuff is in the guest rooms upstairs," Butta told Arnessa and Cenise as he ushered them through the garage into the house. "The kitchen is fully stocked. Make yourself at home." He walked out, shutting the door behind him and leaving the two girls standing in the kitchen entry. The huge gourmet kitchen had marble countertops, a massive stainless steel refrigerator, and a stainless steel double oven built into the wall. A center island with a gas stovetop separated the kitchen from the den area.

"You want something to eat?" Arnessa asked Cenise.

"No," she replied, staring at the floor. "I wanna go lay down. Just feel like when I wake up tomorrow it will all be over." The poor girl's spirit was broken. She'd been violated in the worst way.

Arnessa hugged her little sister tightly. "I'm sorry this happened to you." She began crying.

"There's no reason for you to be sorry. You didn't do anything."

"I didn't protect you."

After a long hot shower Arnessa put on her favorite Victoria's Secret pajamas—a fitted pink cotton T-shirt and a pair of pink-and-white-striped boy shorts. She removed her hairpins and brushed her hair down as she did every night. Instead of wrapping it right back up, she let it hang; the hairpins had been giving her a slight headache.

Arnessa stuck her head into the room where Cenise was staying to make sure she was okay. Her little sister was sound asleep. The attack on Cenise had Arnessa really re-thinking her position in the game. Maybe it *was* time for her to give it up. Although they were often at odds with each other, Arnessa would die if anything happened to her sister. Besides that, she couldn't bear the thought of any-thing happening to herself, which would leave Cenise in the world alone. At the end of the day, they were all the other had.

Hungry, Arnessa went downstairs for a snack. She nearly jumped out of her skin when she saw Butta sitting on the couch. "I thought you were gone."

"Nah, they went ahead without me." He looked up from the book he was reading and could not take his eyes off of her. Butta had never seen her in anything other than the baggy sweats that she wore every day. Now she was stand-ing in front of him in a tight T-shirt that barely contained her 34Ds, which were sitting up with no bra. Arnessa's body was tight, no stomach; she had a nice-sized butt too. Not too big, but not too small either. It had a nice round shape that the shorts were amplifying. He was even more amazed by her luxurious long jet-black hair. He had a thing for hair.

*I knew I should've put on some sweats.* Arnessa wanted to break and run back upstairs, embarrassed to have him looking at her body. Butta sensed her uneasiness and fo-cused his eyes back on the book. Attempting to play it cool, Arnessa headed into the kitchen to get what she'd come downstairs for.

For the first time Butta really looked at Arnessa seri-ously. He saw a female who was doing what she had to do in order to provide for herself and her younger sister. Ar-nessa was so cool and laid back, he often forgot she wasn't a dude when they were around each other. Butta knew that she was tough, but not as tough as *she* would have people think. He could tell that what had happened to Cenise was taking a toll on her already. Arnessa was intelligent and extremely street smart for a twenty-one-year-old chick. She was built for the game, but she was no Kisa Kane.

At any moment the game could destroy Arnessa, and Butta knew it. Look at the effect it had already had on life—her brother, Deon, was dead. Unable to cope with his death, her mother had abandoned the girls.

Although Arnessa was trying to hide her emotions, Butta knew that what had happened to Cenise had shaken her up. Arnessa's vulnerability was like a walking aphrodisiac to Butta. He got up and went into the kitchen, where she stood in front of the refrigerator, holding the door open. The hem of her boy shorts barely covered the bottom of her protruding ass. *Should I cross this line or keep it business?* Butta asked himself, feeling his dick swell. *Nah, let me fall back.* Turning to walk away, he caught another glimpse of her. *Fuck that.* He walked right up on her, and as he reached over her to get a chilled bottle of Evian, he intentionally rubbed his dick against her so she could feel how hard it was. She attempted to move, but there was nowhere to go but into the refrigerator.

Slipping his hand under the waistband of her shorts, he massaged her hip.

"What are you doing?" she questioned, feeling her nipples harden.

"Are you hungry?" he asked, totally dismissing her question.

"Nah, I'm straight."

He pulled her closer to him and shut the door, then

backed her against the refrigerator. Eyeing her luscious body, he noticed her hard nipples. She attempted to walk away. Pushing her back into position, he said a low tone, "Don't do that, ma. You know what I went through walking over here?"

Doing her best to be strong, she asked again, "Butta, what *are* you doing?"

"I can't even front—your ass is beautiful. I mean . . . I knew you were cute. I *been* thinking about getting at you, but I put that shit on hold, trying not to mix business." He took her arm and placed it around his waist.

"Butta, I don't know—"

"You don't know about what? You don't know if you feeling me?"

She diverted her eyes from his.

"No, look at me. Tell me to leave you alone." He ran his tongue up and down her neck. "Tell me to get off of you." Butta slipped his hand down into the front of her shorts and ran his fingers over her swollen clit. "Tell me you don't want me, and I'll stop—that's my word. I won't come at you again."

Without Arnessa saying a word, they both knew that she'd give in.

Taking the lead, he pulled her shirt off. "No more talking." He pulled her shorts down. Kissing her body, he gradually eased onto his knees. "Open your legs, let me show you something."

Doing as she was told, she watched as he licked her clit with the tip of his tongue. She couldn't keep her eyes open as ecstasy shot through her body, a feeling she'd never felt before. Her knees buckled, and she had to grab the back of his head to keep from falling. Licking her clit once more, he said, "You not ready for that." Standing up, he took Arnessa by the hand and led her into the den and over to the couch.

Butta took off his wife beater as Arnessa unbuckled his pants, her hands shaking nervously. He grabbed her hands, "Relax, I got you."

Lying back on the oversized vanilla couch, she asked, "You sure this isn't just a fuck?"

"I wouldn't dare fuck you." He lay between her legs. "I'ma take care of you." Sucking on her lip, he kissed her passionately. When he attempted to penetrate her, he found it difficult. "Are you a virgin?"

"Un-uh," she answered, opening her legs wider, helping him in.

"Damn." He closed his eyes, enjoying the tightness. Arnessa's pussy felt like a hot, wet vise grip on his dick and he nearly nutted. "You sure somebody done been up in here before?"

"Yes, one person . . . three years ago," she replied, a little embarrassed.

Trying to be gentle, he started out stroking her slowly, rolling his hips up and down. He could tell that she was inexperienced, and that turned him on even more. While running his fingers through her hair, he looked into her slanted eyes, "Stay here . . . let me take care of you."

"Why you wanna take care of me?" she moaned.

"It's something about you, plus this shit out here ain't for you."

"I take good care of myself. I'm not a charity case."

"I didn't say you were." He ran all the way up in her and paused. "You don't need to be in the streets beefing with Suef or no other niggas."

"So what you want, for me to give up my blocks to you?"

He gave her a hard thrust. "Let's be real, Arnessa, if I wanted your blocks"—he gave another hard thrust—"I would've had 'em."

At the moment the way that he was sliding his rock-hard dick up and down in her, she felt like he could have whatever he wanted. "I like making my own money," she purred.

"You can keep your money on the street, but you . . . you need to fall back," he said, sliding his hands beneath her ass and lifting her slightly. He spread her cheeks apart and drove deeper inside of her.

"Ahhhh," Arnessa screamed, and her eyes fluttered from the pleasure that he was pounding into her.

He licked her ear, then whispered in it, "I'ma handle that B-more package for you too. You keep sending them chicks down there alone, them niggas gonna take that work and kill them one day." He lifted her legs up over his forearms, going right up the middle.

"Ooh-ooh, oh, *Butta*, wait, stop." Arnessa's body tensed, her legs began to tremble, and her pussy contracted in and out as creamy liquid flowed down, saturating his dick. She was experiencing her first orgasm, and Butta had given it to her; mentally he had her wrapped now.

He pulled out and saw her cream covering his brown dick. "Turn over," he told her. Holding her by the waist, he entered her from behind. She grabbed a throw pillow and bit down on it to keep from screaming aloud. Butta moved her hair out of the way and sucked her neck while sliding in and out of her. "You belong to me now. This is *my* pussy."

Enjoying the long strokes he was giving her from the back, she simply nodded in agreement. Butta ran the tip of his tongue up her spine. Arnessa responded by arching her back and poking her ass out, exactly what he wanted her to do. Beginning to climax, he squeezed her waist tighter, pumping harder and faster, all the while telling her, "Don't no nigga touch what's mine. Understand?"

"Mm, oh, mm," she moaned.

He yanked her hair, thrusting in her even harder, "Did you hear what the fuck I said?"

"Yes," she panted.

Groaning in pleasure, he exploded inside of her. With his dick still in her, he asked, "Whose pussy is this?"

The way he was coming at her was controlling, arrogant, and confident. Arnessa loved it! Hesitantly, she answered, "It's yours, Butta."

Inside a warehouse in Manhattan's meatpacking district, Trenton sat, naked, his hands tied behind the chair, his legs spread apart and each bound to the bottom of a chair leg. His mouth was covered with gray duct tape. When Shawn snatched him out of his car, he hadn't even put up a fight. Instead, he began copping pleas. "You can have my money, just let me go."

"I don't want your money! I'm here for you, young boy." Shawn told him through gritted teeth, then hit him in the face with the butt of his gun.

"So you like delivering messages?" Mannie questioned Trenton as he stood in front of him. "Deliver this then." He lifted his foot and stomped on Trenton's dick. The pain was so excruciating the man nearly blacked out. His brown skin was covered in blood and bruises. "We run those blocks, nigga. Next time you got a message, come see me!" Mannie punched him with the back of a gloved fist, knocking him and the chair over.

Shawn picked up a brick and slammed it into Trenton's face. His jaw split, and he instantly lost consciousness. Mannie looked at Shawn. "What the fuck, man? We not supposed to kill him." They had been beating the living shit out of him for more than two hours.

"That nigga is *not* dead," Shawn laughed. "Throw some of that pig piss on him, he'll come around."

"Man, you tripping. I'm not touching that shit! We done beat his ass enough anyway. He fucked up bad," Mannie said, looking at the blood running from the side of Trenton's face.

Shawn agreed. "Untie his bitch ass, and let's go. I'm starving."

# Chapter 6

Girl, where have you been?" Tasha questioned, opening her apartment door to let Arnessa in.

"Laying low," Arnessa replied.

"Nessa, I haven't seen you in over three weeks! Wait a minute—pause. Are you actually wearing something that shows your figure, and are you carrying a purse?" Tasha asked, examining the pale yellow Juicy sweatsuit that Arnessa had on and the brown leather Gucci bag in her hand. "And your hair is hanging. You look so pretty. What the fuck is going on, bitch?"

"Cut it out, Tash." Arnessa followed Tasha down the hall into the kitchen, where Tasha was cooking. "What's that?

45

It smells good," Arnessa said, taking a seat at the glass dining table.

"I got turkey wings, cabbage, and macaroni and cheese. I know you want a plate."

"Sure do." Arnessa smiled. She loved Tasha's cooking. Without a doubt, the girl could throw down.

"Nessa, how come you don't bring me the B-more package no more? And why them dudes take the trips wit' me and Janine now?"

Arnessa sighed. "You still getting money, right?"

"Yeah," Tasha said, turning to face her.

"Aight then, that's all that matters."

Tasha twisted her lips, "I see laying low ain't changed that slick-ass mouth."

Arnessa knew Tasha had a right to ask those questions, seeing as how *Tasha* was the one stuffing heroin into her vagina three times a week then transporting it down to Baltimore. "My bad, Tash. I'm stepping back from handling the packages personally right now. And those dudes going with y'all in case one of them niggas down there try some fly shit."

Tasha prepared Arnessa's plate and set it in front of her with a glass of her homemade sweet tea, which Arnessa loved. After grabbing a plate for herself, Tasha sat across from Arnessa. "So, bitch, what's going on? You done just up and disappeared."

"I told you, I'm laying low. You know a lot of shit been going down in the streets with Suef."

"You got to come better than that. You done showed up at my door looking all feminine and shit, which I been trying to get you to do for the last two years. Something else is going on with you, *homegirl*."

Arnessa contemplated her answer. *I should tell her—she is my only close friend.* It had been three weeks since she'd gone to stay with Butta. No one else knew about their relationship, outside of Cenise, Shawn, and Mannie—or so she thought. Once Shawn's baby's mother caught wind of the relationship, she and all her chicken-head friends were buzzing.

"I'm staying with Butta now," Arnessa replied.

Looking up from her plate, Tasha asked, "You staying with him, or are you *staying* with him?"

Unsure of what their relationship really was, she answered, "I think we're together."

Tasha's mouth fell wide open, "Are you jayin' Butta, with his *fine, Do-mini-can* ass?"

Arnessa simply blushed.

Tasha laughed. "You finally got you some dick . . . it's about damn time."

The two girls chatted for a little while longer. Then Arnessa had to leave to get Cenise from school. After Cenise's run-in with Trenton, Arnessa began driving her to and from school every day to ensure her safety.

Following Butta's automotive advice for the second time, Arnessa sold her Magnum and purchased a fully loaded black Infiniti FX45. He'd initially told her to get rid of the Magnum in case Suef had any ideas of repercussions against her. A different car would throw him off for a while. Before she'd gotten the FX she'd tried to buy a Grand Cherokee, but Butta, who'd accompanied her to the car lot, changed her mind. "Get you something nice, yo; enjoy your money," he encouraged, knowing the only thing that she cared to splurge on was Cenise.

When Arnessa saw the FX, she fell in love with it, but she didn't feel comfortable with the nearly fifty-thousand-dollar price tag, "Butta, I like it, but it cost too much."

"Ma, if you want that, I'll give you half the money. I think you should have this car, though. You hustle hard for your paper. Treat yourself sometime, baby. 'Cause you can't take it with you."

What she wouldn't treat herself to, Butta did, lacing her with quite a few trinkets and treats. Not because he was trying to spoil her or buy her, but because he wanted her to be more ladylike. Around the middle of her second week at his house, he noticed that she kept all of her small belongings—like her money, license, and ATM card—in her pockets. When he'd thought about it, he'd never seen her carrying a purse. The following evening when she returned to the house, the couch in the den was filled with shopping bags from Louis Vuitton, Gucci, Prada, Saks, and Bergdorf. Each bag contained two or three purses, along with a matching wallet or billfold. A couple of the bags were for Cenise too, who thought Butta was just the coolest.

Later that same night, when Butta came in and got into the bed where Arnessa was lying awake, she told him, "Thanks for the handbags—they're all really pretty. But you didn't have to—"

Cutting her off, he placed a finger across her lips. "You're a lady now . . . my lady."

Lil Wayne's *Receipts* filled the car as Arnessa sat outside of Cenise's school, waiting for her. Without alerting her phone, Butta's voice came over her Nextel speaker. "Ma, where you at?"

Pressing the PTT button on the side of her phone, she chirped him back, "Picking Cenise up from school."

"What else you got to do?"

"Um, I'm running Cenise and her friend a few places."

"Meet me at my people's spa that I showed you on Seventh. Let them take your whip and go."

"Aight," she responded.


Butta closed his phone. "She's on her way," he announced to Kisa, Sincere, and Eisani.

"Now, what is it that you want us to do?" Eisani asked Butta.

"E, she the same girl you picked the handbags out for. I want y'all to take her shopping." Butta pulled two bundles of money, totaling a little over fifteen thousand from the pockets of his jeans and set them on Kisa's desk. "Pick her out some hot shit, yo. I want her to get some fly shit. I'm talking about skirts, dresses, blouses, jeans, shades, shoes—"

Kisa interrupted him, "Butta, you upgrading bitches now?"

Everyone laughed, including Butta. "Come on, Kane, you know it ain't like that."

"I'm fucking with you, b. I can tell you like her, though. I've never heard you talk about a girl the way you talk about this *Arnessa*."

"I know," Sincere interjected, "all he been talking about is Arnessa since he picked me up this morning."

"That's enough, that's enough," Butta said, grinning. "I'm feeling her for real, plus she so cool. I can't wait for you all to meet her."

\*   \*   \*

Once inside the bustling luxury spa, the receptionist led Arnessa upstairs to Kisa's office. When Arnessa entered the room, Butta stood up and pulled her to him, hugging her tightly. He kissed her. "Hey, baby."

"Hi," she said in a low voice, not at all used to being affectionate in front of others.

Proudly, he introduced her to everyone. "This is Arnessa. Arnessa, this is my brother Sincere, his wife Kisa—but we call her Kane—and this is Eisani, she not nobody special."

"Shut up," Eisani told him. Then she turned to Arnessa. "It's nice to meet you."

"Same here." Arnessa smiled nervously, feeling insecure in the presence of Kisa and Eisani. The two of them were beautiful, as exquisitely dressed as if they'd just stepped off the pages of *Vogue*. They both exuded power and confidence without speaking. Feeling inferior to another female was not something that Arnessa was used to.

"We outside when y'all ready," Butta said, walking out with his arm around Arnessa.

As they walked down the stairs Arnessa asked Butta, "Where are we going?"

"I gotta make some runs with Sin; you're going shopping with Kane and Eisani."

Arnessa stopped walking, "Butta, no, I don't know them. You and I can go shopping this weekend. I'll get whatever you pick out," she pleaded.

Standing on the stairs, he rubbed her face and assured her, "That's my family. They going to take good care of you, get you right for our trip."

"What trip?"

"We're going down south next weekend for a wedding."

Apprehensively, she sighed. "If this is what you want."

"It's not just about what I want, Arnessa. It's about pre-paring you—"

"Preparing me for what?" she snapped. "To be a lady?"

"Yes, but no, that's not the only thing. I mean I'm into you—you know that—and I only want to see you shine at anything you do. If for whatever reason we don't work out, I want you to leave me a better woman."

Over the course of the day, while shopping, Arnessa got more than clothes. She gained two new friends. At first appearance she'd thought Kisa and Eisani were stuck up, but she soon learned that they were the exact opposite. She found them surprisingly down to earth and easy to talk to, like the older sisters she'd never had. An added plus was that they both knew what it was like to be in the game.

Arnessa reminded Kisa of herself when she was younger, a wild child, sort of a loose screw. She liked her instantly.

Shopping should have been Kisa's middle name. She was addicted to it. She lived for it, no matter if it was for herself or someone else. Arnessa became Kisa's muse as they swept through every high-end designer and depart-ment store in Midtown. The trunk of Eisani's S550 was filled with so many shopping bags they could barely shut it. By the time they reached the last store, L'impasse, Arnessa and Eisani were exhausted, but not Kisa.

"I hope this is it," Eisani said.

"You don't have to come in," Kisa replied. "I came to get something to wear tonight. Arnessa, you wanna come in and get something for the party?"

"What party?" Arnessa asked, confused.

"My cousin, Kennedy, is having a book-release party to-night at Strata. Butta is coming. Aren't you coming with him?"

"I don't know, he didn't say anything to me about it."

"You don't have to go with him . . . 'cause you're going with us."

A few hours later, the girls were at Eisani's loft having drinks and getting dressed. Eisani and Kisa's younger cousin Tyeis came over to touch up Kisa's hair. She ended up doing Arnessa's hair too. Tyeis's hands were anointed—every time she picked up her scissors or curling iron she created magic. She cut the front of Arnessa's hair into long flowing layers with a straight razor and gave her feather curls around her face.

"Tyeis got your shit looking good," Kisa said as she entered the vanity area of the spacious bathroom and handed Arnessa a caramel martini.

Getting up from the vanity stool, Arnessa took the glass. "I don't know if I can drink this one too. That last one got me feeling a lil' tipsy."

"You don't drink much, do you?"

"Rarely," Arnessa responded with a giggle.

"Sit back down," Kisa instructed, "Let me put some makeup on that cute face." Kisa opened a brand-new box of Bobbi Brown foundation and began applying it to Arnessa's face. "You know, I've never heard Butta talk about a girl the way he talks about you. Hell," she laughed, "I've never really heard him talk about any girl."

"Yeah, right,"

"I'm serious. Trust me, you're special," Kisa said, applying eye shadow to Arnessa's lids. She took another sip of her drink, "Real talk. Butta is a good dude. Most of all he's loyal. Take good care of him, and he'll always take care of you." Kisa gulped the remainder of her martini.

The liquor and the level of comfortableness led Arnessa to disclose something personal to Kisa. Up until now she had no one else to discuss the subject with. "I don't know if I'm doing it for him sexually."

Kisa coughed, spitting out her drink. "Huh?"

"I think he wants me to go down on him," Arnessa said, embarrassed.

"If you don't want anybody else to do it, you better." Kisa laughed.

"It's not that I won't do it . . . I don't know how."

"Hmm?"

"I've only been with one other person."

"No wonder you're so special, that coochie tight," Kisa joked. "I take it you would like a few pointers."

"Exactly," Arnessa replied, blushing.

"Wait one second, I'll be right back." Kisa returned with two bananas and handed one to Arnessa. "Peel this." Kisa proceeded to teach Arnessa how to give a blow job by demonstrating on the banana. She also gave her a few other tips that she guaranteed would drive Butta crazy.

"'What you know about that? Hey I know all about that.'" Arnessa rapped along with T.I. as she walked through Strata with Kisa and Eisani, her newfound friends. It was packed wall to wall. All eyes were on Arnessa as she entered the VIP area, clad in a sleeveless beige empire-waist minidress that looked spectacular against her brown skin. Cut very low in the front, the dress showed off her perfect chest, and the golden brown Dolce & Gabbana peep-toe pumps accented her shapely legs. The four martinis that she'd consumed at Eisani's gave her a burst of confidence and helped her to walk smoothly.

Arnessa looked absolutely stunning. Butta had to do a double take when she approached him. Twirling around and giggling, she asked him, "You like?"

Butta scanned her body from top to bottom, then glanced over at Kisa and Eisani, who had big grins plastered on their faces, proud of Arnessa's new look. Turning his attention back to Arnessa, he pulled her into a big bear hug. "You look beautiful, baby."

She wiggled from his embrace. "I want to dance," she said, moving her hips to the beat.

"Have you been drinking?"

Smiling all silly, Arnessa nodded her head while dancing seductively.

Shawn walked over and stood next to Butta. "My dude, she cleans up very well."

"Yes, she does," Butta said, unable to take his eyes from Arnessa. He wrapped his arm around her. "I'm ready to be out."

"We just got here," she complained.

"*Y'all* just got here; *we* been here. I gotta get you home. You got me wanting to do some things to you," he said, rubbing her ass.

That one touch had her thinking, *Fuck this club shit.* "Aight, but let me go say bye to Kane and Eisani."

Arnessa made her way over to where Kisa and Eisani were standing with Sincere. She paid no attention to the man walking toward her until he shoved her to the ground. He then bent over and asked her, "How's your little sister?" When she looked up, she saw that it was Suef. Before

Arnessa could give any type of response, Sincere came over, laid Suef out with a hard right, and began viciously stomping him. Butta, Shawn, and Mannie quickly followed suit. Eisani and Kisa rushed over, helping Arnessa to her feet. From the corner of her eye, Kisa saw Suef's right-hand man, Abdul, charging toward Sincere. Reacting quickly, she stuck her foot out, tripping him. Abdul crashed to the floor only inches from Sincere's feet. He grabbed Sincere's leg, trying to pull him down. Eisani got a champagne bottle from a bucket nearby and smashed Abdul in the face with it. Sincere turned his attention to Abdul and began stomping on his chest.

Club bouncers pushed their way through the crowd toward the altercation. They stood back for a moment when they saw it was Butta and his crew. If it had been anyone else, they would've picked them up and threw them into the street. Instead, the head bouncer, who they all knew from uptown, walked over to them. "Come on, fellas, that's enough—that's enough."

Suef's reference to her little sister pissed off Arnessa more than being shoved to the ground. It bothered her so much that, as soon as she arrived home, she ran straight upstairs to Cenise's room. Arnessa was relieved to find her sound asleep. In a few weeks Cenise would be graduating from high school. Arnessa was sending Cenise and her best friend, Nomie, to Oakland to spend the entire summer with Nomie's aunt before leaving for college. Both girls would be attending Spellman in Atlanta. Cenise, who had been on the honor roll since kindergarten, had received a full scholarship.

Arnessa was relieved that Cenise was going away because she would be far from the drama that was unfolding daily. Inside, she already knew that once her sister was gone, she was going to miss her tremendously. Arnessa walked over to the bed and stared down at Cenise; for a brief moment it was like looking at her mother. A tear snuck out of the corner of her right eye and slid down her cheek as she thought about how different their lives would've been if their mother, Maria, hadn't abandoned them.

Some days Arnessa longed for her mother, but most days she hated her. She wished her mother had died rather than disappeared. That way she could've just grieved and moved on, instead of being emotionally confused. Every time Arnessa made an attempt to let it go and move on, she thought of her high school graduation, and her hatred for her mother only magnified.

Arnessa never forgave her mother for missing the biggest day of her young life. She vividly remembered walking across the stage, knowing that Maria wasn't there. The hurt she felt was so painful that after the ceremony she'd become physically ill with fever and had vomited through the night.

Wiping her eyes, Arnessa bent over and kissed her little sister's cheek. Deep down, Arnessa hoped that Maria would show up for Cenise's graduation. Pulling the covers up over her sister's shoulder, she thought, *It doesn't matter if she ever shows up . . . I'll always be here for you.*

On the way to her bedroom Arnessa overheard Sincere giving Butta advice, and she stopped to listen.

"You got to get rid of that nigga immediately," Sincere expressed. "From the door when he sent his people at Arnessa's sister, you should've bodied him and the nigga he sent. Fuck all that back-and-forth shit. You forgetting how we do this?"

"Fuck no!" Butta exclaimed.

"Aight, then you need to put a lid on this nigga like yesterday. He young, he disrespectful, and he smelling himself. I'm telling you, handle him before he handle you."

# Chapter 7

D amn, girl, them Pradas is crack," Kisa said, admiring the bright orange sneakers that Kennedy was wearing.

"They are crazy," Eisani added as she and Kisa took a seat on either side of Kennedy on the park bench.

"Un-uh," Kennedy said, pulling her shades down to the tip of her nose and looking over the rim at her two cousins. "Don't be tryin' to gas me up. After you two monkeys turned my party into WWF, then bounced without seeing me."

"That was not us!" Kisa proclaimed with a giggle.

"Whateva, yo," Kennedy stated. "My people told me when one of them niggas went for Sincere, you"—she pointed at Kisa—"tripped him, and ole female Barry Bonds over here smashed him in the head with a Dom P bottle. I swear you two hoes is still hood."

"Bitch, please," Kisa spat, with a smirk on her face. "If your ghetto ass had been over there, you would've been thumpin' right with us."

"And you know this." Kennedy laughed. "But who was that chick wit' y'all?"

"That was Butta's girl," Kisa replied.

"Lil' man know what he doing wit that rock," Eisani said, directing their attention toward Kennedy's son, Jordan, who was playing basketball with two other small boys. Jordan was adorable with his tanned brown skin and wide bright brown eyes. He also had the cutest smile to match them. Kennedy's world revolved around him. Technically, he was not her only child, since she had legal custody of her cousin Nina's kids. Though they now resided with their grandmother, Kennedy still treated them as if they were her own. She communicated with them daily, and when Jordan got something so did they. Each of the children had a special spot in her heart, but Jordan clearly owned it.

"So what time is this bum-ass nigga supposed to get here?" Kisa asked, referring to Brian, Jordan's biological dad.

"Now, and if he don't get here in the next ten minutes, I'm out."

"What did ya mom and them say about Brian meeting Jordan today?" Eisani questioned Kennedy.

"I didn't tell nobody but y'all. I didn't even tell Yatta."

"Why you ain't tell ya sister?" Kisa inquired.

"It's like this, whatever happens here today, y'all not gonna judge me, and I won't have to hear about it no more.

For instance, if this nigga don't show up today, it's no sweat off my back since Jordan don't know why we're here anyway."

"Kennedy, you didn't explain to him that he was here to meet his real father?" Eisani asked, perplexed.

"Sure did not," Kennedy replied, her lips twisted to the side. As she was about to explain her reasoning, a man with medium-length dreads that sprouted wildly from his head approached the three women. Kennedy glanced up at him, then did a double take once she recognized his face. It was Brian. It had been seven years since she'd last seen him. Back then he was slim and kept his hair in a neat low cut. One thing for sure, he was still fine, with baby fine chocolate skin and a perfect square chin. He was iced out and fly in clothes that were not even in stores yet.

There was a brief silence as they just stared at each other. Brian spoke first. "What up, Kennedy? Damn, get up and give a nigga a hug."

"You's a fucking idiot if you think you'll ever get another hug from me in this lifetime."

Kisa and Eisani both burst into laughter.

Brian looked at them. "I see the get-along gang is still together. How y'all been?"

"We straight," Kisa answered for the both of them.

"That's good, that's good." He focused his attention back on Kennedy, thinking she was more beautiful than ever. "Where my boy at?"

Kennedy rolled her eyes in utter disgust. "I don't know where your boy is, but *my* son is over there on the court."

Brian looked over and zoomed in on the little boy who was undeniably his. "Wow, he's a big boy."

"What the fuck was you expecting, a newborn? I mean, he is six years old now, or did you even know that?" Kennedy asked, with plenty of attitude.

"Kennedy, I know I was foul and shit for the way I carried you, but you need to kill that sarcastic shit."

"I need to what?" Kennedy stood up and got in Brian's face, "Nigga, who da fuck you think you talkin' to? I'm not the lil' dumb bitch you used to know. Don't *ever* think you can tell me what to do in your joke-ass life. And you better consider yourself privileged that I'm even here today, allowing you to stand within two hundred feet of my son."

"I see you still sexy as hell when you mad." Brian reached out to caress her face.

Kennedy slapped his hand away. "What the fuck is wrong with you? Don't ever touch me."

*She's about to spaz,* Kisa thought.

Placing her weight on her right leg, Kennedy cocked her head to the side and put her hand on her left hip. "Look, my man, you betta find something softer to play with, 'cause I ain't the one. And since you think I'm such a got-damn joke, let me be clear about a few things before any introductions take place. You see that"—she pointed at Jordan—"that's my heart. And you . . . you're less than dog shit. If you was dying right here and now and the only thing you needed to live was liquid, I wouldn't even spit in your mouth. I'm telling you right now, you got one time to hurt my son with some bullshit broken promise and I'ma fuck your clown ass up. 'Cause when Jordan hurts, I hurt, and whoever hurts us has to deal with *me.*"

Before Brian could respond or Kennedy could continue, Jordan ran up and stood next to his mother. He knew that something was wrong, and at the ripe old age of six he felt like he could protect Kennedy from the world. "Mommy? Who is this, Mommy?"

"I'm your daddy, lil' man."

Kennedy shot him an evil look. "You don't have any right. I got this."

Kennedy's mean expression went from scowling to a warm smile as she looked down at her son. She squatted so that she and Jordan were face-to-face. Suddenly, she became nervous, "Sweetie, you know how Chaz's daughters are like my daughters, but they have a real mommy that they live with too."

"Yes, Mommy." He nodded.

"So you know how Chaz is your father 'cause he takes care of you and spends time of you?"

"Yes, Mommy."

"But you remember how Mommy told you had another daddy too?"

"Yes."

"Well, sweetie, this is him. His name is Brian."

Jordan looked up at Brian, then looked back at Kennedy, "Mommy, if he's my daddy . . . why haven't I seen him before?"

Kennedy looked up at Brian, giving him a smug smirk, then she looked back at Jordan. "Honey, that's a question he'll have to answer."

"Lil' man, you wanna come over to the court with me and shoot around for a while?"

Jordan didn't answer immediately as his six-year-old mind attempted to process what he'd just learned.

"Come on, lil' man," Brian said as he reached for Jordan's hand. "We got a lot to talk about."

Hesitantly, Jordan took Brian's hand. As they walked toward the court, Jordan looked back at his mother. A confused expression covered his little face. Kennedy watched and wondered if she'd made the right decision. Something in the back of her mind told her that she would regret her choice.

The first meeting between father and son lasted two hours. A master manipulator, Brian had little Jordan in the palm of his hand. When it was time to leave, Brian gave Jordan a one-hundred-dollar bill, then attempted to give Kennedy a wad of hundreds. Kennedy handed it right back and said, "We straight, my man, we don't need no handouts."

Chaz wasn't alone when Kennedy arrived downtown at the apartment where she and Chaz resided when they were in New York—Sincere and Butta were there. Moreover, from the looks of things, they'd all finished off a big bottle of Hennessy.

"What up?" Kennedy asked as she walked into the living room.

"What up, Ken-Ken?" Sincere responded.

"What's it do?" Butta said.

Kennedy couldn't help but notice that they all were looking at her a little funny, especially Chaz, who was clearly intoxicated. "Where's Jordan?" Chaz asked Kennedy as she plopped down on the couch next to him.

"He's at Auntie Karen's. She wanted him spend the night before we leave for Charlotte. We can pick him on the way to the airport."

"Aight, aight," Chaz responded very sarcastically.

"It's been real, my dude," Sincere said as he stood up and gave Chaz a pound.

Butta did the same and told Chaz, "Can't wait till that bachelor party next weekend, fam."

"I can't wait neither," Chaz replied, while staring at Kennedy with a snarl on his face. Chaz got up to walk them out. When he came back to the couch, he asked Kennedy, "Where you been all day?"

"Uptown with Jordan."

"What y'all do uptown?"

"I took him to the park, and I got up with Kane and Eisani."

"Who else you got up with, and don't even *think* about lying, 'cause I saw you up in that dread nigga face."

Kennedy's heart skipped a beat. "You followed me?"

"Hell no, I wasn't following you. I met up with Sin, to pick up a wedding gift that I got for ya sneaky ass. He knew that Kane was meeting you at the park, so we came over to surprise you. *But*, to *my* fuckin' surprise, you all up in some nigga's face." He slammed his glass down on the table, shattering it. "You betta start talkin' right fuckin' now, Kennedy!"

"That wasn't some nigga," Kennedy mumbled. "That was Jordan's father."

"Back the fuck up. What you say? I couldn't hear you."

"That was Brian, Jordan's father. He's been bothering me for the last two months to see him. Since we were here, I decided to let him meet Jordan."

"Two months! Two fuckin' months you been talking to that faggot, and you ain't said shit to me? Why da fuck you didn't tell me, huh?" Chaz mushed her head. "You must be fuckin' him." He mushed her a second time, causing her neck to pop back and forth like a spring.

"You buggin', yo." Kennedy stood up. "Don't put your hands on me like that, and ain't nobody fuckin' nobody."

"Bitch, you betta sit your ass back down," Chaz said firmly.

"Who you calling a bitch?"

"You, you *dumb* bitch."

"Fuck you, Chaz."

"Nah, fuck you, Kennedy, 'cause that's how you like a nigga to treat you. That nigga dragged you like shit, and you going behind my back to see him. You a pathetic bitch. I really feel like slapping the taste out your mouth. Since you waited a week before it's time for us to get married to show your true colors, the wedding is off." Chaz grabbed his keys off the table.

Kennedy was shocked at how far out of control things were spinning. She blocked his path. "What's wrong with you? Why are you spazzin'? I've done nothin' wrong. I took my child to meet his father."

"You did everything wrong."

"Like what?"

"Man, Kennedy, get out my way. I don't even see you right now. I'm going out."

"Going out where?"

"Going out to show you that you not the only one that can be sneaky."

"I was not being sneaky, Chaz. I took my son to meet his father—"

"That is not his father! Stop saying that shit!" Chaz yelled in her face. "*I'm* Jordan's father. I love him. I take care of him, and I spend time with him. That pussy-ass nigga ain't never did none of that. He hadn't even seen him before today. That is my child too, and you didn't even think enough of me to consult me before you took him to meet that crab-ass nigga. Fuck all that, 'cause I got my own kids to be a father to. Shit, I spend more time with Jordan than I do with my own girls. I'll get out the way and let dude have his job back."

Kennedy felt like she had been stabbed, and Chaz could see it in her face. "Jordan always gon' be mines. I'll always be his father and be there when he needs me. He don't have shit to do with the games his silly-ass moms play." Chaz pushed Kennedy to the side and headed for the door.

"Chaz, let me explain."

He stopped in his tracks, because all he wanted was an explanation. He wanted to hear her out, but his ego mixed with Hennessy wouldn't allow it. So he told her in a calm, almost nonchalant way, "Nah, you don't have to explain shit now, baby girl. You didn't want to explain it before. At least you didn't lie to me, though, 'cause Sin had already told me at the park that dude was your sperm donor. I only asked you 'cause I wanted to see if you was gon' keep it one hundred or if you was gonna start telling lies in addition to being sneaky."

"Chaz, baby, don't do this—come back," Kennedy pleaded as she tried to keep from crying. "You know we have an early flight back to Charlotte."

He could hear the hurt in her voice, and it was a bit satisfying. He wanted her to hurt too. It was upsetting and a little embarrassing to have learned from Sincere who Brian was. As he opened the door he told her, "Don't worry, I'll be back, maybe . . . If I don't come back, you know what it is."

Chaz drove straight to his baby mother Ria's house in Brooklyn, polishing off a pint of Hennessy he had in the car. By now he was in rare form. Just as he was about to knock on the door, Ria opened it, walking out with three of her friends. They were all dressed in club attire, laughing and chatting. Ria jumped when she saw Chaz standing in front of her. "What are you doing here?" she asked.

"Where in the hell you going, and where my daughters at?"

"I'm going out, and the girls are in the bed. What are you doing here? You not supposed to get the girls till in the morning."

"I can come here when I want. Shit, I pay the bills. Say good night to these whores you call friends. You not going nowhere. I'm tired of you leaving my daughters here while you're out gallivanting all night."

"You must have got me confused with that bitch you're 'bout to marry. Allow me to remind you that you don't run me or shit around here."

"Ria, don't show out, aight? Just do what I said."

Since Chaz had slapped all the fire out of Ria a few years back for cutting Kennedy's face, she had learned not to play with him when he was serious. Ria rolled her eyes and sighed, "I'll get with y'all later 'cause this nigga is trippin'."

"Huh?" the girls squawked in unison. Then one of them said, "What about my daughter, Ria? You promised to pay her for babysitting, and now I'm going to have to take her all the way back to Queens before we go to the city."

"I'll still pay her, and she can spend the night here. Just pick her up first thing in the morning, 'cause I got shit to do."

As soon as her friends were gone and the door was closed, Ria went into mode. "That slut-ass fiancée of yours know you here?"

"Yo, Ria, watch your mouth for real, aight'?"

"Or what?"

He got in her face. "You know I'm not with none of that shit you be on, especially not tonight. I just wanna see my girls," Chaz said, then entered his daughters' bedroom. The two girls were sleeping in twin beds directly across from each other. He stared at them for a moment from the doorway, then walked over and kissed both of them on their cheeks. He always referred to them as his little brown beauties. The both of them were growing into beautiful young ladies. Their cute big bushy afro puffs had been replaced with long straight doobies. Seeing his daughters made him feel a little better, but it did nothing to repair the hurt that he'd experienced earlier.

Chaz made his way into the living room, where Ria was watching television, and sat on a plush oversized brown suede recliner. Ria looked him up and down, her lips twisted to the side. "Why not tonight?"

"What are you bumping ya gums about now?" Chaz asked, irritated just by the sound of her high-pitched voice.

"You said you wasn't for none of my bullshit, *especially* not tonight. It must be trouble on the home front with lil' miss wifey."

"Why don't ya dizzy ass just shut the fuck up sometime."

Ria had no intention of closing her mouth, since he'd ruined her night. "I know that big bubble-butt bitch don't know you over here. I need to call her and tell her to come pick ya drunk ass up."

"The second you pick that phone up, you betta pick up the want ads and get a job to pay your bills. 'Cause you won't get another coin from me."

"And I'll take you right to court."

"Do you, ma!" He laughed. "They can only base it

against my reported salary. Go ahead, so you can get less than a quarter of what I give you now."

His words silenced her instantly.

"Yeah, that's what I thought," he taunted. "Say something else, and watch me take your ass to court for custody. You barely raising them, always leaving them with some teenager while you out gallivanting . . . I guess it's hard being a mother when you in your second childhood."

Ria was on pause for real now; she had run out of slick comebacks. Chaz didn't say anything else. He didn't want to give any more of what little energy he had to battling with another female. The Hennessy along with fatigue were weighing heavily on him. He soon dozed off into a deep, much needed sleep.

Around 1:30 AM, Kisa rolled over in bed and felt that her husband's body was not there. She opened her eyes and sat up to survey the room, then called out, "Sincere."

There was no response. She retrieved her BlackBerry from the nightstand. When Kisa saw the time, she caught an instant attitude. Sincere had promised that he'd be home by midnight, and he had not even bothered to call. Dealing with renovations on their recently purchased four-thousand-square-foot brownstone and overseeing the daily operations of the spa rendered Kisa exhausted most evenings. Many nights Kisa slept so soundly that she didn't notice that Sincere was coming in between three and four. Now that the renovations were complete, along with the bulk of the interior designs, Kisa hadn't slept as hard.

Before calling Sincere to curse him out, she got up and searched each floor of the three-story brownstone. He wasn't there. Kisa called his phone a few times but didn't get an answer. She returned to bed and awaited his call.

Thirty minutes went by, and Kisa's phone had yet to ring. She was steaming. *He thinks it's a fucking game,* she told herself as she scrolled through her phone, stopping at Eisani's name. Kisa sent her cousin a text: *Where you at?*

*We're at Mansion,* Eisani replied.

Kisa texted back: *I'm about to come through.*

After a quick shower, Kisa put on a pair of black short shorts, a black lace push-up bra, and a sheer black peasant top. She completed her outfit with a pair of fuchsia Louboutin peep-toe stilettos. Kisa quickly but flawlessly applied her makeup, unwrapped her hair, and headed down to the brownstone's underground garage.

Kisa cruised toward downtown in her 645i with the top down, blasting Fab's *From Nothin' to Somethin'*. With the wind blowing through her hair, she contemplated not even returning home. *That'll teach him,* she thought, smiling. At a stoplight Kisa looked down at her phone. Sincere still hadn't called back. *I'm definitely not going home.* Kisa really wanted to cut her phone off because she knew that would piss Sincere off, but she kept it on. She knew in her world an emergency was always around the corner.

Kisa found Eisani in the VIP with their cousins from Philly. "Cuzo!" Eisani exclaimed, hugging Kisa with an almost empty bottle of rosé in her hand. "What you doing here?"

"I told you I was coming."

"I thought you was fronting. You know how you do." Eisani grinned. "What up though?"

"My husband showing his ass, so I decided to show mine."

"Oh, so that's it. Hubby got you heated. I knew your ass had to have a reason to be out."

Kisa pointed at the bottle in Eisani's hand, "I need one of those right now."

"It's two fresh bottles on the way out right now."

At first Kisa sat at the table, constantly checking her phone to see if Sincere had called; but after a few glass of champagne she forgot all about that phone and was up dancing with her cousins. Once she'd polished off the rosé Kisa moved on to Grey Goose, her favorite. She was having a great time, and she realized how much she'd missed partying with the girls. It was the most fun she'd had in a very long time.

By 4:00 AM Kisa was twisted, so she opted out of joining Eisani and the girls for an afterclub meal at their favorite diner. Kisa said her good-byes, got into her vehicle, and let the top down. She hoped that the wind against her face would help sober her up for the drive home. Pulling away from the curb, she reached in her bag, grabbed her cell, and checked it for the first time in two hours. "Wow." She laughed at the thirty-one missed calls and ten unread text messages. The phone rang. "Hello," Kisa answered, with a slight giggle in her voice.

"Where the fuck have you been?" Sincere yelled.

"No, the better question is, where have *you* been?"

"Kane, stop playing."

"I'm not playing, and I'm not telling you nothing until you explain what you were doing that kept you from answering my calls."

"I was uptown with Butta gambling."

"Bullshit!" Kisa snapped, and hung up.

Sincere called right back.

"Yeah, nigga, what is it?" she answered.

"I swear to God you gon' make me choke your ass."

"Whatever, my man. Go choke that bitch that kept you from answering your phone."

"You bugging over nothing, yo. I'm telling you the truth. I was gambling."

"If you were just gambling, why didn't you answer your phone?"

"Because I left it in the car; we were standing right outside of the car shooting dice."

"Yeah, right! You know I had a feeling that if we moved back here you was gon'be right back on the same bullshit with these hoes."

"I'm not trying to hear that. Where the hell you at?"

"I'm on the way home."

"And where have you been?"

"Out!"

"Out where?"

"You kill me," Kisa said, "You wasn't worried about where I was at while you were out doing you."

Sincere sighed deeply. He was on the verge of losing it. "I'm not with the games, so cut it out already."

"How cute." Kisa giggled. "Like I said, I'm on my way home. Toodles." She pressed end, tossed the phone onto the passenger seat, and turned up the music.

When Kisa pulled into the garage, Sincere was sitting waiting for her. She opened the door and stumbled out, wearing a silly grin.

"Are you drunk?" Sincere questioned with disgust.

"Are you drunk?" Kisa mimicked, wobbling side to side as she removed her heels. "Do I look drunk?"

"Yes."

"Well, why the hell you ask?"

Sincere lost it. He yoked Kisa up by her shirt. "I don't know what your problem is, but you better check that shit right here."

"Your sneaky ass is my problem."

"For the thousandth time, I was gambling."

"So you say." Kisa yanked away and stormed upstairs.

Sincere followed. "I'm not going to start dealing with your jealous issues again."

"You are the cause of my issues!" she yelled.

"Don't start bringing up shit from five years ago."

"You know the saying, Sin. Once a cheater, always a cheater." Kisa crossed the marble foyer to the second set of stairs.

Sincere jumped in front of her. "I'm not cheating on you. Where is all this coming from?"

"It's coming from your actions. Ever since we got up here, you been out every night. I can't never get you on the phone. What I don't understand is why you trying me like that when you know I'm far from stupid."

"You are tripping over absolutely nothing. I've only been hanging with my niggas, trying to have a little fun before we bring the kids up."

Kisa stood silently, just staring at her husband. He seemed to be telling the truth, but one thing that she knew about him was that he was a beautiful liar. "Aight, whatever." She sighed. "I'm going to bed."

"Nah, you not going nowhere. Where you been with them lil'-ass shorts on?" His eyes zeroed in on her thick thighs, which were causing his dick to swell. Even at his angriest, Sincere couldn't fight off the strong sexual attraction he had for his wife.

"I was at Mansion with Eisani."

"Where else you been?"

"Nowhere."

"I think you been out on some get-back shit."

Kisa twisted her lips. "Don't try to flip this shit on me."

"Take them shorts off."

"What?"

"You heard me." He moved in close. "Take all that shit off."

Blushing, Kisa dropped her purse to the floor, then seductively removed her blouse and shorts. Standing in her bra and thong, she asked, "You happy now?"

"No, 'cause I said take it all off."

Kisa obliged him, taking off the thong first. She slid her bra straps off each shoulder, then turned around slowly, making sure to graze Sincere with her ample ass. "I need you to unfasten this."

Sincere unsnapped the bra, reached around, and pulled it off of her. Cupping her breasts he kissed her shoulders and sucked her neck. The alcohol in Kisa's system intensified every touch and lick. She moaned loudly. Using his body, Sincere eased her over to the staircase. "Get down and bend over."

Kisa knelt down on the third step, bent over, and rested her arms on the sixth step. "Like that?" she purred.

"Just like that." He admired her from behind as he dropped his jeans and boxers to the floor. With his dick at full attention he got behind her, spread her cheeks open, and slid in.

"Hmm," Kisa moaned, loving the sensation that she always experienced when he penetrated her. It never got old.

Sincere swayed his hips back and forth, stroking gradually. Feeling sheer ecstasy, Kisa reached down and massaged her clit to speed up her oncoming orgasm. As his strokes became faster and stronger, she inched away. Sincere pulled her back by her hair. "Stop running and take it," he told her, thrusting harder and licking the back of her neck. Kisa exploded all over him. Her body went limp, but he kept going until she came again. Minutes later, he finally climaxed.

Moving slow, Kisa climbed the stairs to her third-floor bedroom. Completely out of it, she flopped down in the middle of her bed and dozed off.

"Hey," Sincere said loudly, entering the bedroom, "Ain't no sleeping in here." He opened her legs wide.

"No, Sin," she groaned. "I'm tired."

"I don't care. You come in here accusing me of fucking. I'm going to prove to you I haven't been out cheating." Sincere stuck his index and middle fingers into her, tickling her G-spot. Kisa's body responded the way he knew it would. Her back arched up off the bed while her hips bucked rhythmically. Simultaneously, Sincere sucked on her ripe nipples. Shivering and shaking, Kisa came for the third time.

Sincere withdrew his fingers, got on top of Kisa, and pushed her legs back until her knees touched her shoulders. Pressing down hard, he drove deep, pumping rapidly until he came in her. Though she was very satisfied, Kisa was happy that he'd busted fast, because she was exhausted. As soon as he got off her, she rolled over and attempted to go back to sleep. Unfortunately for Kisa, Sincere was not done with her yet. He gave it to her three more times before the sun came up.

Before going to sleep Sincere asked, "Do you believe I wasn't out fucking now?"

Kisa lowered her head to the middle of his body, "Yes, I believe you." She planted a kiss on his soft dick, then looked up him. "Can I please go to sleep now?"

The next morning when Chaz awoke he didn't immediately remember the previous night's events. So naturally, he thought that the person giving him a blow job was Kennedy. Groggily, he moaned, "Hmm, Kennedy."

*No, he didn't just call me that,* Ria thought, infuriated. She jumped from her knees and mounted him. Chaz's head was tilted back, and his eyes were closed. Ria whispered in his ear as she slid down on his dick, "You know that bitch could never suck you off like me."

Chaz's eyes shot open, and instantly everything came back to him. His first instinct was to push Ria off of him; he decided against it, though. The way he saw it, this was one last piece of ass before he tied the knot, and he hadn't been with anyone other than Kennedy in two years. Besides, it had been more than five years since the last time he'd had sex with Ria, and though now they mostly had a hate-hate relationship, after all that time she felt good sliding up and down on him. As Ria worked her hips back and forth, Chaz's eyes rolled behind his head in pleasure. He could feel the pressure mounting inside of him, and he was ready to explode. "Get up, Ria," he muttered.

She didn't move, she wanted him to come inside of her.

"Get up, yo."

When Ria didn't budge, he shoved her from atop of him, but not before the first load of semen was shot inside of her.

"Kennedy, what's taking Chaz so long?" Kennedy's sister Kenyatta asked as they sat aboard the luxury private jet owned by Yatta's husband, Strick. Strick also owned T.O.N.Y. Records, the label that Kennedy and Chaz both were signed to.

"I don't think he's coming."

"What do you mean?"

"Exactly what I said," Kennedy snapped.

"Hold up, why you comin' at me like that?"

"My bad, sis," Kennedy removed her shades, revealing her red puffy eyes. "I've been up all night."

"Have you been crying?"

"Yeah," Kennedy nodded. "Chaz said the wedding is off and left."

"Why?"

"'Cause I didn't tell him I was taking Jordan to meet Brian or that I'd been in contact with him."

"Back up, you let Brian meet Jordan? When?"

"Yesterday," Kennedy responded, then went on to tell her everything that happened.

When Kennedy finished, Kenyatta simply shook her head and said to her, "I thought you learned your lesson a long time ago about being so secretive."

"Apparently not," Kennedy said sarcastically.

Before they could continue their conversation, Chaz's daughters came running onto the jet. "Hey, Ken-Ken," they sang, almost in unison. "Hey, Auntie Yatta."

Kennedy opened her arms wide to embrace the girls, "Hi, Tiki and Chastity."

"Where's Jordan?" asked Tiki.

"He's back there with Jada and them. They're watching *The Incredibles*." Kennedy looked up and saw Chaz standing before her. They looked at each other, and what was only seconds felt like hours.

Yatta stood up and grabbed Tiki's and Chastity's hands. "Come on, girls, let's go back here with all the kids and get you buckled in."

Chaz sat down next to Kennedy without saying a word.

"I didn't think you were coming," Kennedy told him.

"I don't know why."

"'Cause you said the wedding was off, and you didn't come home last night or this morning. Where were you, anyway?"

"I rode around for a while, then I went to the studio." The lie rolled off his tongue naturally, due to the fact he'd been practicing it from the time he'd left Ria's house. "How you feelin'?"

"Tired. Since I didn't get any sleep last night."

"We here now and I'm sober, so let's put it on Broadway. Am I still mad at you? Hell, yeah. I'm nowhere near mad enough not to marry you, never that. Really, I'm more hurt than I am mad."

Kennedy lowered her head and mumbled, "I'm sorry."

Chaz placed his finger beneath her chin and lifted her face up. "Don't be sorry, just don't be deceitful."

# Chapter 8

Kennedy's nuptials were held outside on the lawn of The Green in downtown Charlotte. It was the wedding that every little girl dreams of. The weather was picture perfect, sunny, and seventy-seven degrees. Big pink roses hung heavily around the altar. The smell of fresh grass and the natural fragrance of the flowers filled the air. Kennedy's four bridesmaids, her older sister, Kenyatta; her younger sister, Kneaka; Kisa; and Eisani all wore powder-pink chiffon halter dresses. Chaz and his groomsmen wore beige tuxedos with pink ties. The four flower girls littered the aisle with mounds of yellow roses for Kennedy to step on. All in attendance agreed that Jordan was the most handsome ring bearer they'd ever seen.

A male soloist sang Stevie Wonder's "You and I" as Kennedy walked down the aisle. She was stunning in a strapless ivory ball gown. Her train stretched out almost ten feet behind her. Her hair was pulled back in a neat ball of pin curls, showing off her pristine face. By the time she reached the altar, tears of joy were dropping one after the other. Chaz had to take his handkerchief and wipe her face.

Arnessa sat in her chair, thinking how she had seen weddings only in the movies. She was amazed at how Kennedy just glowed beautifully in her dress. Never giving much thought to marriage before, Arnessa now wondered if she would ever be someone's bride.

Little did she know that Butta was watching her from the corner of his eye, thinking, *In a few years we could be up there.* He couldn't put his finger on it, but something made him feel that Arnessa was that special one. As hard as he tried, he couldn't fight that feeling. For Butta and Arnessa the wedding was the perfect getaway, with all the drama that was unfolding in New York.

Cenise sat to the right of Arnessa, happy to be there. She hadn't wanted to come at first, but Arnessa made her come along for her own protection. There was no telling what could happen if she was left alone in the city. Cenise was elated when she found out that she was going to the wedding of Kennedy and Chaz, two of her favorite rappers.

Kennedy placed her trembling right hand in Chaz's palm, and she began to recite her own vows. "Chaz, you are caring, charming, humorous, and charismatic. You are a wonderful son, a responsible father, and a terrific friend. Chaz, you *are* the man of *my* dreams. I'm so glad that you're mine. My love will never leave you, for it will always be with you, beyond time, space, and throughout all eternity."

It was rare that Chaz shed a tear, unless he was suffering from pain. Kennedy's words had caused a few to escape his eyes. One thing was for sure, she had his heart. Besides his mother, she was the only woman for whom he'd cried. Though he'd performed on stages in front of thousands, he'd never experienced the emotional mix of excitement, joy, and nervousness that he felt as he gazed at Kennedy. She was the only one for him. He'd known it from their first date. Only a few couples could go through the things that they had and come out unscathed. Quickly, Chaz wiped his face, ready to recite the words that he'd been rehearsing for the last week. Before he began, he gave Kennedy's grandmother, Big Ma, a wink. If it weren't for her, the union of Chaz and Kennedy would have ceased to exist. She was the one who'd nursed Kennedy back to health after her breakdown. Big Ma was the one who'd brought them back together once Kennedy was healed. No one was happier than she to see this day.

Chaz gave Kennedy's hand a little squeeze and cleared his throat. "Kennedy, you are the woman I've always wanted but never thought existed. Your loyalty is unquestionable and your beauty undeniable. I admire everything about you—your smile, your intelligence, the glitter in your eyes when you're happy. Not only do I admire you, I value you and I think you're priceless. The love that we have is so rare that I will never forsake it. Nor will I forsake you." A twinge of guilt shot through him as his romp with Ria flashed through his mind. From this day forward he planned never to do it again.

After the exchange of rings, a few rituals, and two songs,

the pastor pronounced them husband and wife. The guests moved over to a beautifully decorated ballroom at the Westin Hotel for the reception. Kennedy and Chaz stayed behind at The Green, taking pictures with their bridal party.

At the reception, everyone enjoyed cocktails and conversing with people they had not seen in a while. Arnessa was standing next to the bar waiting for a drink when Cenise walked up behind her. "Nessa, look who I found," she said with huge grin.

"Who?" Arnessa questioned as she turned around and came face-to-face with Rap and his wife, Jesse. "What's up, yo?" She hugged both of them.

They were shocked to see Arnessa in a dress, with her hair in free-flowing curls. "You look gorgeous," Jesse told her.

"What ya doing down here?" Arnessa asked, genuinely happy to see them.

"What we doing here?" Rap replied. "Shit, that's what I need to be asking. These my people. I guess it's true what I been hearing in the streets then."

"And that is?"

Rap chuckled. "The last time I saw you, I was putting you on to Butta to do some business. Next thing I'm hearing is, dude done wifed you."

All Arnessa could do was blush. "Rap, you know it didn't go down like that. I mean, everything just happened so fast."

"I bet it did," Rap remarked. "Where my dude at anyway."

"He sitting right over there," Arnessa said, pointing toward a table where Butta was sitting with Sincere. "Go holla at 'em, I'll be over there soon as I get my drink."

When Arnessa felt her cell vibrating in her small clutch purse, she struggled to get the clasp open. Upon seeing Tasha's name on the screen, she answered, "Yeah, Tash, what's up?"

"Nessa," Tasha panted, "Bizzy just got merked on my stoop."

"Are you serious?"

"Dead ass."

Arnessa looked over at the table where Butta was seated and saw he was staring directly at her. He was also on his cell, receiving the same information from Mannie. Utter disbelief was the only way to describe what Arnessa was feeling. She swallowed hard, then asked, "What happened?"

"I don't really know—he had just rung my bell," Tasha answered, out of breath from walking fast. "I was on my way down when I heard three shots. They were so loud I knew they were coming from right outside, so I waited about a minute. Then I went and looked out. Bizzy was laid out, yo—blood was everywhere."

"Where you at now?"

"I got the fuck outta there. I knew Five-O was gon' be banging on doors. Since I had this shit on me, I went out the fire escape. I'm on my way up the block to meet Mannie."

"Aight, call me when you get to where you going. And Tasha, be careful."

Butta had made his way over to Arnessa by the time she hung up the phone. "Who were you talking to?" Butta asked.

"Tasha."

"Did she tell you 'bout Bizzy," he asked, already knowing the answer.

"Yeah, she did. Butta, do you think Suef did it?"

He thought about her question before answering, "Anybody could've done it. I mean, we don't know, Bizzy could've had some other bullshit going on . . . but I put my paper on that cocksucker Suef."

Arnessa couldn't digest the fact that she was having this conversation about Bizzy. There was no way that this could be happening. Bizzy was the only person on her team whom she'd known her entire life. They were from the same block, were the same age, had attended the same school since day care. Their mothers had even been good friends back in the day. Bizzy's mother was the only other thing on Arnessa's mind. *She's going to be devastated*, Arnessa thought.

As she pulled all thoughts together, his death became a reality. Suddenly, she didn't feel so well; she had to get out of there before she fell apart. "I gotta get outta here," she told Butta.

"Let's go up to the room," he said, knowing that Bizzy's death had badly upset Arnessa, who was trying her best to hide it. Butta would've waited until the reception was over to tell her if she hadn't heard about it from Tasha. All he wanted was for her to have a good time.

Arnessa didn't feel right taking him away from the reception. "No, Butta, you stay down here with your friends. Besides, I wanna be alone for a while."

"Aight." He kissed her on the cheek. "I'll come up in about an hour to check on you."

Turning around, Arnessa walked briskly out of the ballroom so that no one would see the tears forming in her eyes. She got on an empty elevator, and as soon as the doors closed, she began to cry. Although she was very sad about Bizzy, her tears were not exclusively for him. It was as if the news of his death had taken her back to the moment she'd learned of her own brother's death. She'd reached an indescribable level of vulnerability and was finding it very hard to hold on to what little security she had.

Arnessa was so caught up in her emotions that she'd forgotten to press a floor button. When the elevator doors slid open, Butta was standing right there, looking down at his cell as he made a call. When he lifted his head and saw Arnessa crying, he stepped onto the elevator and pulled her into his arms, hugging her tightly. She sobbed heavily, resting her face in the middle of his chest. He told her, "Ma, you don't ever have to be alone."

The reception was winding down and Kennedy, TaTa, Yatta, Eisani, and Kisa were sitting at one of the round tables, just kicking it. "I'm glad that you at least made it to my wedding," Kennedy said to her cousin TaTa.

"Don't start that mess, Ken. I'm here."

"That's not the point." Kennedy slurred from all the champagne she had consumed. "You were supposed to be a bridesmaid, man. Eisani, talk to your sister."

"I know you don't think I can reason with her?" Eisani questioned, her eyebrows raised, "Everybody knows she's a weirdo."

TaTa playfully threw a flower at Eisani. "You my sister, you supposed to be on my side."

Out of all the cousins TaTa had always been the strange one, but lately she'd been acting even stranger than usual. Her svelte size-twelve frame had suddenly shrunk to a six, and her normally radiant cinnamon-colored skin was now pale and blotchy. Whenever she came around, she was silent and withdrawn. It was clear that something was stressing her.

Maybe it was because she'd been busted for selling two bricks of cocaine to a female undercover cop. There was no way she could ever get them to understand that she was co-operating with the police. TaTa recognized that she wasn't built to do any jail time. The more people she set up, the more time got shaved off her potential sentence. Her aim was to shave it down to zero.

"TaTa, you know not being in the wedding with us was some foul shit," Kisa said.

"How you calling me foul, Kane? Don't nobody know what I'm going through right now."

"Don't nobody know 'cause you don't tell nobody shit," Kisa shot back, rolling her eyes.

"Okay, that's enough, you two," Kennedy said. "Look, Ta, we not your girls. We're your family, and you can always come to us. You acting like you don't know. Now, what's up wit you?"

TaTa sighed. "Kennedy, this not the place to air out my issues. This ya wedding night, ma, let's keep celebrating. I promise in due time each one of you will know what's up with me."

*Chapter 9*

Over the next three months, the number of blood-stained sidewalks and white chalk lines multiplied weekly throughout the blocks of Harlem as a small-scale war erupted between Suef and Butta. Most—if not all—of the casualties were lower-level crew members. What Suef failed to realize was that he was the only one fighting for those blocks because he needed them. Butta's money was long; the cash those blocks brought in was nothing compared to what he made distributing cocaine and heroin up and down the East Coast.

For Butta, it was all about respect. With every passing day he was becoming increasingly annoyed that no one could find Suef. The majority of Suef's team had been murdered or severely injured at Butta's orders. But that wasn't good enough. He wanted Suef dealt with. As long as Suef was alive, Butta would continue to be tense, expecting him to strike at any moment.

Butta also wanted just to kick back and spend some quality time with Arnessa. They'd fallen hard for each other, in spite of the chaos around them. Loving a man was a new feeling for Arnessa, but never having had a real boyfriend left Arnessa confused about how to express her love.

Arnessa was nurturing by nature, and she generally enjoyed having someone whom she could take care of. Every day she cooked, cleaned, and catered to all of his personal needs. Little by little, Arnessa had gone from hustler to a housewife. She enjoyed her new life, but for the most part she found it dull. Arnessa missed the rush of the hustle, the day-to-day grind.

It had been so long since Arnessa had given any thought to what she wanted to do outside of hustling. Watching Kisa run her own businesses was making Arnessa want to become a legit entrepreneur. Quietly, she spent days on the Internet researching the most profitable businesses in the country. She wanted something with long-term income potential, so she decided getting into the real estate market was a good option. Being an agent was out of the question for her, but she loved the idea of buying a property, fixing it up, then selling it. This was a familiar concept for Arnessa. She figured if she could flip weight . . . she could flip properties.

It was a rare night when Butta made it home before midnight and wasn't exhausted. But tonight he and Arnessa lay in bed watching *The First 48*, Arnessa's favorite program. She felt that this was the perfect time to tell him about her business venture. Sitting cross-legged, with her back against the headboard, Arnessa looked down at Butta, whose head was resting on her thigh. "Butta, remember how I was telling you that I wanted to start my own business?"

"Yeah, I remember."

"I've decided to open a real estate investment company."

"You wanna buy buildings and rent the apartments?"

"No, well, maybe that too, but mainly I want to buy properties, fix them up, and sell 'em."

Butta sat up attentively, "It's a lot of paper in that type of business if you do it right. Let me get in."

"Wow, this is too funny." Arnessa laughed.

"What?"

"You're the second person I've told about my business idea, and just like the first person you want in."

"Who's the first person?"

"Kane."

"I should've known that girl had an ear for a good business deal."

"Plus she already plugged me to some good connections to help get me started."

He wrapped his arm around her and pulled her down. "That's what's up. I think your company will be a success."

"You do?" Arnessa gushed at his encouragement.

"Yes, you're smart, ambitious, and we both know you're capable of running a business."

No one besides her brother, Deon, had ever paid Arnessa such nice compliments. Inside, Arnessa was beaming. Her eyes scanned his face, and her fingertips caressed his chin as she simply smiled at him.

"What you smiling at?" Butta asked.

"You. I . . . ." She hesitated. Although they'd been together a little over six months, she still found professing her feelings aloud difficult.

"I what?" Butta nudged.

Looking toward the ceiling, Arnessa searched for the correct words. "I'm still getting used to the whole relationship thing. Lately, there have been times when I wanted to tell you . . . I love you."

"I love you too, baby."

"Do you really?"

"Yes, I love you. I love you very much. It's something about you." He began kissing her, adoring her sumptuous lips. Before Arnessa, Butta hadn't cared too much for kissing, but with Arnessa, he couldn't kiss her enough.

Tossing her leg atop his body, she straddled him and nibbled his earlobe. She knew his body well and understood exactly where to kiss, massage, and suck. Butta's dick stiffened beneath her. "Hmm, what's that?" she purred, moving from his ear to his neck, then down to his bare chest, where she circled his nipples with her moist tongue. Lying back, Butta enjoyed the immense pleasure that Arnessa was giving him. With his guidance she'd become a superb lover. Arnessa pulled his boxers off and wrapped her hand around his dick, steadily jerking it up and down while looking up at him. She licked her lips teasingly.

"Stop playing, girl; let me get some of that mouth."

Arnessa licked his penis slowly. "Tell me you want it."

"You know I want it."

Clasping her mouth around the head, she sucked firmly as she took more and more of him in. Bobbing her head up and down, she tightened her jaws while jerking him with her hand. Arnessa had become a professional, courtesy of the skills Kisa had shown her.

"Umm, baby," he moaned as she began to deep throat him while performing swallowing motions that created intense pressure and extreme satisfaction at the same time. It felt like she was making love to him with her mouth. He removed the clip from her hair. His body shivered in delight as he grabbed a fistful of her long mane. Arnessa knew that he was about to explode, so she pulled back, letting his dick slip from her mouth slowly.

"Why you stop?"

"Now, now, I can't just let you lay back and have all the fun." She smirked as she crawled onto him and began riding him. Butta was elated that Arnessa was becoming less inhibited. He was even happier that it was with him. He had awakened things in her mentally and physically that she had never known existed. Picking up the pace, she rode him till they both climaxed.

Butta slapped her ass. "That was good, lil' mama."

"I know," she said cockily as she rolled off.

"What you mean, you know? Come here." He pulled her body close to his, squeezing her tight. Her back was against his chest, and he rested his chin in the crease between her neck and shoulder. As they both began to doze off, he told her, "I really do love you, Arnessa. You do know *that*, right?"

"Yeah I know . . . but do you know you're the first and only man that I love?"

"I do now," he responded, with a little sarcasm.

"Now that you know, don't hurt me."

The next day, Arnessa had lunch with Kisa and Mrs. Spencer, a client from the spa. Along with her husband, Mrs. Spencer owned a successful contracting firm that had locations in six states on the East Coast. Arnessa observed while Kisa did most of the talking on her behalf. Using her most proper voice, Kisa effortlessly negotiated a deal to use only Mrs. Spencer's company for all of Arnessa's real estate investment projects in exchange for a modest discount. Watching Kisa spew out numbers without blinking or stumbling only reassured Arnessa that she'd made the right decision by going into business with Kisa.

Arnessa glanced down at her vibrating cell phone, which rested in her lap. It was the fourth phone call from an unfamiliar Atlanta number. *This can only be Cenise or Nomie,* she thought; she knew no one else in Atlanta. But where were their cell phones? Excusing herself from the table, she answered the phone as she entered the bathroom, "Hello?"

"Arnessa," a tearful voice spoke.

"Nomie?"

"Yes."

"What's wrong? Why are you crying?"

"It's Cenise . . ." Nomie paused.

Arnessa's heart dropped to the pit of her stomach, "What happened to my sister, Nomie?"

"She got knocked."

Breathing a little easier, Arnessa asked, "For what, fighting? I told y'all not to go down there with that rowdy shit."

"Nah, Nessa, they got her for trafficking."

"Trafficking what?"

"Cocaine," replied Nomie.

Pain shot through Arnessa's head. "What you mean *cocaine*? What the hell y'all into down there?"

"*I'm* not into nothin', Nessa, I swear. It's that dude, Black, that Cenise be messing wit'. I told her after she made the first couple of runs not to do it no more."

"What run?"

"From back home to down here."

This was a lot for Arnessa to process, and too much was being said over the phone, "That's enough talking on this line; where they holding them at?"

"Cenise is the only one that's locked up, and she's in Greenville, South Carolina."

"So where this Black nigga at? He better be on his way to fucking bond her out, I know that."

"I tried calling him, but every number Cenise gave for him is disconnected."

Arnessa was becoming more pissed with each answer. "What's his real name?"

"We don't know," Nomie answered truthfully. "Everybody down here call him New York Black."

"That's every dark-skinned New York nigga name when they outta town. How come Cenise didn't call me?"

"She said she been calling the house, but she couldn't get you. I had her on three-way the first few times I called you. I think she had to get off the phone."

"The next time she call, hit me if for any reason I don't answer. Make sure you tell her to keep her mouth closed."

"Are you okay, dear?" Mrs. Spencer asked, upon Arnessa's return to the table. She noticed the sweat stains on the younger woman's beige silk blouse and her smeared mascara.

"I'm okay. My food just didn't agree with me." Arnessa smiled weakly.

Kisa instinctively knew that Arnessa was lying, not to mention that her hands were trembling. "Mrs. Spencer, I know you have another meeting. I'll take care of the check,"

Kisa suggested, wanting her to leave quickly so that she could find out what was really up with Arnessa.

"Thank you, Kisa," Mrs. Spencer said, getting up from the table. "Arnessa, I hope you feel better. Talk to you soon, ladies."

"Bye," they said in unison as they watched her walk away. As soon as Mrs. Spencer was out of hearing range, Kisa turned to Arnessa. "What's up with you?"

Still in disbelief, Arnessa shook her head. "That was Nomie on the phone. She said Cenise got knocked for trafficking coke."

"Are you serious?"

Arnessa nodded.

"We can go to the airport and take a flight to Atlanta and get her out."

"She not even in Atlanta, yo; she some place I've never heard of called Green something, South Carolina."

"*Greenville?*" Kisa's eyes widened, hoping that she hadn't heard correctly.

"Yeah, that's the place."

"Oh no!"

"Why you say it like that?"

The waiter walked over to return Kisa's credit card; she signed the receipt, giving him a generous tip. "I don't want to scare you or jump to any conclusions," Kisa told her as they got up from the table, "but that is the absolute worst state to catch a drug charge in. Niggas be getting ten years for an ounce of blow." Kisa dialed a number as they walked out of the restaurant and across the street to the parking garage.

"What it do, mama?" Kennedy answered.

"You in Charlotte?"

"Yeah."

"You still cool with that bondsman chick?"

"Who, Dreann? Yeah, we straight, why?"

"Hold on, Ken," Kisa said as she fished through her purse for the parking stub. Once she'd located it, she handed it to the young parking attendant who was openly admiring her.

"You gorgeous, yo; what's your name?" He moved in close. Something he shouldn't have done.

Kisa couldn't stand for strangers to get in her personal space. That type of thing made her extremely uncomfortable, "I'm telling you now, get *out* my face and go get my fucking car before it be a problem," she said, staring him down. Sensing her seriousness, he walked away mumbling obscenities. Kisa returned to the phone. Kennedy was laughing, "What's so funny?" Kisa asked.

"You," Kennedy replied. "You always breaking on people."

"Whatever, that bum-ass nigga was all in my face drooling. Anyway, I need you to check with your girl and see if she do bonds in South Carolina."

"Who in the world got locked up down there?"

"Cenise, Arnessa's little sister."

"The one that was at my wedding?"

"Yeah, her last name is Binds. Find out what her charges are and the amount of her bond, and we'll put it in your account."

"I'm on it."


A half hour later Kisa was sitting on a stool in Butta's kitchen when Kennedy called back. "Kane, Cenise's charge is felony cocaine trafficking, two hundred to four hundred grams. Her bail is a hundred stacks. I already gave Dreann the ten percent. I'm going to ride down there with her to pick her up."

"I'll probably fly down with Arnessa tonight to pick her up."

"You know Chaz and I are flying back tonight. I'll see if I can get her on the flight with us."

"That will be good. Hit me back and let me know, so if you can't, we can go ahead and make arrangements." Just as she was hanging up the phone, Butta came in, followed by Sincere, Mannie, and Shawn.

"What's the word on baby girl?" Butta asked

Kisa told him everything that she'd gotten from Kennedy.

"This shit is crazy," Butta sighed after hearing the update, "Where Nessa at?"

"She went up to take a shower; this is stressing her."

"I already know. Cenise is her life," Butta said, heading for the stairs.

Shawn walked over to Kisa all smiles. "Sis, what up?"

"What do you want, *Shawn*?"

"You remember back in the day how all of us would be in one place like this, and you'd whip up one of them bangin' meals."

"I remember vaguely," she joked.

"Come on, Kane, cook something for us."

"I don't cook no more, ask Sin."

"Picture that," Mannie chimed in as they all laughed.

"Shawn, that chick you call your girl still won't cook for you?" Kisa asked, smiling mischievously as she hopped off the stool. "If my husband will accompany me to the store, I'll throw a little something together." Without waiting for

Sincere's response, she grabbed her purse and his hand and walked toward the door.

Upstairs Butta pushed the bedroom door open a little and peeped inside, Arnessa was lying in the middle of the king-sized bed with her back to the door. She was wearing a white terry-cloth robe. Her freshly shampooed hair was wrapped in a white towel. A small packed duffel bag was at the foot of the bed. Butta lay down behind her and wrapped his arm around her, pulling her close to him. "You okay, baby?"

When she didn't respond, he peeked over her shoulder to see if she was awake. Arnessa stared blankly at the wall. She looked brokenhearted. "How could she do this to me, Butta?"

"I don't know, Nessa."

"This feels so crazy. It's like I don't even know my little sister. I can't believe she let some piss-ass nigga gas her. Now, *she* sitting in a cell, and he in the fuckin' wind." Water filled Arnessa's eyes. "I know she scared out her mind."

"It's gonna be aight," he assured her, kissing the back of her neck. "Kane said Kennedy already paid Cenise's bond and is on the way to pick Cenise up."

Arnessa sat up, "I need to get dressed so we can get to the airport."

"Nah," he pulled her back down onto the bed, "Cenise is gonna fly up with Kennedy tonight. You need to relax." He turned her around so that they were now facing each other. Her face was streaked with tears. Butta removed the towel from Arnessa's head, and her damp hair fell across the pillow. Using the end of the towel, he wiped her face. Arnessa slipped one arm beneath him and the other around him.

She planted her head firmly into his chest and wept silently until she fell asleep.

Later that night Arnessa awoke to the laughter and music that were coming from downstairs. Butta was no longer next to her. Arnessa slipped on a white tank top and a pair of gray sweats and went downstairs to see what was going on. She found everyone sitting around the massive dining table. Eisani had also joined the group. In the center of the table were the remnants of what Kisa had prepared: king crab legs, jumbo shrimp, rice, and seafood salad, along with a few top-shelf liquor bottles.

Butta rose from his chair when he saw Arnessa; she waved him back down and sat on his lap. "You feeling better," he asked her.

"A little. Has Kennedy or Cenise called?"

"They'll be here soon. You ready to eat? Kane fixed you a plate. It's in the kitchen."

"Maybe later. I don't have an appetite right now."

Butta's phone rang. "Let me up, Ness." He walked through the kitchen and out to the garage. When he came back in, Kennedy, Chaz, and Cenise were with him. Cenise stood off at a distance while everyone else exchanged greetings.

"Thanks for getting her out," Arnessa told Kennedy as they embraced.

"You don't have to thank me. It was no problem. Baby girl is shook up, though, especially since she can't get in touch with ole dude."

Cenise walked over to Arnessa, expecting to receive compassion and comfort from her big sister. Unfortunately, when Arnessa looked at Cenise, all she felt was anger and rage. Neither sister said a word. They just stared at each other. Unable to match Arnessa's gaze, Cenise looked away first. Suddenly, Arnessa slapped Cenise, knocking her to the floor. As Arnessa advanced toward her to hit her again, Butta grabbed her from behind. "Nessa, what's wrong with you?"

"What's wrong with me?" She tried unsuccessfully to free herself from his grasp, "Ain't *shit* wrong with me! What's wrong with this little ignorant bitch?" she demanded, pointing at Cenise, who was being helped up by Kisa. Everyone else looked surprised at how Arnessa was handling her sister.

No one was more shocked than Cenise, though. "Why'd you hit me, Nessa?" she cried. "Why?"

"Why? Why? Why were you on the highway with that nigga's coke."

"'Cause I love him," Cenise sobbed.

"You can't be serious. You don't even know his name, *stupid*."

"And he paid me."

"Paid you what?"

"Two Gs a trip."

"What the fuck is two G's to you, Cenise? That was your monthly allowance in high school. You not talking to no dummy, aight? All this is about trying to impress a bum-ass nigga."

"You don't even know him," Cenise countered

"Apparently, you don't either, and if he gave half a fuck about you, he wouldn't have left you for dead. You can't tell when a muthafucka is using you?"

Already embarrassed, Cenise was now pissed at Arnessa for going at her in front of everyone. Mustering up some nerves and twisting her neck, she told Arnessa, "I don't know why you all in my shit. Just six months ago you was moving more coke and dope than Jeezy rap about."

*Hmm, let me get out of the way 'cause she 'bout to beat da shit out of this girl,* Kisa thought, just as Arnessa broke away from Butta's grasp and rushed Cenise. Arnessa grabbed her by the neck and slammed her into the wall. Cenise's slanted eyes became wide as golf balls as she tried to breathe. Arnessa tried to fight off the tears, a battle she quickly lost as they spilled from her eyes, "What I did, I did for us. I hustled every day for you so that you could have the best. I put myself on the line for you. Now you might've thrown it all away for a *boy*."

Realizing that she was choking her sister, Arnessa stepped back. Sobbing and gasping for air, Cenise crumpled to the floor.

Arnessa looked down at Cenise, "Everything is a wrap for you now."

"The police said that I could cooperate."

"*Cooperate!* Ha!" Arnessa laughed insanely, "Did you go to the police academy? Do you have a uniform in your closet I don't know about?"

Scared, Cenise shook her head. "No."

"Well then, you don't work for the fuckin' police! Yeah, you done jumped in this game feetfirst wit'out a damn clue, and like it or not, it's rules to this shit. Rule number one, no snitchin'. Now, if you want to break that rule, I suggest you pack up the little bit of shit that *I didn't* buy and get the fuck out. I don't support no rats."

Cenise sat there with the most hurtful expression on her face. The only person she had in the world had just given a harsh ultimatum. Arnessa knew her delivery was cruel and rapid, but so was the game. She also knew that the game didn't give a fuck about nobody. The room was so quiet that if a piece of tissue had dropped, everybody would've heard it.

Arnessa watched Cenise as she contemplated her very limited choices, "I bet the game don't look so good from the inside, do it, lil' sis?" Arnessa chuckled. "It's a major decision, ain't it."

Reluctantly, Cenise agreed by nodding her head.

"What you gonna do?" Arnessa asked.

In a low whimper she answered, "I'll let you handle it."

Arnessa replied, "You've made the right choice." Arnessa turned to go upstairs. She stopped and looked back at Cenise. "Welcome to the game, lil' mama."

*Chapter 10*

**D**amn, bitch, you's a winna," Suef grunted as the chick on top rode him wildly, her warm juices running down his dick. "Keep fucking daddy just like dat, Rellie."

Rellie rolled her eyes, and not in pleasure but at how wack he was. *If this nigga would just shut the fuck up sometime, he'd be straight,* she thought. She began moaning like she loved it, completely gassing his head like she had done to so many others before him. "Fuck 'em, rob 'em, and get ghost" was her motto for men.

She kept her ear to the streets at all times and knew who was getting that paper. Rellie had been hearing a lot of chatter about Suef, so she made her way back to her birthplace of New York City just to get at him. She'd robbed and set up so many hustlers and thugs on the East Coast that she could never rest easy on that side. So Rellie had made Houston, Texas, her home.

Any dude who wasn't on point with his shit became a victim as soon as she laid her venomous eyes on him. Once they got a taste of that sweet snapback-comeback pussy, it was a wrap. They'd practically give her whatever she wanted, just to stay around. The problem was, she didn't want their crumbs; she wanted the whole cake. Many men had awakened after mind-blowing sex with Rellie to find themselves tied up, their jewels gone, and their safes cleaned out.

Rellie was not the prettiest chick either. In fact, most thought she was just average. Standing at five feet three inches, she was petite, with extremely fair skin that bordered on pale. She kept her fire-engine-red hair blended with only the most expensive extensions. With a mouth full of exquisite porcelain veneers, her smile was worth twenty thousand, literally. When she covered her body in the high-priced designer labels, diamonds, and her favorite stilettos, she went from average to the baddest bitch moving.

When Suef saw her in all her shining glory, he nearly tripped over himself to get at her. After spending only a few days with Suef, Rellie knew where all of his stashes were since she was always cooped up in the house with him. She couldn't help but wonder why he rarely left his apartment in Brooklyn, especially when he was supposed to be the man uptown. From doing some serious ear hustling, Rellie learned about the war that was ensuing between Suef and Butta. Rellie couldn't help but feel like a pot of gold had fallen in her lap, knowing that wherever Butta was, Sincere was nearby. She finally saw her chance to seek revenge against the person she hated most: Kisa Montega.

After Suef climaxed, she got up, not caring whether she came or not. Most of the time Rellie felt like she did a better job of making herself nut with her vibrator than any man ever could. She crossed the room naked to grab her cigarettes from the dresser and sat on a bench at the end of the bed. "What's good wit' ya family?" she asked Suef as she lit up.

"Lil' cuzo is on point, as usual. He ready to get this shit poppin', yo. We gon make them pussy-ass niggas pay for every nigga of mine they done took out. I still want more payback for that bullshit they did to my man Trent."

"What happened with that bitch sister down south?"

"Cuzo said she made bail, but that don't matter," Suef chuckled, sounding so grimy. "In that racist-ass state, she is finito, baby; they giving niggas a hundred years down there for a gram or two."

"Suef, listen, I know these muhfuckas. When we get at them, we got to go hard and correct the first time. We can't give them no time to regroup. Something needs to happen soon, before they figure out you set that lil' chick up."

"Trust me, baby, they not gon' put that shit together."

Rellie cut him off. "See, you lost already by underestimating them. Now, I don't know nothing about this chick Arnessa but what you told me. What I do know is that Butta, Sincere, Kisa, and even that slut Eisani are far from dumb. So once you get your foot on their throat, you gotta keep pressing till they're dead."

"It carries how many years?" Arnessa questioned to make sure she was hearing the lawyer correct. Maybe it was his deep southern drawl that had her thinking she'd heard him wrong. She, Cenise, and Butta were having a meeting in the office of Barry King, the top narcotics defense attorney in Greenville. Prior to their meeting, Cenise had made her first court appearance. It had been two weeks since her arrest, and she'd been formally indicted for trafficking two hundred to four hundred grams of cocaine.

"The charge generally carries a mandatory twenty-five years," he repeated. Instantly, Cenise burst into loud sobs and tears. "Now, sweetheart, calm down," King told her, giving her a Kleenex. "I told you what the charge carries . . . Cenise has a few things working in her favor. She's still young enough to be charged as a youthful offender, and she doesn't have any priors. In a quick chat that I had with the solicitor, he let me know that he just may agree to dropping the charges down to possession and one year in prison, followed by home incarceration for a year. The home incarceration will be contingent upon Cenise establishing a physical residence here in South Carolina."

"A year in prison?" Arnessa perched forward in her chair. "She can't do no year in prison. Look at her." She pointed at Cenise, who was crying out of control, "She's not built for time. It's her first offense. Can't she get some type of intense probation, or just the house arrest?"

"Calm down, Ness," Butta said, patting her thigh. "Mr. King, what do you feel Cenise's chances are if she goes to trial?"

"Not good, since the state will more than likely call the confidential informant who tipped the police off about Cenise. And if it—"

Arnessa cut him off. "I thought this was a regular traffic stop?"

"Turns out the police were tipped off. Everything is here in the motion of discovery." He handed Arnessa the paper so that she could read it. "Like I was saying, if we take it to trial and lose, I can promise you the state of South Carolina *will* hand down the harshest sentence allowed."

On a beautiful sunny autumn morning, from a chair across the room, Butta watched Arnessa while she slept. Rays of sunlight crept through the blinds and kissed her skin, giving her an angelic glow. Butta was absolutely gone over Arnessa; he couldn't recall ever feeling anything close to what he felt for her. It had been three weeks since their meeting in South Carolina with Mr. King. Arnessa had been in a terrible funk since then. Butta knew that the thought of Cenise having to spend one day, let alone one year, in prison was killing Arnessa.

Butta tried to be there for her as much as he could. He desired with all of his might to comfort her and give her the stability that she'd been lacking. A few things were getting in the way, such as the fact that no one had been able to find Suef. Then there was Nichelle, a chick who'd been down with him for years. Butta and Nichelle had had a sexual relationship but were never a couple. He used her house to stash large amounts of cash and keys to various safes. All of her bills were paid by Butta. As far as other men were concerned, Nichelle could date who she wanted. Butta only had one rule: She couldn't bring them into the apartment.

The understanding between Butta and Nichelle had been working fairly well, until Nichelle found out about his relationship with Arnessa. She'd known about plenty of Butta's girls, but she could tell that this one was special.

Butta barely came around anymore, and when he did, it was only to put money up or take it out. She really knew something was up when he stopped having sex with her.

Butta felt that something was different about Nichelle. She began to nag him for time and throw herself at him, things she'd never done before. At first he couldn't understand where she was coming from. Then one day he looked into her eyes and could tell she was jealous. Butta knew from past experiences that jealousy had the power to corrupt people and affect their decision-making process. He decided to eliminate Nichelle's role in his life before she made any stupid decisions concerning his money.

Butta got up from the chair and sat on the edge of the bed next to Arnessa, who was beginning to wake up. She opened her eyes and saw Butta's face. "Morning." She smiled and wiped the sleep from her eyes.

"Good morning, princess. Did you sleep well?"

"Yes, Butta."

"Do you have a passport?"

"Yeah. Why?" Arnessa quizzed.

"Sincere invited us to Turks and Caicos with him and Kisa. We leave the day after tomorrow."

"I can't up and leave Cenise—"

Butta placed his forefinger over her lips, "No excuses. We're going. You need a vacation. *We* need a vacation somewhere that we can relax without looking over our shoulders. Besides, Eisani said Cenise could come stay with her while we're gone. Speaking of Cenise, you need to stop being so cold toward her."

"You think I'm being cold?"

"You're not being yourself. You're not being comforting or nurturing, the things that she relies on you for. The two of you barely talk around here." Butta pushed a piece of stray hair from Arnessa's face and stroked her with his fingers. "I know you're still hurting, ma, but you have to put your pain and anger aside and be as normal as you can with her. In less than six months she's going to prison, a place that will change her forever. So you have to step up now."

Arnessa understood exactly where he was coming from, and she lowered her eyes, nodding in agreement.

Butta looked down at his ringing cell phone. "I gotta get out of here—Mannie's downstairs. What you doing today?"

"I'm going out with Kisa to check on some projects and new properties."

"Aight, I plan on coming in early so we can hang out." Butta leaned down and gave her a kiss, "I love you."

Arnessa held his face in the palms of her hands and just stared at his face for a moment. He was so perfect to her. She didn't want to let him go. She gave him another kiss, then pressed her cheek against his. "Butta, I love you so much."

He responded, "I love you more than you know."

"Where's Shawn?" Butta questioned as he climbed into Mannie's Tahoe.

"He said he's going to meet us at Nichelle's. I think he was laid up with that jump-off."

"He is so wack for this shit."

When they arrived outside Nichelle's tenement building, Mannie asked Butta, "You want me to come up with you?"

Giving it a little thought, Butta replied, "Nah, it shouldn't take me but like twenty minutes to clean out the safes."

"Hit me when you ready, I'ma go around the block and

check on Dee and my daughter. I haven't seen them in two or three days."

"Mannie, get right back, yo. I'm trying to get my shit and leave. I'm not trying hear this bitch up in here breaking." He grabbed two empty duffel bags and exited the vehicle.

"I got you, my dude." Mannie assured Butta as he pulled away from the curb.

As soon as Mannie walked through the door of his daughter's mother's apartment, she went nuts. "You come for your shit, I hope, Mannie," she said in her heavy Panamanian accent.

"I didn't come home to hear ya mouth, Dee."

"Dis not ya home, Mannie. You neva here," she said as she grabbed a trash bag of his clothes and tossed it in his face.

Dee's performance had Mannie wishing that he hadn't stopped by. Although she was a small size six, Dee was a fireball. Mannie grabbed her before she could toss another bag at him. "Chill out, yo." He squeezed her arm. "Dee, chill before I kick the fuck out your little ass." Once Dee relaxed, Mannie began trying to make her understand why he was away so much. A conversation familiar for both.

"Baby, you know it's a lot going down right now. I'm in the gutta trying to keep food on the table to feed you and our baby. I could come through the crib more often, but when you be spazzin' on me like this . . . it make me not even wanna come by."

"But, Mannie, we neva see you anymore."

"It's not going to be like that much longer Dee, I promise. Where my little girl at?"

"In her crib sleeping."

Mannie went down the hall to his daughter's pink nursery. He bent down and kissed her forehead. Mannie was still amazed at how much his six-month-old daughter looked like Dee. She was the only thing that could make the killer in him fade away. Looking down at his daughter, he decided he wanted to be home. He looked over at Dee, who was standing in the doorway. "You got some of that fish I like?"

"Yes." She beamed, hoping it meant that he was going to sit and stay awhile.

"Start cooking," he said as he exited the room. "I'll be back in 'bout two hours."

"No, no, no," Dee yelled, running past him and blocking the front door. "No, Mannie, you think you so slick. I not stupid; you leave you no come back."

"I'll be back, ma, that's my word." He pressed his body against hers and squeezed her butt. "I'm definitely coming back for some of this." Mannie licked her ear and told her, *"Dame un beso."*

Dee did kiss him as he requested. "I guess I'll let you out, but if you don't come back . . . I put all your things in the street."

Mannie's phone began vibrating as he fished it out of his pocket. He said, "Aight, Dee, open the door, this is probably Butta."

Dee unlocked the three bolt locks and turned the knob. When she pulled the door back, she froze as she came face-to-face with a masked man. Mannie, focusing on his phone, looked up just in time to see the muzzle of the masked man's chrome gun. Mannie reached for his own gun in the small of his back, but there wasn't enough time. The masked man had the drop on him. Dee screamed as the heat of a bullet grazed her ear and slammed into Mannie's throat. Blood sprayed from his neck as his body dropped to the floor. Dee continued to let out shrill screams. She thought she was in the middle of a nightmare.

"Shut the fuck up, bitch." The man slammed Dee's head against the wall, knocking her unconscious. Then he stood over Mannie, who was barely holding on. The man removed his mask to reveal his identity. Mannie's eyes bulged wildly when he saw Trenton's face. The man's face was still scarred from the savage beating that he'd received from Shawn and Mannie months earlier. Trenton smiled evilly down at Mannie. "You told me the next time I had a message to bring it to you right. Here's the message, faggot," Trenton squeezed the lever pumping two bullets directly into Mannie's face. He picked up Mannie's keys and cell phone then fled the apartment.

Hurriedly, Butta filled the second of the two duffel bags with stacks of cash. He'd hoped to be done before Nichelle came home, but he wasn't so lucky. Just as he dropped the last stack of cash into the bag, he heard the locks turning on the front door. *Fuck*, he thought as her stilettos clicked against the hardwood floor. Butta zipped the bags and headed out of the room with hopes that there would be no major confrontation.

Nichelle greeted Butta with an icy glare. Standing five feet nine, she had an ultraslim frame. Her flawless skin was the same color as rich chocolate, and her long brown hair flowed down the middle of her back. She looked like a life-sized black Barbie doll. Nichelle glanced at the bags that Butta held in each hand, "It's like that?"

"Like what?" Butta responded dryly.

"You were just going to take everything and not say a word."

"It's a lot going on outside right now. I'm moving things around till stuff blow over. I left some money in your top drawer. Enough to pay ya bills for a year and then some."

Nichelle shook her head with a slight giggle then told him, "You must think I'm a fool. The real reason you taking that money up outta here is 'cause ya girl don't want you around me. You betta remember who been down with you. That's how dudes do, though—get a whiff of some new young pussy and forget about the bitch that's been ridin' with 'em."

"Not for nothin', my girl don't even know you exist. Plus right now, I'm not trying to even hear that bullshit you kicking." Butta walked past her, heading toward the door.

"So you just gon' disrespect me and not acknowledge what I'm saying to you. That's okay, 'cause niggas like you always get it the same way they give it."

Butta spun around, "Are you threatening me?"

Smirking at him, she folded her arms across her chest. "Take it how you want it."

Dropping the bags, Butta moved toward her and grabbed her face with one hand. He squeezed her cheeks tightly between his thumb and fingers. "You must be really feelin' ya'self coming at me like that, 'cause you know I don't hit bitches. Before you get too comfortable with that notion, you betta know I got somebody to handle my light work." Butta shoved her away by her face.

The thrust caused her to lose her balance and fall to the floor. As Butta picked up the bags, she yelled behind him, "What you gonna do, go get ya girl?"

Ignoring her, Butta left the apartment and went down-stairs. When he got down there, Mannie's truck was double-parked in front of the building. Butta made his way out, "Open the tailgate," he said, pointing toward the rear of the truck. The darkly tinted window rolled halfway down, and a shiny chrome pistol pointed out. There was no time to break and run before the first bullet hit the right side of his abdomen. Butta crumpled forward when the next bullet hit right below his collarbone and came out his back, shattering the door behind him. Three more bullets hit his midsection before he fell face-first onto the concrete.

Trenton hopped out of Mannie's truck and into a white rental Toyota Camry that pulled ahead of him. When the Camry pulled away, as if on cue, Nichelle stepped through the completely shattered door. Pieces of glass crackled beneath her shoes as she moved with caution to avoid falling.

Nichelle politely stepped over Butta's body and grabbed the duffel bags. She struggled with one because the strap was stuck beneath his body. After a hard snatch she retrieved the bag. The weight of the money made the bags tough to carry, so she had to cradle one and drag the other to her car, where she tossed them in the trunk. She never bothered to call 911 and slid into her burgundy Lexus 430. Nichelle gave Butta one last look and smiled, then drove away.

Lying on the sidewalk with his life seeping away, Butta thought back to a conversation he'd had with Sincere. It was when he first came home from prison, before Sincere and Kisa moved back to New York. During the conversation, Sincere had tried to convince Butta to move down to Charlotte. Sincere's attempt proved futile, as Butta told him, "I was born in Harlem. I was raised in Harlem. I'm gon' die in Harlem."

There was no doubt that Butta had meant those words; he just hadn't meant for them to come to fruition so soon.

# *Chapter 11*

"What up, Sin?" Kisa answered her phone.

"This is my fourth time calling you. Where you at?" Sincere questioned frantically.

Kisa heard the urgency in his voice. "I'm uptown. I just dropped Arnessa off at her car. What's wrong?"

"Go back, get her before she pulls off, and then come to St. Luke's."

"What happened?"

"Mannie is dead, and Butta's been shot. He's in critical condition and is in surgery."

"Oh God," Kisa exclaimed. "When?"

"I don't know everything, just get her and get here. You strapped?"

"Yes."

"Kane, you gotta be on point for real, 'cause I don't know what the fuck is going on."

"I got it, Sin, I got it. I'm on the way." She pressed the end button as she turned her Mercedes G wagon back onto the one-way street where she'd left Arnessa only moments earlier. Arnessa's vehicle was still parked in the same spot on the left side of the street. The car that was driving ahead of Kisa pulled alongside Arnessa's SUV. It slowed to a complete stop when Kisa saw a black handgun emerge from the driver's window. She could tell by the size of the hand and wrist that the person holding the gun was female but not much else.

Out of natural reflex Kisa grabbed her Glock .380 from her purse. She threw her car in park and quickly got out of the truck. Just as the unknown female was about to squeeze the trigger, Kisa let off a shot. It hit the rearview mirror, knocking it clean off. The driver was so startled that she dropped her gun and sped off.

"Kane!" Arnessa called out to Kisa from behind. She was standing on the stoop of a gray brick tenement building with Tasha next to her. "Who were you shooting at?"

"Someone I thought was about to shoot you. Where were you?"

"I went upstairs to Tasha's for minute."

"Get in my car. We gotta get to the hospital. Butta's been shot."

Arnessa heard Kisa's words, but they didn't sink in right away. Seconds later they clicked, and she felt as if her world was coming apart. *Don't flip out,* she told herself. "Is he alive?"

"Yes. Sincere said that he's in surgery."

"What happened?"

"I don't know. All I do know is that Butta was shot, and Mannie's dead."

"Mannie's dead?"

"Yes, Nessa, now come on—we have to get there."

Tasha grabbed Arnessa gently by the elbow. "Do you need me to come with you?" she asked with great concern for her friend.

"Yes."

Arnessa was heartbroken once she arrived at the hospital and learned of Butta's life-threatening condition. She sat in the waiting room between Kisa and Tasha with her head buried in her lap, sobbing uncontrollably. Inside, Arnessa ached horribly. She couldn't grasp why so much was happening to her.

Sincere sat across the room; next to him sat Shawn, who was trying to explain what he knew. Shawn blamed himself. "If I had been on point, Mannie wouldn't be dead, and Butta wouldn't be in there shot the fuck up!"

"You don't know that," Sincere said. "If you had been, then you might be dead just like Mannie." Sincere was furious. Mannie was one of his closest friends, and Butta . . . Butta was his brother. Sincere's mother Lena had raised Butta since he was nine years old. "Y'all been playing with this nigga far too long," he told Shawn in a stern but low voice. "The games is over. When I see that nigga, I'ma lay his faggot ass down."

"Fuck," Shawn said, looking at the entrance of the waiting room. Sincere followed Shawn's gaze and saw Nichelle entering the room. They both glanced over in Arnessa's direction; her head was still down.

Sincere leaped from the chair in an effort to get her out of the room before Arnessa caught wind of who she was. Part of Nichelle's purpose for going to the hospital was so Arnessa would find out about her. She knew exactly why Sincere was moving in her direction. To ensure she accomplished her mission, Nichelle kicked her performance into high gear immediately. She dropped to her knees and began to wail loudly, "Where's my Butta? Did they kill my Butta? Somebody please tell me he's okay."

"He's alive, Nichelle," Sincere said as he helped her up.

For a moment Nichelle was stuck. *How the fuck did he survive all them shots.* The other purpose of Nichelle's visit was so that no one would suspect her involvement. She didn't know what to do now, but for the moment she had to play it off. "So my baby's going to be okay?"

Sincere noticed Kisa was standing next to him. *Here we go,* Sincere thought.

Kisa was extremely disgusted by Nichelle. She was one person whom Kisa had never cared for. "You need to raise up outta here with all those theatrics. Butta's *girl, Ar-nes-sa,* is going through enough right now. She don't need to hear ya wack ass up crying over what is not yours."

"Butta's girl? You must be done fell and bumped ya head 'cause I'm Butta's girl, and I been his girl for years," Nichelle said with emphasis. She looked Kisa up and down, trying to contain her envy. Kisa was radiant in a winter-white silk balloon-sleeve blouse, matching wool high-waist trousers, and gray leather boots. Outwardly, Nichelle loathed Kisa. Inwardly, she wanted to be her.

"Just 'cause he stash money at ya crib and you done made some runs for him don't make you his girl. Plus you don't even like dudes, you fuckin' dyke!" Kisa shot back.

Nichelle folded her arms and sneered at Kisa. "You acting like you his bitch, all up in my face with this rah-rah shit. What's the problem? Ole girl can't fight her own battles?"

Before Kisa could respond, Arnessa got up and stepped in front of her. With a tear-soaked face Arnessa told Nichelle, "Obviously, you don't know shit about me, so let me make a few things clear to you, *ma*. Don't ever mistake my sadness or what I'm going through right now for me being a punk, 'cause I'll stomp the fuck outta you in this hospital."

"I doubt that very much," Nichelle spat.

"Well, buck then, bitch, I dare you," Arnessa warned. She wanted Nichelle to try her; at that moment she would've loved nothing more than to unleash her frustrations on Nichelle's face.

"Chill, Nessa, chill," Sincere said, stepping between the two women. "Shawn, walk Nichelle downstairs. I'll be down in a sec."

Reluctantly, Nichelle proceeded to walk out with Shawn.

From the corner of his eye Sincere could see Kisa scowling at him, "Why you telling Arnessa to chill? That whack bitch came up in here being disrespectful. And what are you going downstairs for?"

Sincere pulled Kisa by her arm into the hallway and told her, "Pipe ya lil' red ass down, aight. From what Shawn told me, Butta had a lot of paper stashed in homegirl's crib. For right now I gotta play neutral so I can get Butta's money out of her spot."

Kisa rolled her eyes. "Don't play nothing with that simple bitch, for all y'all know, she probably set him up."

"Kane, let me handle this, aight?"

"Whatever, Sin." Kisa went back into the waiting room and sat next to Arnessa.

"I'm going to get Nessa something to drink," Tasha said to Kisa as she rose from her chair. "Do you want anything?"

"Yeah, can you bring me a ginger ale, please?"

"Sure."

Kisa looked at Arnessa. "You okay, sweetie?"

"To tell you the truth . . . I don't know. So that was Butta's other chick in the flesh, huh?"

"Nichelle is nothing to Butta."

"Come on, Kane, I'm far from naïve."

"Don't do this right now."

"Don't do what? Deny that I'm hurt that she showed up here."

"Fuck Nichelle or any other bitch that might wanna come at you when your dude is down."

"But—"

"But what? Arnessa, I've been here before, okay. Therefore, you can't tell me shit. You been riding with him through the good. It's your duty to ride through the bad, even when people are throwing dirt from all sides. Butta is back there shot up, and if he was locked up, I would be telling you the same thing—fuck all the bullshit. As wifey, you got one job, and that's to hold him down."

"Nichelle, we gotta get that money out ya spot so Butta's connect can be paid." Shawn said as they stood in front of the hospital.

"There's no money in my house. Butta took it," she lied through her teeth.

Sincere walked up. "Butta took what?"

"She's saying Butta got his money already," Shawn commented in a tone of disbelief.

Sincere eyed Nichelle for moment. *Kisa might've been*

*right 'bout Nichelle setting Butta up,* he thought. "Come on, let's go."

"Go where?" Nichelle questioned, afraid that they suspected her involvement.

"To check ya car then ya apartment," Sincere responded.

"You can check whateva you want." Nichelle shot back with confidence, knowing that they wouldn't find the money because she'd already hidden it at a home she'd recently purchased on Long Island. No one, including Butta, knew about the house. "My car is parked up on 116th."

As the trio walked up Amsterdam, they suddenly found themselves under attack as bullets flew at them. Shawn and Sincere both pulled out their guns as they ducked behind an illegally parked cab. Nichelle ducked down and crawled until she was out of the line of fire, then got up and ran.

When Shawn stood up and fired a few shots, he saw the two men who were firing at them but couldn't make out their faces. He ducked back down and yelled over to Sincere, "I don't know these niggas."

Sincere raised up, firing off a few shots. He caught a glimpse of the two but didn't recognize them either. Shawn stood to let off another shot, but was shocked when he saw one of the men aim his gun at the other and shoot him in the head twice.

"Oh shit," Shawn gasped.

"You hit?" Sincere asked.

"No, but dude just shot his boy in the head."

Sincere peeped over the trunk of the taxi and watched as the man took the gun out of the dead man's hand. "What kind of shit is these niggas on?" The man then ran back to the opposite side of the street and got into a waiting burgundy X5. Sincere looked at the female who was driving, "I know that chick," he mumbled, trying to remember where he knew her from.

"Sin cut ya phone off and drop it in the gutta."

"For what?"

"'Cause we gotta be out."

Sincere complied easily, for he knew the drill all too well when it came to being on the run. He wanted badly to call Kisa, but there was no time. With sirens approaching in the distance, they sprinted the two blocks to Shawn's Navigator. Shawn drove straight to a monthly parking garage, where they abandoned the truck for Shawn's dark blue Maxima. It was the 2002 model, but it was in mint condition and reserved for moments like this.

When Eisani and Kennedy arrived at the hospital, they practically ran into the waiting room. Kisa could tell by their faces that something else had happened, "E, what's wrong?"

"You tell me! What the hell popped off outside?"

"How should I know?" Kisa replied. "We been up here all night."

"Well, some dude is outside with his head blown the fuck off, and the jakes is on their radios saying Sincere and Shawn are suspects."

Kisa stood. "Say what? That's impossible, Sin and Shawn was just here." She went to her purse and pulled out her BlackBerry. She dialed Sincere's number and waited for it to ring, but it didn't. Instead, it went straight to his voice mail. She tried his number once more, only to get the same results. Instantly, she became afraid. *This can't be happening now.* Just as much as she was fearful, she was frustrated. They'd just settled into their new brownstone, and Lena was due to arrive the next day with Kai and Christen.

"Mrs. Montega," a male voice spoke.

"Yes," Kisa looked up and saw a detective she was all too familiar with.

His name was Mike Santangelo. Years earlier, he had been one of the officers on Sincere's payroll. Santangelo was accompanied by his new female partner, Detective Sorcosky, a white woman about medium height with a solid build, reddish-blond hair, and green eyes. The moment Sorcosky spotted Kennedy, she zeroed in on her and smiled at the thought of being able to finally send her to prison. "Ms. Sanchez, we meet again. It seems like whenever there's ongoing criminal activity, you're never far away."

A couple of years had passed since Sorcosky, along with twenty federal agents, had burst into Kennedy's album-release party and arrested her and Yatta. The charges were later dismissed, but Kennedy's hatred for Sorcosky was still fresh. "Agent Sorcosky, it has been a while, and you still look . . . worn out." Kennedy smiled. "This must be some serious shit for the FBI to be here."

"I'm not FBI anymore. I'm NYPD. *Homicide*."

"Congratulations on your promotion," Kennedy said sarcastically. "Man, I can only imagine whose life you fucked up to get promoted from Federal Bureau of Investigations up to the New York City Police Department."

Sorcosky would've liked nothing more than to smack the smirk off Kennedy's face. "This must be the rest of your drug-dealing family. The only one missing is your sister Kenyatta."

Kennedy, now eight weeks pregnant, was easily annoyed and feistier than usual. "I see that strap you wear at night still has a hard-on for me." She smiled. "I'm outta here. Something about pigs just makes my skin crawl."

"Mrs. Montega, I need to see you out here, now." Santangelo said with authority. Then he said to Sorcosky, "Let me talk to her alone."

Sorcosky eyed him suspiciously but complied.

When Kisa stepped into the hallway, Santangelo let the formalities go. "Kane, where the fuck is Sincere?"

"Santangelo, you ought to know me better than that. If I knew where my husband was at, I'd die before I'd tell you."

"I'm trying to look out for him."

"Yeah, right." Kisa waved her hand and turned to walk away.

"There's a witness who says she saw Sincere and Shawn execute the guy out there."

She turned around. "Who's the witness?"

With a sly smirk he replied, "Now, *you* ought to know *me* better than that."

Kisa knew that meant the information was going to cost her. "I know you very well, and I know what you like, so holla at me."

"Another detective took her statement before I arrived and took her down to the station. Once I get the information, I'll get back to you."

Kisa entered the waiting room as Butta's doctor was leaving. "What did he say?" she asked Arnessa.

Visibly upset, Arnessa couldn't talk, so Eisani answered. "Butta made it through surgery. He's still in critical condition, and to give his body time to heal, they put him in a medically induced coma."

Kisa squatted down in front of Arnessa and held her hands. "Sweetie, Butta's going to be all right. You gotta be strong."

"I don't know if I can right now."

"Yes, you can, 'cause we got you." She gave Arnessa a hug. "Eisani and I have to leave for a while. I'll be back, but first . . . I have to find my husband."

# Chapter 12

"Y ou will never believe who I ran into at the hospital," Kennedy said as she walked into Yatta's lavish forty-five-hundred-square-foot Manhattan apartment. The place was exquisite, just like the other four homes that Strick and Yatta owned.

"Who?" asked Yatta, floating through her home in a long champagne-colored silk robe with a dry martini in hand, like the millionaire wife that she was. Yatta was very petite, with long, naturally curly hair. She slightly resembled Jada Pinkett.

"That bitch, Agent Sorcosky!"

"Are you serious? What was she doing there?"

"Get this: She's a DT now, for the city."

"How the fuck did that happen?" Yatta asked as they took seats in the family room.

"Hell if I know, but that bitch was poppin' shit and everything, talking about this must be ya drug-dealing family." Kennedy mimicked Sorcosky, "The only one that's missing is your sister."

"No, she didn't."

"Yes, that bitch did."

Yatta chuckled. "Anyway, how's Butta?"

"I didn't even find out 'cause once I ran into Sorcosky, I burned it up. I'm going back over there when I leave here . . . just waiting for the jakes to clear out, which will probably be never, since some dude got merked outside of St. Luke's, and they think Sincere and Shawn did it."

"They got way too much shit going on already since they moved back. Anyway, how are you?"

"I'm okay, always tired. You know how the first couple of months are."

"When are you going to tell Big Ma and Mommy that you're pregnant? I'm getting enough of them calling me, talking 'bout they dreaming of fish and asking me if I'm having a baby."

"I'm going to let them know next month."

"Where's Jordan?"

"Brian took him to a Knicks game."

Yatta sipped her martini. "How's that going with him and Brian?"

"It's going pretty good since we moved back here. Brian's been coming to get him almost every day." Kennedy felt her purse vibrating. She reached in and retrieved her ringing cell phone. She smiled wide when she saw, HUSBAND displayed on the screen. "Hey, baby," she answered.

"What you doing?" Chaz asked.

"Sitting here talking to Yatta."

"Where y'all at?"

"I'm at Yatta's."

"You close—swing by the studio and pick me up. Let's go get some dinner. I know you hungry." He laughed.

"Oh, so you got jokes?" Kennedy could hear Strick in the background. "What did Strick say?"

"He said you need to come in here and lay down some tracks before you get all fat and can't fit inside the booth."

"Tell him I said shut up before I put my sister on him."

"He said bring your sister—she don't run nothin'!"

"I sure will." Kennedy pressed end. "Yatta, put on some clothes. Your husband poppin' big shit."

"Call up there again, you fuckin' flashlight cop," Ria barked at the security guard who sat behind the tall wooden and gold-trimmed desk in the lobby of the building that housed Strick's recording studio.

"Miss, I'm sorry," the young Puerto Rican guard said, "but he said that he will call you later."

"I don't give two shits what he said. You pick that damn phone back up, tell him I said it's very important and that I'm not leaving until he comes down." Ria was sick of Chaz avoiding her. Ever since she confessed that she'd gotten pregnant from when they'd had sex before his wedding, Chaz would barely take her phone calls or speak to her when he picked up their daughters.

The guard picked up the phone to call upstairs once more and told the receptionist, "Could you tell Chaz that his visitor is still here and she refuses to leave until he comes down?"

Once the receptionist relayed the message, Chaz got on the phone. "Son, listen, I don't mean to be rude, but do your job, yo. You security. If she won't leave, put her ass out." He wanted Ria gone before Kennedy arrived, in order to avoid a major confrontation. Chaz knew that Ria was primed for the event. He was surprised that Ria hadn't called Kennedy to tell her about the night that they'd slept together, which she had been threatening to do. Ria had him stressed. The situation was wearing on his nerves daily.

The guard placed the phone back on the hook. He inhaled deeply because he knew what he had to say was not going to go over well. "Miss, he's not coming down. You need to leave now, or I will have to escort you from the premises."

"Escort me from the premises! Muthafucka, I wish you would bring ya faggot ass from around that desk," Ria barked in her nasally voice and heavy Brooklyn accent.

While Ria continued to loudly belittle the young guard, Kennedy and Yatta entered through the automatic revolving door. They were talking and laughing. However, as soon as Kennedy heard Ria's voice, her stomach turned, "This bitch," Kennedy sighed.

"Who is that?" Yatta asked, not recognizing Ria from behind.

"Ria with her dumb self," Kennedy stated with disgust.

"I swear if she say something to you, *I'ma* duff her," Yatta said.

"Please, she don't want it with neither one of us."

They strolled by, totally ignoring Ria as she continued to yell obscenities at the guard. Kennedy simply waved at the guard. He pressed the button without hesitation, allowing them to pass through the turnstile. This further infuriated

Ria, who then turned all her attention and rage toward Kennedy, "I know you see me, you high sididdy whore."

Yatta advanced in Ria's direction with her fist balled, but Kennedy pulled her back. "I got this," Kennedy said. "You must be feeling yaself today, you wack-ass, bum-ass bitch. Do like the man said, get the fuck up outta with that stalker shit."

"You got me twisted," Ria retorted. "I don't have to stalk the man that I already got two children by and one on the way." Ria opened her full-length sable coat, revealing her protruding belly.

Kennedy's eyes locked in on Ria's stomach, "Come again?"

"Oh, you heard me the first time. This one"—Ria pointed at her abdomen—"is his too."

The guard's mouth dropped. Yatta looked at Kennedy, who had a weird look on her face while silently staring at Ria's stomach.

"You're expecting again? Me too." Kennedy smiled. "That's what's up. Congratulations," she said, then proceeded onto the elevator.

Upstairs in the spacious studio, Strick was sitting at the sound board with an up-and-coming producer and an engineer. Chaz stood inside the booth, laying down verses for a new single. A few of the label's artists and staff were sitting around on couches, along with the usual groupies and do boys. When Kennedy breezed into the room, everyone greeted her, but she didn't respond. She opened the door that led to the other side of the glass. "Kennedy," Strick called out, "what are you doing? We're in the middle of a song." He looked back at Yatta, who was standing in the doorway. Yatta shook her head and ran her finger across her throat, as if to say, Just leave it alone.

"Kennedy, I was recording. What's up?" Chaz asked, removing his large headphones. It was hard for him to read her face since it was blank.

Calmly, Kennedy spoke, "I just saw Ria downstairs." She paused to study his reaction. He had no immediate one, so Kennedy continued, "She was more than happy to let me know that she's pregnant."

Chaz didn't utter a word.

"That's not it, though—she says it's *yours.*"

The whole room gasped. They'd heard everything courtesy of the mic, which was on. Strick looked back at Yatta, who was standing in the same spot with her mouth twisted to the side and her arms folded across her chest.

Still quiet, Chaz's eyes shifted around the booth but never landed on Kennedy.

"I need you to look at me, 'cause I'm wondering why you on mute. At this point, you should be saying Ria buggin', she ain't having no baby by me. I haven't fucked her. Instead, you not saying shit!" Kennedy's voice got louder with each word. "Why the fuck is that, Chaz?"

Opting not to tell a lie that would just morph into another lie, Chaz told her, "'Cause. I don't know."

Kennedy let out a slight chuckle, then turned serious. "You don't know what?" She wanted to hear him say it.

"I don't know if it's my baby or not."

Kennedy felt like a grenade had just exploded on her heart. She dropped her head and stared at her feet. Then suddenly she reached up, palmed the microphone that hung from the ceiling, and slammed it into the side of Chaz's head, knocking him off balance. He stumbled to the side. Kennedy jumped on him, hitting with a barrage of hard punches as both fell to the floor.

Strick jumped up, "Everybody out! Now!" he yelled. While everyone ran from the room, Yatta rushed to the booth. Kennedy and Chaz were now on the floor. Kennedy was still hitting him while he tried vigorously to get her under control without hurting her or the baby.

"Kennedy, stop before you hurt the baby," Yatta screamed while trying to catch her sister's flailing arms. Even though Yatta was small, she was strong. She bear-hugged Kennedy from behind and dragged her off of Chaz.

Kennedy kicked him hard in the thigh with the stiletto heel of her boot as she was being pulled away.

"Yo," Chaz screamed, "You wilding now, kicking me with them sharp shits! Calm the fuck down already."

"Fuck, nigga, you better be glad I ain't stab ya nasty ass." Kennedy tried to rush him before he stood all the way up, but she was unable to free herself from Yatta's grasp.

"Kennedy, chill before you hurt the baby," Yatta reiterated.

"Yeah, cut that shit out, you gon' mess around and miscarry," Chaz added.

"And why the fuck would you care? You got another one on the way. You bum-ass dirty-dick-having nigga!"

"I don't even know if that's my baby. She could be lying. Did you think about that?"

"Who cares if it is yours or not? That don't change the facts! You still fucking that slut. I can't believe you broke our vows for her. The same bitch that had my face sliced open. Fuck that—the same bitch that burned you!"

"I didn't break our vows . . . this happened before we got married, when I was tight with you about Brian. That's the only time something happened with me and her since I've been with you."

"You must think I'm stupid now. You been fucking her. I've just been too foolish to see it." Kennedy could feel tears stinging the backs of her eyelids, but she refused to let them out. "You are so whack for doing this shit to me. I've been nothing but loyal to you, and this how you choose to play me?" she screamed loudly. "Having a baby on me with that slut whore of all bitches?"

"Kennedy, listen—"

"For real, for real, I don't wanna hear shit you gotta say no more, my man, 'cause now I don't even see *you*, nigga." Looking over her shoulder, she told Yatta, "You can let me go. I'm done here."

Slowly, Yatta released her. Kennedy snatched her purse from the ground. Her disgust for Chaz was written all over her face, and she made no attempt to hide it as she stormed out of the room.

Chaz knew that to go after her at the moment would be useless. He decided that he'd give her few hours to calm down before going home and trying to rectify the situation.

For hours Kennedy aimlessly drove her black-on-black BMW 645i through the city. The man whom she had vowed to love forever had hurt her in the worst way possible. Kennedy thought that she was reliving a nightmare. She prayed that someone would wake her up.

As the sun crept up over the city, Kennedy made her decision. She knew in heart that she loved him too much to leave him, but she had to make him feel the pain she was feeling. Not by sleeping with another man, because there was no other man she desired. Kennedy wanted only him. Kennedy decided to take away something that he deeply desired, which was to have a baby by her. Chaz wanted nothing more than to have a biological child by Kennedy.

When the abortion clinic opened at nine that morning, Kennedy was there. From the time she walked through the doors her mind was in a thick fog, as if she were detached from herself.

While administering the local anesthesia, the nurse attempted to make small talk with Kennedy. She heard the nurse's voice but couldn't decipher her words; they all sounded like blah blah blah to Kennedy.

Kennedy showed no remorse for the child whom only twenty-four hours prior she had looked forward to birthing and showering with love. She lay emotionless as the doctor vacuumed the fetus from her uterus. The pain, hurt, and anger had completely numbed her. Not only had it numbed her, it had smothered her judgment.

Once the procedure was finished, she remained at the clinic for the required one-hour post-abortion observation.

After the hour was up, Kennedy limped out of the clinic. She went to the Duane Reade on the same block and filled the pain prescription that the doctor had given her.

When Kennedy got into her car, she retrieved her Treo from the glove compartment. She had missed more than eighty calls. All of them were from either Chaz or Yatta, although the majority of them were from Chaz. Knowing that Jordan was secure with her aunt Karen, Kennedy powered the phone off and tossed it onto the backseat.

Kennedy drove straight to the Parker Meridien hotel and got a suite. She took two Vicodin and fell into a deep comatose-like sleep. Kennedy slept all day and night, waking only to take the medication. She woke up the next morning, feeling hazy. A long, piping-hot shower cleared her mind a little. After lying around dozing for most of the day, she made the crucial decision to go home that evening.

Exhausted from searching the city for Kennedy, Chaz lay across the couch watching SportsCenter, one hand stuck down in his pants and the other dangling over the edge of the couch holding the remote. He was just about to reach for his phone to try Kennedy's cell once more when he heard the locks on the front door turning.

Knowing it could only be Kennedy, he sat up promptly. When she strolled through the living room, he asked, "Where you been?"

Totally ignoring him, with her lips pursed and nose in the air, Kennedy walked on toward their bedroom.

*Oh, she trippin' hard, like she didn't hear me.* Chaz jumped up and followed her. "Yo, I know you vexed wit' me, but you still my wife. Answer me when I'm talking to you."

"You can't be serious." Kennedy rolled her eyes.

"I'm dead serious! Where da fuck you been, Kennedy? I mean, you could've at least answered your phone, if just to say, I'm aight, but I'm not fucking with you."

Kennedy stared at him coldly as she undressed but didn't mutter a word.

"So you just gon' ignore me?"

Kennedy remained silent as she pulled out a pair of pajamas from her dresser drawer and slipped them on.

Chaz understood fully where she was coming from, so he said, "I know you're hating me right now . . . but you at least owe me the right to know you're okay, *especially* when you're carrying *our* child."

"If the baby is all you're worried about, then worry no more, my man." Kennedy smirked evilly as she climbed up into the middle of the king-sized bed.

"What you mean by that?"

"It means you don't have to worry 'bout *our* baby anymore, 'cause *our* baby no longer exists."

"No longer exists?" Chaz questioned, confounded by her statement. "What the fuck does that mean, Kennedy?"

"It means I had an abortion, Chaz."

"I know you playing with me." He almost laughed.

"Nah, I ain't playing. I'm dead ass, my man."

Chaz stared at her, stunned. He was frozen in denial. His heart crumbled. "You killed our baby? How the fuck could you do some foul shit like that?"

"How could you do the foul shit that you did?" Kennedy snapped, rolling her neck, "You done lost all rights to question anything I do. Go question your bum-ass baby mother."

"I know this shit with Ria is messed up, and it's hurting you, but you're dead wrong for aborting the baby. Our baby. My baby."

"So the fuck what—I had an abortion. You got another baby on the way with your broke-down loser baby mother. Obviously, you didn't need one by your wife." Kennedy pulled the covers back and stretched out, her back to him.

Chaz stood in silence, looking at her, and anger began to consume his body. He yanked the covers off Kennedy and snatched her out of the bed by her neck, tossing her onto the floor. "Get the fuck out of my bed," he yelled. "Get up out my house, yo. You got me fucked up if you think you gonna stay here and you done killed my seed." Chaz began pulling her clothes from the dresser drawers and throwing them at her. He went into her walk-in closet and began snatching her clothes off the racks.

Kennedy scrambled to her feet. "You want *me* to leave you, fuck-ass nigga?" she shouted, running up on him. Kennedy grabbed her clothes from his hands. "I'm not going nowhere, nigga. My name is on this mortgage too. *You* get the fuck out. You started all this shit. You fucked that dirty whore baby mama of yours and got her pregnant again. So you go be with her and ya ready-made family."

Chaz grabbed Kennedy by the chin with one hand and squeezed her face hard. "This ain't no negotiation, you self-ish-ass mean bitch! Get ya shit and get the fuck up outta here."

Kennedy looked him square in the eyes and told him, "Like I said, I'm not going anywhere. If you want me outta here, you going to have to kill me, then drag my dead body *outta* here."

# Chapter 13

**M**ommy, Mommy, Mommy," Kai said, shaking Kisa as she slept on the couch.

"Yes, Kai, what do you need, baby?" Kisa asked groggily, her eyes closed. It was the first little bit of sleep that she'd gotten in the two days since Butta had been shot. Much hadn't changed. There was still no word from Sincere and Shawn. Frustration was eating away all of her patience.

"I want my daddy now." Kai whined, which she'd been doing since she'd arrived with Lena and Christen the day before. They had come up so that Kisa could get them registered to attend school starting right after the Christmas break.

"Kai, I told you, your daddy had to go out of town on an emergency trip."

"Call him, Mommy."

"I can't. His phone isn't working."

"I don't believe you."

"Go sit down, Kai," Kisa said through clenched teeth.

Kai stomped her tiny feet and yelled out loudly, "No!"

Kisa leaped from the couch and grabbed Kai by the collar of her Dora pajamas, "I don't have no patience for little fresh-ass seven-year-olds right now. Your daddy is not here to protect you from a whipping. So I suggest you do what I say when I say it, or else I'ma get my belt and tear your little behind up! Do you understand me?"

Like her mother, Kai was stubborn, so she didn't respond at first.

"You betta answer me, little girl," Kisa said with a hard scowl on her face.

With tear-filled eyes Kai nodded her head up and down. Kisa released her grip, and Kai scurried away, her long thick pigtails bouncing up and down as she cried for her daddy.

Kisa was about to return to the couch when the intercom rang. *Lord, please don't let this be the jakes again.* The police had trampled through her home the day before in search of Sincere. She was pretty sure that they were still lurking around the block, hoping to catch Sincere slipping.

Kisa pressed the talk button on the intercom, "Who?"

"Eisani."

Relieved to hear that it was her cousin, Kisa buzzed her through the main entrance to the brownstone. Then she hurriedly ran down one flight of stairs to open the front door.

As Eisani stepped inside she asked, "Who's here with you?"

"Just the kids. Lena's at the hospital."

Eisani pulled a small UPS box from her oversized black Gucci bag. "This came to my house for you this morning."

A Virginia address was on the return label. Kisa pulled back the flap on the open box; inside was a Boost prepaid phone. She looked up at Eisani, "You think it's from Sincere?"

"More than likely," Eisani responded as she reached for the doorknob. "Kane, I gotta go see if I can get some more of Butta's money off the street for Arnessa."

"Aight, be safe." Kisa shut the door behind her then plopped down on the first step of the staircase in the foyer. She pulled the phone out and powered it on. *Am I supposed to wait for him to call me*, Kisa wondered. After a few minutes and no call, Kisa clicked on contacts, where a number was displayed with no name. She pressed the talk button and held her breath as the phone rang.

Sincere answered, "Kane?"

When she heard her husband's voice, tears slid from her eyes and she exhaled. "Baby, are you okay?"

"I'm good, ma, what about you?"

"I'm better now that I'm talking to you." She smiled inwardly.

"How's Butta?"

"He's listed as critical but stable. They have him in a medically induced coma. Your mother and Arnessa are at the hospital now. So what happened the other night? The jakes are saying y'all killed dude execution style."

"Baby, we didn't even merk that nigga!" Sincere exclaimed. "His own man laid him out!"

"Well, they have a witness that says otherwise."

"Who is the fucking witness?" Sincere questioned, feeling as if this was only becoming worse by the second.

"I don't know yet. I'm waiting for Santangelo to get back to me with the info."

"Where did you see Santangelo?"

"He came to the hospital. He's on some type of narcotics-homicide task force now."

"There was a girl driving the car that the dude got in. She looked so familiar, but I can't think of where I know her from." Sincere paused, attempting once more to recollect. "Anyway, has Nichelle been back to the hospital?"

"Not at all," Kisa replied. "Ain't nobody seen that bitch since that night; for all we know she could be the witness."

"She might be, but besides all that, she got Butta's paper, and half of it needs to go to his connect. That bitch was tryin' to say Butta had already got his money out, but Shawn told me that's what Butta went there for when he got shot."

"Sin, I told you that bitch was greasy a long time ago. She can be bought too easy, and people like that don't have loyalty to nobody. Only loyalty that chick got is to money. There's no telling how deep she tied into this shit."

Sincere sighed. "You right. Have anybody seen that punk-ass nigga Suef?"

"The streets is still quiet on that nigga. Mannie's funeral Mass is in two days."

"This shit is so fucked up, we can't even be there for my people's funeral. Ma, I'm sorry to put this on you, but I really need you to straighten this out so we can get back."

"Sin, you don't have to be sorry about nothing, and you know I got you." Kisa assured her husband, while simultaneously trying to assure herself that she was ready for this uphill battle. "I already took some paper to your lawyer. You need money?"

"Nah, I got some from the house before we got on the road."

"I figured I knew them stacks looked a little light. It's straight where you laying your head?"

"It's not home, but it'll do. Did Terry come through?"

"Yeah, he's got two guys watching over Butta. He got dudes at both ends of our block, and he's coming over soon so I can take the kids out to Jersey to that fun center place."

"Yo, I forgot the kids was coming up. They been asking for me?"

"Kai is buggin' me for you. Chris is doing the normal wanting to be up under me. With all this going on, I'm not even going to register them for school. I'ma just send them back down with Lena."

"I miss y'all already." His words were doused in pain and regret. "I wanna come home to my family."

Kisa choked back her tears. "We miss you too, sweetie. I'ma take care of everything so you can come back to us. I love you."

"I love you too."

Spending time at the fun center with Kai and Christen took Kisa's mind off of the looming chaos. Kisa cherished her two children. For hours she ran around with them, playing games as if she were a third child.

"I'm beating you, Mommy, I'm beating you." Christen screamed joyfully as he watched his red sports car zoom past Kisa's car on the screen. He had to sit on the edge of the seat just so he could reach the pedals in the race-car booth.

Of course Kisa was letting him win. She loved the way his soft brown eyes lit up when he was happy. With his freshly cropped Caesar, Christen was absolutely gorgeous. Kisa knew that in a matter of years she would be running the girls off of her doorstep. He was such a momma's boy, and he had Kisa wrapped around his tiny little finger.

When GAME OVER displayed across the screen, he said in his cutest voice, "Let's play again, Mommy!"

"No, Chrissy, that was our third time." Kisa slid out the booth and extended her hand to him. "Plus we have to get ready to leave so we can make it to the movies."

He put his hand in hers and hopped down. "Is Daddy going to be at the movie?"

Kisa's heart sank. She wanted to break down, but she kept up a solid front for her kids, "No, sweetie, he won't be there this time, but when he gets back, we'll go again."

"Okay, Mommy," was his only response as he skipped off in the direction of Kai and Big Terry. He was so much more laid back than Kai and easier to deal with. Kai, much like Kisa when she was younger, was a handful.

"You wanna go to the movies in the city or out here?" Terry asked as he steered Kisa's champagne-colored Benz wagon out of the parking lot.

"We're going out here," Kisa said from the backseat. "Go up to the light and make a left."

"I don't need you giving me directions," Terry joked. "I know my way around Jerz."

"Yeah, yeah," Kisa replied, smiling.

Terry was like a protective uncle to her. She loved him like a blood relative. He was a big teddy bear, but his scrap game was serious, and his aim with the burner was official too.

They'd been through a lot together. While Sincere was doing his bid, it was Terry who protected Kisa after she was robbed and beaten during her first pregnancy. He even drove her to the hospital when she went into labor with Kai.

He loved to remind her of that night. "Just like when you called yourself, telling me the quickest way to Harlem Hospital, from Esplanade of all places! And I been in Harlem my entire life." He burst into laughter as if it tickled him just to tell the story. "What killed it, though, is that the hospital is ten blocks straight down Lennox."

"Oh, don't act like that, Terry." Kisa giggled joyously. "I wasn't too sure if you knew anything that night, the way ya big tough ass nearly passed out when you seen that my water had burst all over the carpet."

That fond trip down memory lane came to an abrupt halt when the rear window of the wagon shattered to pieces. *What the fuck?* Kisa thought, while immediately springing into action. She unfastened Kai and Christen's seat belts, tossed both of them to the car floor, and threw herself atop them. She hovered over her children as bullets pummeled the car. The only thing on her mind was protecting her kids from the oncoming bullets.

She was so focused on her children, that at first she couldn't hear Terry repeatedly calling, "Kane! Kane!" He yelled while weaving the car from side to side on the dark two-lane street, trying to avoid the hail of bullets. "Kane, where's ya burner?"

Kisa reached beneath the front passenger's-side seat, where she kept her Ruger SR9. She leaped back onto the backseat with her knees planted firmly and began returning fire rapidly. Unable to get a clear shot on the gunman, who was shooting wildly from the passengers-side window, she aimed for the front of the car. Her bullets ripped through the car's engine with precision.

The next two shots she fired blew out the tires of the gunmen's car. She watched as the car spun out of control then slammed into a tree. Her heart pounded heavily in her chest as she tried to catch her breath.

Before she could even recoup her breath, she felt her own car careening off the road. "Terry!" she screamed out, as her body flung helplessly against the door.

The car came to a sudden halt as it slammed into a ditch. Kisa checked her kids to make sure that they were okay. They were fine but a bit shook up.

"Terry, are you okay? What happened?"

Terry was unresponsive. As Kisa peered closer, she gasped when she saw the gaping hole in the back of his head. "Oh God, he's dead," she muttered. *Don't fall apart now, bitch.*

She looked down at her children. Kai was holding her baby brother tightly while her eyes were transfixed on Kisa in disbelief.

"Kai, listen to Mommy. We're okay, baby."

Her daughter stared at her blankly.

"I need you to stay down here and hold on to your brother. Do not get up until Mommy tells you to. Understand?"

Kai slowly nodded her small head in agreement.

Kisa climbed over the seat. She reached across Terry's wide body and opened the driver's door. With a rush of adrenaline, she pushed Terry's lifeless body from the car.

Kisa slammed the door and threw the car into reverse. She grabbed her handbag from the backseat and retrieved the Boost phone that Sincere had sent her.

As she put the car in drive and sped away, she dialed Eisani's number.

"Hello?"

"E, this Kane. I got instructions, you ready?"

"Give 'em to me, ma," Eisani said, responding to the seriousness in Kisa's tone.

"Call dude from Hunts Point with the wrecker service. Tell him to bring a tarp and meet me at the Hilton by Short Hills. I'll be parked in the back. I need you to go to the hospital and get Lena and bring her to the Hilton, 'cause I gotta put her and my kids on the first flight out of Newark." Kisa inhaled. "Tell Arnessa to make arrangements to get Butta on that medical flight, as we discussed. Make sure that she understands whatever the cost, we got it. E, I need this shit done like twenty minutes ago!"

"Cuzo, I'm on it. Like an hour ago!"

"E," Kisa called before she could hang up.

"Yeah?"

"We need to get Mish up here."

"You sure?" Eisani quizzed.

Sternly, Kisa replied, "E, *call Mish*."

# Chapter 14

I wanna make a toast," Suef said, raising a champagne glass in the air. A ten-carat wide-band platinum bracelet dangled from his wrist, sparkling wildly every time the light hit it. Sitting at the head of a long table, he was dressed dapperly in dark slacks and a matching button-up shirt. Rellie stood immediately to the right of him, wearing a tight mint-colored minidress with camel-colored stiletto pumps. His younger cousin lil' Black stood to the left. "A toast to showing them old clown-ass niggas who really run this city!" Suef boldly shouted. "Manhattan is ours!" The ten men, including Trenton and Abdul, clapped and cheered. At the moment Suef felt like the Nino Brown and Scarface characters whom he'd idolized since childhood.

Rellie watched Suef's act with a blushing grin. Despite how hard she'd tried to fight it, Rellie had fallen for Suef. She broke her number one rule: no falling in love. After some hard thinking, Rellie decided that it just might be time for her to settle down. Who better to do it with than Suef, a man on the come-up, well on his way to being the kingpin.

Over the years she'd amassed a small fortune by robbing drug dealers. So if Suef didn't work out for her, she had her own money to fall back on. Not to mention that if she and Suef went their separate ways, she'd rob him blind.

When he finished addressing his team, Suef slipped his arm around Rellie's waist and whispered in her ear, "My niggas is cool and all, but together . . . me and you, we could take over the world."

"Let's not get ahead of ourselves. We need to first finish what we started," she said with a solemn expression.

"You still trippin'?" Suef questioned. He knew that she was upset because Kisa hadn't been killed.

"I want that bitch dead, Suef."

"You saying that like my people didn't try. Those niggas was two of my best hitters. They both died trying to merk that ho. Stop sweating that shit, 'cause in a minute, Kane, Arnessa, and anybody who wit' 'em gon' be dead."

"How did it go?" Kisa asked Eisani and Arnessa as they entered a downtown apartment that Arnessa and Kisa had recently renovated to place on the market. Instead of selling it, they were now using it to lay low.

"It didn't go," Eisani responded.

"Why? What happened?"

"Juan won't fuck with us. He says we're too hot right now."

Kisa picked up a box of Virginia Slims off the coffee table. She pulled out one of the long skinny cigarettes, lit it, and took a drag. Normally, Kisa regarded cigarette smoking as a filthy habit, but stress now had her smoking a pack a day. She preferred to smoke some good purple, but getting high wasn't an option. There was too much going on, and she needed to be on point at all times.

It seemed like every day a new issue popped up, blindsiding her. The day before one of her credit cards had been declined when she attempted to pay for some toiletries. Then she tried two other cards, to no avail. When she tried her bank card, it was also declined. Given the amount of money she had in her bank account, she knew that there was no reason for her debit card to ever be declined. Kisa literally ran to the nearest Citibank to find out what was going on.

The bank manager studied the computer screen with a nervous expression on her face. "Mrs. Montega, I regret to inform you that your accounts have been frozen."

"Frozen? For what?"

"It looks like a judge issued a warrant. We had no choice but to comply."

She placed a call to her attorney after leaving the bank and found out that the police had her accounts frozen in an attempt to get Sincere to come out of hiding. Things were going to hell with each passing minute, but nothing could deter Kisa. She'd survived much worse situations.

Kisa had already taken a large sum of cash from both her home and office safes. She needed to come up with a plan to make money, thinking that since she'd used her money to pay off Butta's tab with his connect, Juan, in return Juan would front her some cocaine.

Kisa tapped her cigarette against a beautiful black glass ashtray, blew smoke from her nose, and said to Eisani, "I'ma pull some cash together just to buy some from him."

"Kane, he not gonna sell to us either. Juan said you need to chill for a minute, let some of this shit die down. He said you got too much heat on you."

"Who Juan think he is now, Dr. Drug-Dealing Phil? I don't need advice from him. I need work from him. Matter of fact, fuck him. I still got other people I can reach out to." Kisa put her cigarette out. "Have you heard anything on Nichelle yet?"

"Yeah," Eisani replied. "Her dumb ass still right here in New York. She bought a house out on L.I. and copped a new BMW drop. Not only that, she clubbing every night in the city, balling out of control, buying the bar out."

"Nichelle is more of a foolish bitch than I thought. Can you find out where the house is?"

Eisani smiled, "I already know."

"Good, when Mish get here tonight, we gon' get at Nichelle ass and get that paper back. Once we do that, I'll be able to make some real moves."

Later that evening Kisa with Arnessa and Eisani picked Mish up from LaGuardia Airport. From there they headed straight to Long Island in search of Nichelle's home. On the way they devised a plan for getting inside the house. It was a simple plan, but with Mish as an unfamiliar face, they were sure that it would work.

They quickly found Nichelle's two-story home, thanks to the truck's navigation system. Mish approached the house alone and pressed the doorbell. Moments later, Nichelle answered the door, wearing a pair of sweats and a T-shirt, "Yes, can I help you?" she asked Mish.

"I'm already lost, and now my car has conked out on me up the street. Plus the battery is dead on my cell. I just need to use a phone to see if I can get my auntie to pick me up."

Fooled by Mish's exaggerated southern accent and plain clothes, Nichelle offered, "Come on in, you can use my phone."

Little did Nichelle know she had just welcomed a cold-blooded murderess inside of her house. Standing five feet eight inches tall, with a slim frame, copper-colored skin, and natural blond hair, Mish was the definition of an exotic beauty. It was her magnificent looks that helped her in succeeding as a professional hit woman. The majority of her victims were betrayed by her beauty.

"Thank you so much," Mish said, stepping inside. "This is my first trip to New York, and I've heard such terrible things."

Nichelle led Mish to the den area, where a DVD was playing, "It's not that bad at all, especially out here on Long Island. It's quiet. You can have a seat. I gotta run upstairs to get my cordless."

When Nichelle was out of sight, Mish quietly tip-toed around the house, peeking to see if anyone else was there. She hurried back to the couch when she heard Nichelle's approaching footsteps.

"Here you go." Nichelle handed her the phone.

"Thanks." Mish took the phone and dialed an automated customer-service line and pretended to talk to her aunt. She kept her fake conversation brief. She hung up the phone then told Nichelle, "My auntie says she doesn't live far from here. If you don't mind me waiting here for a few minutes, she's going to call your phone back when she gets up the street to my car so I can walk up there to meet her."

"Sure, you can wait here. I'm not doing anything special."

"One more thing, and I promise I won't bother you anymore."

"What is it?"

"Can I please use your bathroom?"

"Yeah, it's back there," Nichelle said, pointing over her shoulder.

Mish stood up with the phone still in her hand and walked behind the couch, where Nichelle was sitting, and headed toward the bathroom. Quietly, she doubled back. Nichelle was so into her movie that she didn't hear her coming. Mish crept up behind Nichelle and slammed the phone into the side of her head, knocking her unconscious. Mish quickly leaped over the couch and began hog-tying Nichelle with some thin wire that she pulled from her pocket.

Once Mish had finished tying Nichelle, she ran upstairs, checking every room to make sure that no one else was there. Mish then placed a call from her own prepaid cell to Kisa's. "K, we're ready."

Moments later Mish opened the front door, allowing Kisa, Eisani, and Arnessa to enter.

"Damn, Mish, you done killed her already?"

"She not dead, just out cold. Watch this." Mish picked up a tall glass of chilled soda off the coffee table and tossed it on Nichelle's face.

Coughing hard, Nichelle regained consciousness. "What tha?" She looked up, shocked to see Kisa, Eisani, and Arnessa standing over her, all three dressed in black and wearing black latex gloves.

Kisa smiled at her, "What's wrong, Nichelle? You look

like you've seen three ghosts. You thought we'd be dead by now, didn't you? Or you didn't think we'd find you all the way out here on Long Island?" Kisa asked sarcastically. "You got to be more careful 'bout who you let in ya house."

"Eat me, bitch." Nichelle growled.

Arnessa lifted her foot and kicked Nichelle hard with her Nike boot, "Shut up, slut!"

The pain Nichelle felt from the kick was horrendous, knocking the breath out of her. That didn't stop Nichelle from poppin' shit once she caught her breath. "What's the matter, Arnessa . . . jealous of Butta's real woman," Nichelle taunted.

Arnessa gave her a swift kick to the chin, "Didn't I say shut up!"

"Hold up, Nessa," Kisa spoke. "I know you wanna get her as bad as I do, but let's handle b-i first." Kisa squatted down in front of Nichelle. "We're just here for Butta's paper and a little info. You can make this go by quickly, or you can drag it out."

"That's my paper, bitch!" Nichelle snapped.

Kisa slapped her with the back of her hand, "Somehow I knew you was gonna be a hard bitch to work with. E, tear this place apart. While you look for the money, we're gonna tear her ass up until you find it."

"That's what it is," Eisani said, leaving the room and heading for upstairs. She knew by how easy they were able to get into Nichelle's home that she was simple. She went to the most logical place first—just where she knew a simple person would hide money—the bedroom closet. After knocking over a few shoe boxes, Eisani located a duffel bag filled with money.

Meanwhile, downstairs, Kisa and Arnessa took turns

wailing punches on Nichelle. Mish looked on. The punches didn't stop Nichelle from running her mouth, though. With a bloodied nose and swollen lip, she jeered at Kisa, "I know why you so mad at me." She coughed. "'Cause Sincere loved the way I sucked on his big dick while Butta hit me from behind. You know, on all those late nights when he was hanging with Butta when y'all first moved back." Nichelle cackled, amused by her own lie. "But what he really loved . . . was the ménages with my girl Shaunta and me."

Sincere's history with women made what Nichelle was saying believable. Nichelle didn't get the rise she expected out of Kisa, who just stared at her blankly. Arnessa, on the other hand, reacted, slamming Nichelle's head against the wooden floor. "Damn, bitch, do you ever shut the fuck up?"

Eisani reentered the room, "I got it," she said, holding the bag. "Let's be out."

Nichelle locked eyes with Kisa, "I'ma see you, bitch."

"I really doubt that." Kisa smirked.

Something in Kisa's face and statement scared Nichelle as she watched everyone leave the room except Mish, who was carefully wiping down anything she had touched prior to putting on gloves. When she finished, she flipped Nichelle onto her stomach.

"What are you doing now?" Nichelle questioned.

Mish didn't respond. Quietly, she pulled a straight razor from her pocket, squatted down over Nichelle's back, pulled the woman's head back, and, with precision, sliced Nichelle's neck wide open.


"What's the total?" Kisa asked Eisani, who had just run the last stack of cash from the duffel bag through the money counter.

"Two hundred seventy-five stacks, mama."

"Two hundred seventy-five thousand? That's all? Shawn said it was supposed to be like six hundred Gs. What the hell did Nichelle bum-ass spend three hundred twenty-five thousand on that quick."

"That car, that house, and all that expensive-ass furniture. Plus I told you, the bitch was balling out of control in the club."

"I got to get some work and flip that immediately." Kisa sighed. "Santangelo wants one hundred stacks for the info on the witness."

"One hundred thou? Are you serious?"

"Yeah, man, he got my back against the wall. He know I'll do anything to get Sin outta this shit. Sin better be glad I'm not no fucked-up bitch, 'cause if I was I would leave his ass out to dry."

"Why would you say something like that?" Eisani asked, eyeing her like she'd lost her mind.

"I forgot you were upstairs when Nichelle basically said she's been fucking Sincere and Butta." Kisa filled Eisani in on exactly what Nichelle had said.

"And you believed her?" Eisani quizzed.

"I don't know."

"Come on, Kane, what you mean you don't know. That bitch said that just to get at you."

"But what if she didn't?" Kisa said, thinking of those nights over the past months when Sincere had stayed out with Butta. Kisa picked up her vibrating Boost phone. "Speak of the devil." She got up, went into the bathroom, then answered the phone, "You gonna live a long time."

"That means you must've been talking about me," Sincere said. "I hope it was good."

"It was what it was," Kisa said cynically.

Sincere picked up on the cynicism and the dryness in her voice. "I don't know what that mean. Anyway, what's going on now? You made any progress?"

"A little, I got that paper from Nichelle. Over half of it wasn't there, of course."

"So what else you gotta do?"

"I'ma try to flip it once or twice, then holla at Santangelo."

"Did Mazzetti say when he'll be able to get the bank accounts unfrozen?"

"He can't. He said the judge's order is airtight. They'll unfreeze them in six months, or if and when they catch you. Whichever happens first."

"What's going on with you? How you holding up?"

"I'm good, yo," Kisa said, voice dripping with attitude.

"Yo, what's really wrong with you? I been peeping ya lil' snotty-ass attitude since we got on the phone."

Kisa tried to hold it in, knowing that it wasn't the time to be arguing over what some broad had said. Although she could hold her own better than most dudes, she was still a female with emotions and sensitive feelings, especially when it came to her husband. "You'll figure it out when you come back and I'm done with you."

"What?" Sincere barked. "What the fuck are you buggin' about now?"

"I'm buggin' about you! Like why the fuck you still can't keep ya dick in your pants?"

"I'm on the run. I'm not fucking nobody! What the hell is wrong with you?"

"You might not be doing nothing right now, but you was fucking Nichelle. She told me all about you, her, and Butta's little sex parties."

"I know you bugged out now. I ain't never in my life touched Nichelle. I'm hanging up, yo, 'cause you sounding real stupid right now."

"You bet not hang up on me—"

"How dare you come to me with that dumb shit when I'm on the run for my life?" Sincere said, cutting Kisa off. "I don't care nothing about what some grimy, money-grubbing bitch said to you. Hoes *been* coming at you. You should be used to it by now. If you not, then man the fuck up, 'cause I don't have the time or patience for no dumb shit right now." He slammed the phone closed, then opened it and cut it off.

Sincere looked at his phone. He contemplated calling her back to smooth the situation out because he understood the immeasurable amount of pressure that she was under. At the same time, he was under more pressure than she was. It was Sincere who was facing possible life in prison for a murder that he didn't commit. His thoughts were, *Fuck her. I'm not catering to that petty shit tonight.*

"Who was you screaming on?" Shawn asked, shutting the door to his bedroom, where he'd been laid up with a chick he'd met the day before.

"Kane." Sincere sighed, shaking his head. "She bugging out 'cause Nichelle said that we was having sex."

"You and Nichelle?" Shawn questioned, his face twisted.

"Yeah, man . . . and Kane listening to her like a dumb ass."

"Did you tell her it was a lie?"

"Of course I did. Then I let her have it for even coming at me like that."

"Did she believe you?"

"I don't know . . . I hung up on her. Man, right now, I don't care what she believes."

"Hello? Hello?" *I know he didn't hang up.* Kisa pressed the send button twice to redial his number. Instead of Sincere's voice, she got his voice mail. After the beep Kisa went bananas, letting all her pent-up frustrations go.

"Nigga, I know you didn't hang up on me 'cause I'm questioning you. I can question you whenever the fuck I feel like it. You must've forgot, but let me remind you right now, I'm all you got. Therefore, when I ask you, fuckin' answer. You probably was fucking her—that's why you was acting so defensive of her at the hospital that night."

Kisa inhaled to catch her breath. "Since you wanna handle me like some little bitch you fuck with, I'ma do everything I have to do to get you home, 'cause you're the father of my children . . . but when you do return, don't expect me to be here for you anymore."

*Chapter 15*

A conservatively dressed Kisa stepped out of the back of a chauffeured Lincoln Town Car in a navy Prada skirt suit and wool trench. "I'll be ready in half an hour," she told the driver, who held the door as she exited the vehicle. Kisa walked up the stone and brick stairs to one of the largest private residential buildings in Manhattan. It took up more than half the block.

Moments after pressing the bell, the butler opened the door. "Good morning, Mrs. Montega. The lady of the house is expecting you. This way." He motioned with his white-gloved hand.

"Thank you." Kisa stepped onto the marble floor of the huge foyer. The inside of the home was decorated beautifully, with million-dollar paintings and antique furniture. Everything in the house epitomized old, long money.

The butler led Kisa into a study, where the walls were lined with first-edition leather-bound books. Kisa handed the butler her coat and took a seat on a beige floral couch.

"Would you like a drink?"

"No, thank you." Kisa smiled.

"Lady Alexandria will be in shortly."

Seconds later, Alexandria, an average-height Caucasian with striking beauty and a mean figure entered the room, followed by one of her six maids. "Kisa, darling, it's been too long," she said in her fake British accent.

Kisa stood up, thinking, *She need to cut it already.*

Alexandria kissed Kisa on each cheek, then hugged her. She stepped back and gave Kisa's suit a once-over. "Prada, very nice. I have two myself."

"It's always a pleasure to see you too, Alexandria."

The pair had once rolled hard together. They'd met years earlier, when Kisa transported coke for Sincere and Alexandria worked for a Colombian drug lord whom Sincere would sometimes cop from. Alexandria went on to marry that drug lord, who was later killed by a rival.

After her husband's death, Alexandria took over his cocaine empire. She amassed hundreds of millions of dollars yearly, all the while pretending to be a young rich British socialite. She shared diplomat status with her parents, which came with certain privileges—the greatest being immunity from US laws.

Kisa studied her one-time friend, who was dressed expensively yet tastefully. She had to admit that Alexandria was refined, trading in her I-wanna-be-down-with-the-uptown-black-chicks look for one of a world-class traveler.

"Sit, sit," Alexandria told Kisa. "We have so much to catch up on. Can Clara get anything for you?"

"No, Alex, I'm okay, I don't have much time," Kisa replied, wanting take care of what she came for.

"That will be all, Clara."

The maid exited the room. As soon as the door closed, Kisa looked Alexandria in her sky-blue eyes, "I understand you gotta keep up your little front, but you need to cut the extra shit out."

"Whatever are you talking about, sweetheart?"

"That right there . . . that dumb-ass accent. Your parents might be from England, but bitch, you straight out of New York."

Alexandria couldn't help but laugh. Then, in her real accent said, "Kisa Kane, you still my homegirl. Ain't nothing changed about you."

"That's the Alex I know." Kisa reached out and exchanged a pound and real hug with Alexandria.

Alex sat back and pushed her perfectly straight blond hair behind her right ear. "I hear you and your people have quite a mess going on uptown."

"It's not one that I can't clean up," Kisa stated confidently.

"How is Butta doing with his sexy self?"

"The doctor said he's pretty much out of the woods. He's been in a medically induced coma since he came out of surgery. With everything going on, we had to get him out of here, before they tried to finish him off."

"Wow. So what's the business? I know this isn't a social call."

"I need some work."

Alex eyed her for a moment. "I thought you were out the game."

"I thought I was too. I'm back due to circumstances beyond my control. But trust me, it's only temporary."

"Temporary, you say," Alex remarked, having heard that many times before. "How much work you need?"

"I need fifty bricks." It rolled off Kisa's tongue effortlessly, as if she were ordering fifty cheeseburgers. "I'm sure I got the money for twenty-five. I need you to toss me the other twenty-five."

"All I have until my next shipment is fifteen. I'll give those to you for two hundred eighty-five K."

"Damn, Alex, I can't get 'em for fifteen stacks a kilo?"

"I can show you some love on the next go-round. I gotta charge you that 'cause the person that's waiting on the same fifteen pays twenty-two K for each. I'm letting you get them 'cause we go back."

Kisa sighed and opened her large Hermès bag. She placed twenty-eight ten-thousand-dollar stacks on the cocktail table. Then she counted off another fifty one-hundred-dollar bills. "That's two hundred eighty-five thousand."

"Where do you want them delivered to?"

Kisa scribbled down an address on a piece of paper and handed it to Alexandria.

Alexandria glanced at the paper. "They'll be there in an hour." She smiled.

*At this point, fifteen is better than nothing,* Kisa thought, riding in the back of the Town Car after leaving Alexandria. If the cocaine was strong, like she knew it would be, she knew just who to call. Kisa scrolled through her contacts until she came to Kennedy's name.

"Yeah, what up?" Kennedy answered.

"Cuzo, what's good wit' you?"

"Nothing," Kennedy dragged, "*at all.*"

"Why you sound like that?"

"I'm going through it right now."

"What's wrong?"

"Chaz is gone."

"Gone where? On tour?"

"Nah, he gone gone."

"Why?"

"He tried to put me out, and you know it wasn't going down like that."

"Like what? Kennedy, you not making any sense. Why did he want to put you out?"

"'Cause I had an abortion."

Kisa was baffled. "You were pregnant?"

"I *was.*"

"So you really had an abortion? Did you fall and bump ya damn head?"

"No, I didn't bump my head. I just gave him what his nasty hand called for. That nigga got his baby mother pregnant."

"Kennedy, I don't care if he got your *sister* pregnant. We don't abort our kids. What the fuck? You going crazy again?" Kisa hated that she'd said the crazy part, seeing how Kennedy's mental issues were a sensitive topic. "My bad, Ken."

"No need to apologize, 'cause I'm straight. Ain't nothing seven thirty about me. I had to show that nigga he's not gonna have his cake and eat it too."

Kisa shook her head. "Do you hear yourself, Kennedy? You sound like you buggin' again." This time Kisa didn't take it back. "Man, I'll talk to you when I see you. I need you to do something for me. I'm coming through to scoop you in ten minutes. Be ready."

Disgust was clearly displayed upon Kisa's face when Kennedy got into the car, her hair pulled back in a ponytail and her eyes shielded by big sunglasses. Beneath her floor-length chinchilla, she was dressed modestly in a brown V-neck sweater, 7 jeans, and brown Gucci sneakers. She saw the way Kisa was looking at her. "Kane, you don't understand."

"Then make me understand."

"Look, Ria stepped to me, informing me of her pregnancy. I asked Chaz about it. I didn't like his answer, so I did what I had to do."

"What exactly did that bum-bitch Ria say?"

Kennedy told Kisa everything that had happened on the evening of the confrontation with Ria. When Kennedy finished, Kisa asked her, "So why didn't you punch Ria in her face for being disrespectful?"

"'Cause she's pregnant."

"I wouldn't give a fuck. That's the problem with pregnant hood rats—they always bumpin' they gums. Thinking 'cause they pregnant can't nobody touch 'em. I will two piece a pregnant chick upside her head with the quickness, and it won't hurt the baby at all. Getting back to you, though, I'ma say this, then leave it alone. Yeah, Chaz was dead wrong for even jayin' her, but you real foul. You crossed the line."

"Yeah, yeah, whatever you say," Kennedy replied, rolling her eyes, then changing the subject. "What you need me to do for you, Kane?"

"You'll see when we get there."

Just as Alexandria promised, the package arrived at the small Upper East Side studio, where Kisa had requested it be sent.

"What's in the box?" Kennedy asked while watching Kisa use a box cutter to open it.

"Fifteen bricks."

"Huh?"

"There are fifteen kilos in here that I need you to put your magic touch on."

"Why do you have it?" Kennedy questioned.

"'Cause I need to flip as much cash as I can in order to take care of a few things. In case you haven't heard, the police froze all of my accounts . . . personal and business."

"Kane, you don't have to go this route. I can give you money until this thing passes."

"Kennedy, you can't give me the type of paper I need to work with. All I need you to do is stretch this coke out for me as far as you can." Kisa looked up from the box and noticed the worried look on Kennedy's face. "I'm only gon' flip the paper a few times, then I'm out."

"That sounds good, but you know as well as I do, you can choose to step back in the game, but you may not have the luxury of choosing how or when you step back out."

Kisa rolled her eyes toward the ceiling, "Look, Kennedy, I don't need you to be my life coach today. I *need* you to cut this coke, so I can get that guap. Either you gonna help me, or you not. I can do it myself, or get somebody else," Kisa bluffed. Kennedy had the meanest whip game. She could take one kilo of top-quality cocaine and turn it into three kilos.

"You already knew before you asked me that I got you. Go to the store and get the stuff so I can get started. You know the ingredients."

"Yeah, I know." Kisa smiled. "They already in the cabinet over the sink."

It had been more than six years since Kennedy had cut cocaine for anyone. She still had the golden touch that plenty of coke dealers used to love and pay for. It took all day, but by late that night Kennedy had turned those fifteen kilos into twenty-five.

Between Eisani, Arnessa, TaTa, and a few of Butta's customers, Kisa smashed those twenty-five kilos in less than forty-eight hours. A few days later she was right back at Alexandria's to re-up for thirty more kilos, and Kennedy was right there to stretch them out. From that point it was business as usual, and much like Kennedy, Kisa hadn't lost her touch either. Kisa was back in the driver's seat controlling the wheel, and it felt good. She adored the power. Chasing cash was an extreme rush for Kisa, and adrenaline pumped through her more rapidly with every dollar that she made.

It had been nearly two weeks since Arnessa watched Butta's medical flight take off, carrying him to Charlotte, North Carolina. She was heartbroken about being away from him, but she knew Lena was with him, so she took comfort in that.

Arnessa was finding it hard to maintain in the face of so many adversities. She was still trying to come to terms with her baby sister going to prison. She was hustling again, and on a level much higher than she had been before. And there was Suef, of course, who was probably still gunning for her. Everything was draining all of her energy and taking over her mental capacity.

Just when Arnessa was at her breaking point, she got a call from Lena informing her that the doctors would soon be ready to bring Butta out of his medically induced coma.

The following day, Arnessa called US Airways to purchase tickets for the next plane to Charlotte for Cenise and herself. If possible, she wanted to be there when Butta opened his eyes.

Cenise had been acting so secretive and sneaky for the past two weeks that there was no way Arnessa could leave her behind. Even though Cenise would've been at the apartment with Kisa and Eisani, Arnessa knew that there was too much going on for them to keep a watchful eye over her.

Arnessa was packing her things in preparation for the trip when she realized the diamond bracelet Butta had given her was missing from her wrist. She searched the room where she slept, to no avail. When she didn't find it there, she headed for Cenise's room.

Arnessa was about to call Cenise's name as she approached her sister's door, but stood back and listened when she heard Cenise talking on the phone.

"If my sister knew I was still talking to you, she'd break my neck," Arnessa heard Cenise say. "I can't keep meeting up with you."

*I know she not talking to that nigga.* Arnessa wanted to bust into the room and yank the phone, but she played it cool and continued to listen.

"Black, I can meet you one last time, but this is it. I can't keep going against my sister for you. When you left me for dead, she had to pick up the tab on my bail and my lawyer and everything."

Arnessa didn't hear Cenise say anything for a few seconds and assumed Black must've been talking. She had already made up her mind that she was going to follow Cenise so she could find out who Black was.

Cenise began speaking again. "Yes, I love you. I wouldn't

be wearing the charge if I didn't. Just meet me uptown at Jimbo's on 145th and Lennox."

Arnessa turned and tiptoed up the hall toward the living room, where Kisa was counting money and Mish was reading a magazine. Arnessa grabbed the keys to the Denali and her coat. Quietly, she told them, "I need y'all to come with me. I'll explain when we get outside."

Without one question, they picked up their coats and followed her out the door. "This little dingbat bitch is going to meet that dude Black," Arnessa told them once they were on the elevator.

"You *lying*," Kisa said.

"No, I'm not, I heard her on the phone talking to the nigga with her stupid self. Apparently, this isn't the first time she done met up with him either. That's okay, 'cause I'ma hop on both they asses, but I'm really gon' put it on her retarded ass."

"No, you not," Kisa informed her.

"Why not?"

"'Cause you gon' fall back and peep what's really going on. Didn't you and Butta say that y'all felt like he might've set her up on purpose?"

"Yeah," Arnessa replied.

"Let's find out who he is first, then maybe we can find out who he down with and go from there."

When the elevator doors opened up to the basement parking garage, Mish told them, "Go ahead in the truck, I'ma take Eisani's bike." She had a feeling that something just might pop off and she would need a quick escape.

Cenise was glad that Arnessa and Kisa left before her. She was getting pretty tired of their questioning her every little

move, like she was eight instead of eighteen. She was cool
with sharing an apartment with them, but she was really
tired of Kisa being up in her mix. Cenise often felt like,
Who died and made Kisa the boss? She just didn't like the
fact that Kisa could detect her bullshit much easier than
Arnessa.

Hurriedly, Cenise slipped into her favorite jeans and
boots. She didn't want to take the chance of their coming
back before she could get out the door. Standing at the mirror, she quickly took out her doobie pins, unwrapped her
hair, and made sure her lip gloss was popping.

Whenever she was in Black's presence, she always felt
the need to look her best, even after he'd shit on her when
she got arrested. It was like he had a hold on her that she
couldn't shake off. She was so green to the game that she
didn't realize how he was manipulating her.

Whenever Black wanted her to do something for him,
he would fuck her real good while spitting wonderful game
to her. Like many females, she confused it all with love.
Sadly, for Cenise, the very person who she thought loved
her was secretly plotting against her.


"What tha hell?" Arnessa questioned aloud, sitting in the
driver's seat of the Denali and watching four guys getting
out of a navy-blue Escalade in front of Jimbo's. She had
a perfect view from where she was parked on the uptown
side of Lenox Avenue.

"You know them?" Kisa asked.

"You don't know who dude is with the mink jacket on?"

Kisa looked at him but still didn't recognize him. She
thought he was doing too much with three platinum chains
around his neck and big iced-out medallions hanging from

each one. The diamond bezel on his watch was huge, noticeable even from across the street. His eyes were covered in the latest Gucci frames, a Yankee cap sat cocked on the right side of his head, and he wore diamond earrings the size of quarters in each ear. "Nah, I don't know him," Kisa replied.

"That's Suef. You don't remember him that night from the club?"

"I didn't really see him that night, everything happened so fast." Kisa looked back in his direction, frowning, "So this clown-ass nigga is Suef? This the nigga causing all the ruckus, looking like a fucking idiot with all that extra shit on."

"Yeah, that's him, and I wanna know why he here."

"Nessa, you know why he here. This shit ain't no coincidence. He the one who set baby girl up. Who them niggas wit' him?"

"The slim one is Trenton—that's who ran up on Cenise that time. Dude in the black is Abdul; you should remember him from the club—he the one you tripped. I don't know him, though," Arnessa said, pointing at the fourth guy.

"Yo, I put money on it dude is Black," Kisa said, noting his very dark complexion, how cute he was, and that he was obviously the youngest of the four.

They watched as the guys stood outside talking, and then Trenton and Abdul got back into the Escalade, leaving the unknown guy and Suef behind. It seemed as if Suef was trying hard to explain something to him. When Suef was done talking, he playfully slap-boxed with the young guy, gave him a pound, and got back in the truck. Arnessa's eyes trailed the truck as it made a right onto 145th. "I hate that muhfucka," she mumbled. "I can't wait for him to get laid down."

"Butta should've have laid his ass down from the door," Kisa insisted, "instead of all that back-and-forth mess over some petty-ass blocks that Butta didn't even need."

Minutes later Cenise came bopping up the opposite side of the street.

"Look at dumb dumb." Arnessa pointed her out to Kisa. "Her damn head so far in the clouds she don't even know what she walking into."

Cenise spotted Black in front of Jimbo's, and her heart sped up as it always did. She thought he was so fly standing there in a baggy pair of Red Monkey jeans and a yellow leather jacket.

"What up mama," Black asked as she approached.

"Nothing." Cenise smiled, smitten.

Black pulled her into his arms, hugging her and kissing her.

"That's definitely Black." Kisa said, nodding her head up and down.

Arnessa's blood boiled with anger as she watched Cenise walk into Jimbo's with Black. "How could she be so stupid? I mean, I know she don't have a clue that this dude is down with Suef, 'cause neither did I. But why would you still be communicating with a nigga who deaded you when you got locked up with his work?"

"She fucked up off of him. You know all in love and shit," Kisa said. "I'm not feeling this, though. We don't know what these niggas is up to. They could be trying to kidnap her. Call Cenise and get her out of there."

Arnessa dialed Cenise's number.

"Hello?" Cenise answered.

"Where you at?"

"In Queens with Nomie," Cenise lied.

*Little lying bitch*, Arnessa thought, becoming more angered by the second. "I need you to come home now."

"Why? We just got here."

"Look, it's an emergency. Some shit done popped off."

"Aight, I'll be there." Cenise sighed, and hung up the phone.

"You'll be where?" Black questioned.

"I gotta go home now."

"Why? You just got here."

"I know, but I gotta go. My sister needs me. She's all I have, you know?" Cenise remarked sarcastically.

"You still on that? Come on, I told you I been taking a lot of L's lately. When I get back on my feet, I'ma give you the bail money back and help with your lawyer. I'ma take care of you while you bidding. Then when you come home, I'll have stacks waiting."

Cenise slid out the booth and got to her feet. "We can discuss all that later; right now I gotta go."

"At least let me give you a ride. My cousin will be back with my truck in a few minutes." Black followed her.

"Nah, I'm good, I'll take a cab."

As they stepped out onto the sidewalk, Black grabbed Cenise by the arm and spun her around. "What's up with you, b? Why you acting like I can't know where you live now and shit?"

Black's behavior was disturbing to Cenise. A sudden sense of danger came over her; she tried to ignore it but couldn't. Cenise yanked her arm away from him. Scrutinizing him with her eyes, she asked, "Why you so pressed to know where I live?" Cenise didn't wait for him to answer and walked to the curb to flag a cab. Immediately, one pulled alongside of her. Cenise opened the door, but before getting in she turned to Black, "We don't need to do this again. You don't owe me anything. I'm straight." She got in and shut the door.

As the car pulled away, Black took out his cell and made a call.

"Wonder who he's calling," Arnessa said, still watching from across the street. "You think they were planning to do something to her?"

"Maybe, but whatever they got planned is about to be ruined." Kisa pressed the PTT button on her phone, "Mish?"

"Yes, mama," Mish replied, sitting on the all-black Kawasaki Z1000 a few cars behind Arnessa and Kisa.

"You see the dude twelve o'clock in the yellow leather."

"I see him."

"Get 'em."

Mish stuck the phone in the pocket of her black leather Vanson jacket. She shot up Lenox and across 145th Street, right past Black, who was on the phone. Her little frame on the magnificent bike with the chrome double piping intrigued him. *Damn, I wonder what she look like under that helmet,* Black thought. He was about to find out as Mish made a U-turn at the end of the block and slowly headed toward him.

Mish stopped in front of Black. His anticipation turned to shock then to fear when she raised her nine. Mish looked directly at him then rapidly squeezed off three shots, hitting him once square in the center of his forehead and twice in the chest.

Bystanders scattered in every direction and took cover

while Black lay on the ground, his eyes wide open. Blood poured profusely from his head, mouth, and chest. His bright yellow jacket was completely covered red with blood. Satisfied that he was dead, Mish made a left at the light, escaping across the 145th Street Bridge.

"What's up, Nessa?" Cenise asked, full of attitude as she stood in the middle of the living room. She had her hand on her hip as Arnessa, Kisa, and Mish entered the apartment. "I've been waiting here for three hours on you. I thought it was such an emergency."

Arnessa didn't say a word. She walked over to her sister and jabbed her twice in the face with her left fist. Cenise didn't know why Arnessa was jumping on her again, but this time she didn't back down. Cenise swung back wildly. Unfortunately, she missed.

"Oh bitch, you fighting back!" Arnessa hit Cenise with a hard right in the mouth, busting her bottom lip open. Cenise lost her footing and fell back onto the couch. Arnessa hopped right atop of her. She pinned Cenise down by the neck with her forearm. "How long have you been meeting that nigga behind my back?"

"I don't know what you're talking about," Cenise panted.

Arnessa slapped her. "I *saw* you with him. Now you answer me, and if you lie, I'm going to stomp you out like a bitch in the street. Have you ever brought him here?"

"No."

"Did he ever drop you off here or anywhere near here?"

"No, you told me not to bring anyone here."

"You better not be lying to me, 'cause your stupid, sucka-for-love ass done put all of us in danger." Arnessa removed her arm from Cenise's neck and stood up.

"What are you talking about?" Cenise questioned, rubbing her neck with one hand and holding her swelling cheek with the other. "Black doesn't want to hurt me. He wants me to move in with him, and he wants to start paying back the money you spent on my bail and the lawyer."

"And your gullible ass believed all that bullshit he was feeding you?"

"Why does it have to be bullshit? You're not the only one that can have someone love you. Black loves me, and you can't stand the thought of that."

"You are such a foolish little girl," Arnessa responded, slightly hurt by Cenise's accusation.

"If you were me and Butta was Black, you would've worn the charge too."

"We could never be in the same situation 'cause Butta wouldn't dare set me up."

"Black didn't set me up. One of his workers snitched."

"And your naïve ass ate that shit up right along with the rest of it. Well, I hope he told you that he runs with Suef."

A perplexed expression came upon Cenise's face. "What are you saying?"

"That you may have been walking into a trap, you idiot, every time you lied and went to meet up with him. You think you know everything, but you don't know shit. Them niggas could've kidnapped you. They could've followed you back here and merked all of us."

Cenise was shocked. She felt numb on the inside. This would be the second time that she had been violated in some way by Suef. Tears crept from the corners of her eyes. A sobbing Cenise dropped her head into her lap. The person who she thought was her first love turned out to be nothing more than part of a scheme to hurt her sister.

\*　　\*　　\*

"I want that gutta bitch and her little sister delivered to me," Suef spoke solemnly to Abdul and Trenton. The expression on his face was like stone. Wearing nothing but a pair of basketball shorts, he sat slumped down in a red leather overstuffed chair. It crushed him to deliver the news to his grandmother that one of his cousins had been murdered. He could still hear her cries to the Lord playing over and over in his head.

Black, known to his family as Rico, was Suef's baby cousin. He looked up to Suef, wanting to be just like him. He constantly pestered Suef to get down with his team. Suef would give Black jobs that kept him out of harm's way, like setting up Cenise. It was the last thing that Suef thought would get his little cousin killed.

"That bitch agreed to meet Rico just so they could kill him." Suef looked at Trenton and Abdul, who were standing before him like soldiers at attention. "I don't care what has to be done or who has to be paid, but I want that low-life, grimy, slut Arnessa and her sniveling rat sister dead. Go, and don't come back without results."

As the pair exited the room, Rellie walked in carrying the glass of Courvoisier that Suef had requested. "You're gonna have to eat something," she said, handing him the glass. "You can't keep consuming liquor without eating. This is like your fifth or six glass."

Suef turned the glass up and gulped it down. "Bring me another one."

"I'm not. You need to pull yourself together. I'm not one those people who are afraid to say I told you so when something goes wrong. I told you that they would figure out that you set that girl up, and yet you continued to toy with them."

"I wasn't toying with them. We were gonna snatch Cenise up and hold her, or at least follow her back to wherever they staying. The little bitch didn't stay but a few minutes. That's how I know she only came to set him up."

"That plan didn't work now, did it?" Rellie snapped.

"What perfect plan do you suggest?"

"I suggest you let me handle it. I'll bring them bitches out of hiding."

Rellie's feistiness was normally a huge turn-on for him, but not in his grief-stricken state. Suef rose from his chair and stood toe to toe with her. He stared down into her eyes for about thirty seconds without speaking. Of course Rellie, who never met a fight that she backed down from, matched his stare. When he finally spoke, he told her, "Since you got all the fucking answers on how to get at these hos . . . you in charge for now. So let's see what the fuck you can do that I can't."

"Fuck putting money on their heads. I'm going to show you how to get immediate results." Rellie turned and left the room. Hurrying out of the front door and then down the stairs, she made it out of the building just in time to catch up to Trenton and Abdul. "Yo," she called out just as they were approaching their truck. "Hold up a minute."

"What is it, Rellie?" Abdul asked.

"Look, we gon' do this shit my way."

Trenton cut her off. "What you mean, your way?" he questioned saltily. He didn't care too much for her anyhow, and he damn sure hated when she gave them orders. To him, she was a money-grubber and Trenton couldn't understand why Suef couldn't see that.

Trenton's dislike for Rellie was proudly reciprocated by her. Being the sociopath she was, she knew how to put all emotions to the side and take care of business. "Look, *Trenton,* I know for your own ignorant reasons, you don't care for me. Not for nothing, I can't stand you either, but I'm out here for Suef."

"Y'all cut that bickering," Abdul said, ready to get into the car and out of the cold, "Rellie, say what you gotta say."

"Suef has agreed to try things my way for a while. So fuck that putting-money-on-their-heads shit. Kane's people gon' be hard to get next to, but go to whoever Arnessa is close to and torture them muhfuckas until they tell you where she is . . . or better yet, kill 'em. That will bring that bitch out." With an evil smirk, Rellie turned walked back toward the building.

Trenton looked at Abdul and said, "Man, I swear that bitch got ice in her veins."

*Chapter 16*

"Oh my God! Who is this?" Kennedy rolled over as she awoke and grabbed the phone off her nightstand. She was extremely tired from being up all night cutting coke. Without looking at the caller ID she answered groggily, "Hello?"

"I know you still not asleep at one in the afternoon."

Kennedy instantly recognized her aunt Karen's voice. "No, Auntie, I was just laying down for a minute."

"Laying down, my ass. I been calling you for the last hour. Get out of that bed and get up here. Your baby needs you."

Kennedy sat straight up. "What happened? Is Jordan okay?"

"He's fine. His feelings are just hurt cause that good-for-nothing daddy of his just stood him up for the third time this week."

"How come you didn't call me the first time he didn't show up?"

"The first two times he called saying he had to take care of some business. He promised Jordan that he would pick him up this morning so that they could spend the whole day together. That nigga hasn't showed up, and he won't answer my calls."

"I'm on my way." Kennedy hung up the phone, furious. She tried calling Brian a few times herself, but of course he didn't answer. After a quick shower Kennedy rushed to her aunt's Bronx home. Jordan had been staying with Karen ever since Kennedy had had the abortion. She needed time to get her head together; besides, she didn't want Jordan to know that she and Chaz were separated. Jordan didn't mind staying with Karen. He actually loved it since her grandkids were always there.

The first thing Kennedy noticed as she approached her aunt's building was Chaz's car. *What is he doing here?* Kennedy parallel parked and got of her car just as Chaz was coming out of the building holding Jordan's hand.

"Mommy!" Jordan yelled, and took off running toward Kennedy. He wrapped his little arms around her, hugging her tightly.

"Hi J," Kennedy said, squeezing him back. "I missed you."

"I missed you too, Mommy."

She pulled out of his embrace and squatted down so that they were face-to-face, "Are you okay, sweetie?"

"Yes, Mommy."

Kennedy noticed that Chaz had Jordan's bag in his hand, "Where are you two going?" she asked Jordan while giving Chaz a cold stare.

"We're going to Auntie Shorty's house. You wanna come too, Mommy?"

"No not this time, sweetie." She smiled.

Chaz opened the back door of his truck. "Come on, Jordan, we gotta go."

Jordan looked back at Chaz. "Okay." He turned back to Kennedy. "Bye, Mommy."

Kennedy hugged him once more. "Bye, baby, I love you."

"I love you too, Mommy," he replied before skipping off to get in the truck. Silently, Chaz buckled Jordan in and closed the door, then proceeded to walk to the other side of the truck.

"So you just going to leave without saying anything to me?" Kennedy questioned. It was the first time that she'd seen him since they'd fought about the abortion three weeks earlier.

"I don't have shit to say to you," he replied, glaring at her callously.

"You betta have something to say to me, and you taking my son."

"Whatever," he replied, blowing her off. Chaz got in his truck and drove off, leaving Kennedy standing there.

Steaming mad, Kennedy stormed inside her aunt's house. Karen was sitting on the couch in a silk floral housedress folding clothes. She was a tall pretty lady, with the most magnificent skin, the same color as raw brown sugar.

"What the hell, Auntie?"

"I know you must've hit your head on the way through the door, cursing at me," Karen said, looking at Kennedy like she'd lost her mind. "You know you not too grown for me to bust your red ass."

"My bad, Auntie, but why did you call Chaz? You knew I was coming."

"I called him when I couldn't get you at first. But why wouldn't I call him?"

"Because, it isn't any of his business."

"Chaz is Jordan's father, so it is his business."

"He's his stepfather," Kennedy corrected.

"No, no, my dear, he's still Jordan's father, regardless of how you feel about him. Jordan would've been just fine if Brian's deadbeat ass never walked into his life. Chaz is always there for him. He calls him every single day, and he's up here to see him every other day. I don't know why you think everybody revolves around how you feel from day to day." Karen stood and picked up a stack of folded clothes.

Kennedy grabbed a stack and followed her aunt into the bedroom. "Look, Auntie." Kennedy paused for a second to choose her words carefully. She knew better than to get slick at the mouth with her aunt, because it would be nothing to Karen to pop Kennedy in the mouth with a hard backhand. "Auntie, all I'm saying is, just let me handle anything regarding my child first."

"You could've handled it first, if you would've answered your phone. I guess you so tired from putting in work with Kisa. Oh, don't look so shocked. I may have left them streets behind long ago, but I still got people out there who keep me posted." Karen placed the clothes in a drawer and walked over to Kennedy, getting up in her face, "Now Kisa is family, and I love her just like you, but you don't need to get caught up in all that stuff she got going on. You made it out, Kennedy. You got a good career. There is no need to get back into all that mess and risk losing everything that you gained."

Kennedy handed Karen the clothes from her arms, "Auntie, I hear you, but it's not even like that. I'm just there to give Kisa support."

"My ass you are! I know she's moving bricks, and I'll bet the house that you stretching them."

Standing there silently, Kennedy didn't confirm nor did she deny the accusation.

"Oh, now all of a sudden you mums a word, so I must be right. I tell you this, all that time you're spending on so-called supporting Kisa . . . you need to be trying to work things out with your husband."

"Auntie, you wouldn't be screaming work it out if you knew what he did."

"Whatever he did must not be all that bad. I don't see you falling over yourself to file divorce papers."

The house phone rang out, halting Kennedy's response.

"Answer that," Karen told her while she continued to place clothes in the drawer.

Kennedy picked up the phone, "Hello?"

"Hey, Karen, this Brian. I was trying hard to get there, but I got tied up with some business."

"No, muhfucka, it's not Karen. This is Kennedy, and didn't I tell your trifling ass from the fuckin' door not to play with my son's feelings?"

"Kennedy, don't start breakin' already, man. I got a lot going on."

"Ain't none of it more important than my son." Kennedy stopped short when she heard a female voice in the background.

"Brian," the voice said, "can you call housekeeping for some extra towels?"

At this point Kennedy was livid. "I know you ain't laid up at a hotel with a bitch."

"If I am? Who the fuck are you to say something?" Brian snapped. He was getting tired of what he deemed as Kennedy's I-rule-the-world attitude. As far as he was concerned, she should've been happy that he even came into Jordan's life.

Kennedy removed the phone from her ear and looked at it in disbelief. *He done lost his mind.* "Let me explain something to you, you fuck-ass nigga. I can say whatever I wanna say when my son's feelings is involved."

"Not to me you can't."

"Yes, the hell I can. Nigga, you ain't nobody. You ain't neva been shit, and you ain't ever gon' be shit, and since you wanna play games with my child then pop shit to me, you won't see him again till I *say so*. When I think he's old enough or mature enough to deal with your bullshit, that's when you can have a relationship with him. I don't care if that means you have to wait until he's in his twenties."

"You can't do that. I can see him when I get ready. That's my son too."

"Watch me," Kennedy spat.

"You ain't said nothing, bitch. I'll take your evil ass to court."

"For what?"

"Custody of my son," Brian said, just to spite her, knowing that custody was the last thing he wanted.

"Go ahead and try, you fuckin' idiot. Your name isn't even on the birth certificate. Remember you wasn't there for his birth, just like you not here now. Trust and believe

Jordan is straight like muhfuckin' nine fifteen cause his real father, Chaz, came through and scooped him. No matter what's going on, he's always there."

Even as foul as Brian had been toward his child by neglecting his fatherly duties for seven years, he hated the thought of another man taking his place in his son's life. He was jealous of the relationship that Jordan had with Chaz. He hated even more when Jordan talked about Chaz in a glorious light. Kennedy's words crawled right beneath his skin and shot anger all through him. "Fuck you and your husband. Fuckin' lame-ass rapper. I'ma take my son just so he don't grow up to be like that herb."

"Any more conversation with you would just be wasted seconds of my life." Kennedy sighed. "Do what you feel you need to do in order to soothe your ego, you fuckin' loser." She slammed the phone down.

"This ho is really trying me," Brian said to himself, steaming mad at the way he felt Kennedy had just disrespected him.

"Who you talking about?" his female companion asked, walking out the bathroom wrapped in a towel.

"My baby mother. She's a dumb fuckin' bitch, yo. Here I am trying to do right by my son, and she stay coming out her mouth fly. That's okay, 'cause I'ma punish her. I'm going to show who the loser is."

*I knew he was gonna go to sleep,* Chaz thought, looking at Jordan through the rearview mirror. A smile came across his face as he remembered how Jordan's face lit up when he'd arrived to pick him up from Karen's house. Chaz absolutely loved Jordan and was highly disappointed by the way Brian was handling him. Chaz was more than upset;

he was so pissed that if he saw Brian, he would duff him on sight. He knew firsthand how it felt to have a deadbeat father, an issue that he still struggled with as an adult. Chaz vowed to himself, regardless of the outcome of his and Kennedy's relationship, he would always be there for Jordan.

Jordan was still sound asleep when Chaz pulled up in front of Shorty's suburban New Jersey home. *I'm not going to wake him*, Chaz thought when he opened the rear passenger door, unbuckled Jordan's seat belt, and picked him up. Carefully, Chaz placed Jordan's head upon his shoulder, then tried to shut the door quietly. The thud of the heavy truck door closing awoke Jordan, "Are we at Shorty's yet?" he asked groggily.

"Yeah, champ, we're here, but you can finish your nap."

"I'm not sleepy anymore."

"Well, you can get down and walk then." Chaz laughed, placing him on the ground. "You are getting to be one heavy little dude. Look at this little tummy," Chaz said, tickling him.

Jordan giggled joyfully while panting, "Stop okay stop."

Chaz gave in to his pleas. "Aight, stand still, let me tie your sneakers.

"Chaz,"

"Yeah," he answered.

"I'm glad you're my dad," Jordan said with the sincerity of an adult, and then he wrapped his small arms around Chaz's neck and squeezed tightly.

Chaz was rendered speechless for a moment by the huge lump in his throat. He swallowed hard as his heart melted and a tear snuck out the corner of his eye. "Jordan, I'm very glad to be your dad," he managed to get out while warding off the tears that wanted to come flooding out.

"Jordan!" Shorty's six-year-old son yelled as he came running out the front door, followed by Tiki and Chastity.

"What's up, Marquis?" Jordan asked, pulling out of his embrace with Chaz and running over to Marquis. The two little boys dapped each other up as if they were grown men while Chaz kept his back to them in an attempt to compose himself.

"I got the new NBA live," Marquis told him, smiling hard.

"Yeah!"

Tiki and Chastity hugged their stepbrother at the same time. "Hey, J," they both sang out, grinning ear to ear.

Marquis pulled Jordan out of their grasp. "Come on, let's go play." They ran off with the girls tagging along behind.

Tiki stopped, then turned around. "Hi, Daddy."

Chaz spun around. "Hey, Tiki baby."

She waved at him, smiling, before catching up with the rest of the kids.

"Slow down," Shorty told them as they ran past her. "What up, lil' bruh." She held her arms open to hug him as he walked through the door.

He squeezed her tight and pecked her on the cheek, "Hey, sis."

"Come on, I was back in the kitchen cooking." Chaz followed Shorty and took a seat at the center island. "So, how are you doing?" Shorty asked, stirring a pot of marinara sauce.

"I'm good," he replied quickly.

"You're talking to me, Chaz. You don't have to front."

"I'm not fronting at all."

"Have you at least talked to Kennedy?"

"No. I saw her when I was picking up Jordan, but I didn't say shit to her."

"And why not?"

"Fuck Kennedy! She shouldn't have did what she did."

"No, you shouldn't have did what you did, nigga," Shorty rolled her eyes. "You hurt her bad."

"She hurt me too; she killed our baby."

"Get over it, Chaz, 'cause honestly, I can't say that I wouldn't have done the same thing if I were in her situation."

"Why, though? Tell me what does aborting a baby resolve."

"It doesn't matter what it resolves. Kennedy wasn't thinking about a resolution. The girl doesn't even believe in abortion. She did that shit out of a broken heart. Finding out that Ria is pregnant, which may very well be a lie, crushed her."

Chaz was confused. "What you mean, it may be a lie?"

*Let it go,* Shorty told herself as she turned her back and reached into the cabinet. "Nothing." She grabbed a box of thin spaghetti and opened it.

"Yo, you can't say shit like that then back down. Now tell me what's up."

Shorty was very hesitant about telling her brother what she knew, or at least what she thought she knew. She broke the bundle of spaghetti in two and dropped it all into a pot of boiling water. Turning to face Chaz, she simply peered at him for a few seconds. "I heard something a couple of weeks ago. At the time I chopped it up to some he said/she said mess."

"What was said?" Chaz interrupted anxiously.

"Lamisha's cousin, Twin, saw Ria at a club out in Vegas. Twin told Lamisha that Ria's stomach was flat as a board. Not only did she not look pregnant, but she was drunk and dropping it like it was hot all night."

"Impossible," Chaz scoffed. "You've seen Ria—you know how big her stomach is."

"Yeah, well, I thought I knew, until I saw her today."

"What happened today?"

"I finished my shopping sooner than I expected, so I dropped by Ria's to pick up the girls an hour and a half early. When I rang the bell, she answered the intercom but didn't buzz me in. Then it took her like five minutes to come down and open the door. When she finally came down, she was sweating, acting nervous, and her stomach looked very lopsided."

"Lopsided?" Chaz frowned.

"Very lopsided," Shorty exclaimed with a raised brow. "She damn near pushed the girls out the house with their bags, then tried to shut the door. I stuck my arm out to keep her from closing it. I was like, Is everything okay? She said yeah, so I started asking her questions about the baby. I asked her did she know if it was a girl or a boy. She said she hadn't had an ultrasound yet."

"Hold up," Chaz cut in. "Ria said she didn't have an ultrasound?"

"That's exactly what she said."

Chaz's suspicions grew immediately. "This is some real live bullshit. Ria text me two or three weeks ago saying she was having a boy."

"Well, I'm telling you that's what she said. By then, she was looking real suspect, 'cause ain't no way she damn near six months and hasn't had an ultrasound. I asked when her due date is again. Her answer was something totally different from what she said in the beginning. She was in such a rush to get me out of there, she didn't even send any of Chastity's asthma medicine."

Quietly, Chaz just stared at the ceiling. With each thought he became angrier. Shaking his head, he looked at his sister. "Ria has done some crazy shit, but she not crazy. I know she not crazy enough to play with me like this," he said, more to himself than to Shorty. Chaz retrieved his cell from his pocket and scrolled down to Ria's name. "Nah," Chaz said, putting the phone away. "I'm going over there." He hopped off the stool and stormed out.

Shorty slammed the long wooden spoon down, splattering red sauce on the stainless steel stove, and chased after her brother. "Chaz, no! You don't need to go over there and start buggin' out." She caught up to him and grabbed his arm just as he reached the door. "Chaz, just wait till Mom gets here in a little bit to stay with the kids, and I'll go with you."

Chaz looked down at Shorty's hand on his arm then up into her eyes. His glare was so serious and cold that she slowly let her hand slide off his arm. Regretfully, she watched as Chaz left. Shorty ran to the kitchen, grabbed the cordless phone, and called her mother, Sal. "Ma, how much longer will it be before you get here?" Shorty questioned before Sal could even say hello.

"Not long. I'm still at the salon, but I'm almost done."

"What is almost?" Shorty demanded, a few decibels below yelling.

"I'm getting combed out. Is something wrong?"

"Yes! So hurry."

"Is it my grandbabies?"

"No, It's Chaz."

Sal held up her hand to signal her stylist to stop combing, "Did something happen to my son?" Sal questioned frantically. "Is he all right?"

"Chaz is fine, but I told him that stuff I heard about Ria not being pregnant. Now he's on the way over to her house. I wanna catch up to him before he does something crazy."

"I'm on the way, baby," Sal snatched the styling cape from around her neck. "I gotta go," she told her stylist, handing her a one-hundred-dollar bill. Sal dashed out of the salon, not bothering to wait for the forty dollars in change.

Shorty paced the kitchen floor, waiting for Sal to arrive. It felt like it was taking an eternity for her to get there. Shorty called everyone from Strick to Chaz's friends and cousins who stayed in Brooklyn. Unable to reach any of them, she resorted to her last option and dialed Kennedy.

"What up, sis?" Kennedy cheerfully answered, always happy to hear from her sister-in-law.

Shorty inhaled deeply, then quickly exhaled her response. "Ken, I know you not feeling Chaz right now, but please, for me, I need you to go to Brooklyn and stop him . . ."

Kennedy's signal on her cell faded for a few seconds. "Can you hear me, Shorty?"

"Yeah."

"Well, I couldn't hear you. My phone was breaking up. What were you saying? Stop Chaz from doing what?"

"I need someone to stop him from hurting Ria."

"You can't be serious, Shorty," Kennedy said fighting back the urge to laugh. "You know there is not much at all that I won't do for you. I'm so done with your brother and his baby mama. I refuse to ever get caught up in their domestic issues, especially when it doesn't involve me."

"It does involve you," Shorty replied.

"How?"

"'Cause the reason you got that abortion might just be a lie."

"What are you talking about?"

Shorty gave Kennedy the brief version of the story as quickly as she could. The more Kennedy listened, the more she cursed herself for killing her child based on Ria's antics. She felt that if Chaz had simply cheated, with time she could've gotten through it; but having a baby on her was something that she just couldn't rationalize. Learning that there was even a remote possibility that Ria was not pregnant infuriated Kennedy. "Say no more, sis," Kennedy told Shorty, "I'll go out there, and if it turns out that gutta bitch did fake this pregnancy . . . your brother is not the one you have to worry about." Kennedy terminated the call and looked over at Eisani, who was driving, "Take me to Brooklyn, E."

"Who?" Ria questioned, pressing the listen button on the intercom.

"It's me, buzz me in." Chaz responded, trying not to sound anxious.

*What the fuck is he doing here,* Ria wondered. Ria knew Shorty suspected something by the way she'd looked at Ria's stomach and asked all those questions. *I know Shorty done said something to Chaz with her hating ass. I can't let this fall apart now. I'm too close.* "I'm busy; besides, the girls aren't here."

Thinking fast, Chaz replied, "I know. Shorty called. She said you forgot to pack Chastity's inhaler."

Ria released the listen button to go and check. All of Chastity's asthma medicine was sitting on the kitchen counter. *He's telling the truth. Maybe Shorty didn't tell him anything,* Ria thought. *I'm still not letting him up, just in case she did.* Ria went back to the intercom. "I'll be down in a second, okay?"

"I need to come up," Chaz responded, "I'm leaving for a six-week tour in two days. I want to give you some money for the girls."

Her greed took over, and she lost focus, just like Chaz knew she would. Any suspicions that she had about him popping up went out the window. Ria pressed the release button, giving him access to the building. As Ria made her way down the hall, she stopped to check her reflection in one of the many mirrors that lined the walls. She made sure her hair was perfect, smoothed her maternity shirt over her bulging belly, then unlocked the door and opened it halfway.

Chaz furiously kicked the door all the way open and rushed through.

"Take that shirt off, right fucking now." Chaz demanded, not bothering to shut the door behind him.

*Oh God, he suspects something,* Ria thought, trying not to panic. "You must be crazy. I'm not taking shit off! Get out!" she screamed, backing up.

"You don't wanna take it off? I'll rip it off." Chaz advanced on her so quickly that she stumbled backward and nearly fell on her bottom. Chaz caught her by the collar of her shirt just before her body hit the floor. With one hand he tore the shirt from her body. His jaw dropped at the sight of the fleshlike, skin-toned pregnancy suit strapped to her body. Chaz stared down at her silently for a few seconds, then abruptly grabbed her by the neck.

"I hate you." He squeezed tightly, applying intense pressure to her throat. Ria squirmed beneath him as she tried unsuccessfully to pry his hands from her neck. "Kennedy killed my baby because of you." He slammed her head against the floor.

"Let me help you with that." Kennedy smiled at an elderly woman who was struggling to get a red shopping cart filled with groceries up the steps of Ria's building. Looking at Kennedy's and Eisani's gorgeous faces, along with their immaculate appearance, she did not feel threatened, as she usually did when approached by younger people.

"Thank you, sweetie," she replied with a smile.

"Go ahead and get the door. We got the cart," Eisani assured her.

The lady unlocked the door, stepped inside, and held it open for the girls. "You girls must be friends of Ria," she commented, since she knew the other two elderly tenants in the three-story walkup.

"We're more like family," Kennedy said with a wink.

"Thank you for your help; my apartment is over here to the right."

"You're welcome," Kennedy rolled the cart over and sat it next to her door. She ran to catch up with Eisani, who was already halfway up the first flight of stairs. As they came upon the second flight, Chaz could be heard angrily yelling obscenities. They rushed through the wide-open door and promptly began trying to get Chaz off Ria. Eisani wrapped her arms around his waist and pulled with all her strength.

Kennedy dropped to her knees next to Chaz. She grabbed his wrist. "Stop it, Chaz! Let go, you're gonna kill her."

Yielding to Kennedy's words, Chaz snapped out of his trance and released Ria. Ria quickly scrambled from beneath Chaz, coughing and gasping for air.

Kennedy glanced over at Ria and saw the pregnancy suit attached to her body, "What the fuck?" she shrieked. *This is a new low,* Kennedy thought, *even for this crazy bitch.* Then it dawned on Kennedy that she had had an abortion based on a lie that Ria perpetrated so callously. Rage engulfed Kennedy's body, causing her to tremble. "Get your trifling ass up," she said to Ria.

Still reeling from getting choked only seconds earlier, Ria did not respond to Kennedy's demand.

"I said, get up," Kennedy screamed. She grabbed Ria by what was left of her shirt, pulled her onto her feet, and threw her against the wall. "Take this shit off." Kennedy ripped the straps of the pregnancy suit from Ria's shoulders. The fake belly and breasts fell to her feet.

Ria shoved Kennedy away, "Get off me, bitch." The last thing Ria was going to allow was someone coming into her home and playing her, especially if that someone was Kennedy Sanchez. Standing in a bright yellow bra and a pair of black 7 maternity jeans, she told Kennedy, "Oh, so you wanna pop off, bitch! Put your hands on me and shit in my house! Well, pop off, bitch. Let's go. I been wanting to drag ya high-yella ass."

"You want to, but you can't. That's why you ain't did shit about it," Kennedy replied, advancing on her.

Ria opened her mouth to spew a quick comeback, but Kennedy stopped her with two hard left jabs. Ria bounced right back with her own left to Kennedy's jaw. It didn't pack the same power as what Kennedy threw out, but then again Ria didn't have the same rage boiling inside.

For the first minute of the fight they matched each other punch for punch. It pained Eisani every time Ria landed a punch. She wanted so bad to jump in, but she also knew that Kennedy didn't want that. Standing next to Eisani, Chaz cheered loudly and boldly against the mother of his daughters. "Beat her ass, K," he yelled, preparing to jump in if Ria began getting the best of Kennedy.

Four minutes into the fight, both girls were exhausted, and it showed in their movements. Kennedy, who seemed to have a little more energy due to her anger-fueled adrenaline, was ready to finish her opponent off. She got her chance when Ria swung at her with a sloppy right. Kennedy ducked, scooped Ria up by her thighs, and slammed her onto the floor. She straddled Ria's body, pinning her to the floor. Kennedy unloaded a flurry of punches directly to Ria's face.

"NYPD!" a middle-aged white officer announced vociferously as he rushed into the apartment, followed by his partner, a younger black female. They bumped past Chaz and Eisani to get to the altercation.

"Break it up," the female officer barked, pulling Kennedy from atop Ria.

The male officer knelt down to check on Ria, her face covered in a mixture of blood, mucus, and tears. "Ma'am, are you okay?"

Disoriented, she nodded yes.

"I need a bus," the officer said into his small shoulder radio. He proceeded to help Ria off the floor and onto the couch.

Standing in the middle of the floor, his partner began assessing the situation. "Who lives here?" she asked.

"I do," Ria replied groggily, holding her rapidly swelling face.

"Do any of them live here?" she asked, with a wave of a hand in the direction of Kennedy, Chaz, and Eisani.

"No."

"Did you invite them?"

"The only person I invited in was my daughter's father. We were arguing, when she"—Ria pointed at Kennedy—"came in and attacked me."

"Would you like to press charges?"

"Yes," Ria replied solemnly, while beaming on the inside.

The officer turned her attention to Kennedy. "You are considered a trespasser on these premises; therefore, I have to place you under arrest for assault and battery."

Kennedy viewed one minute in jail as being in there too long. When her bond was posted a few hours after her arrival, she wasted no time moving quickly to collect her property. After receiving her things, Kennedy was shocked to find Chaz sitting on a bench waiting for her. "What are you doing here?" she asked with a slight frown.

"I bailed you out," Chaz replied, rising from his seat. "That's what I'm doing here."

"Where's Eisani?"

"She said something about going to meet Kane. I told her to go ahead. I can handle getting my wife out of the bing."

Silence.

Neither knew what to say, an incredibly awkward moment for the couple.

"Thanks for bonding me out," Kennedy said, breaking the silence. "I guess I'll see you . . . later." She walked past him toward the exit.

"You want a ride?"

"Nah, I'm straight," she replied over her shoulder.

Chaz caught up to her. "I didn't ask you if were straight."

"My man, I'm good. I still know how to catch a cab."

He grabbed her by the arm, turning her body to face him. "Kill that stubborn shit. It's just a ride."

"The nerve," she said with a smile, "of you to talk about me being stubborn. This afternoon you didn't have a word to say to me. Now you're full of conversation."

"Things change."

"Nah," Kennedy rolled her eyes toward the ceiling to divert any tears that were trying to escape. "Nothing has changed." She snatched her arm from his hand. Kennedy pushed the door, flinging it open. She stepped out, greeted by the flashing lights of the paparazzi. They'd been camped out since the news of her arrest went across the wire. Kennedy covered her face with her hands so the bruises and scratches couldn't be captured. This was the downside of being a celebrity.

"Fuck," Chaz mumbled, stepping out behind her. He pulled his fitted Yankee cap low and wrapped his arm around Kennedy, bringing her in close to him. "Keep your head down," Chaz instructed. "My truck is across the street."

The paparazzi, made up of about ten photographers, two camera operators, and three reporters, surrounded Chaz and Kennedy as they attempted to get to the truck. They were shoving microphones at them and yelling out questions: "Why did you savagely beat the mother of your husband's children?" "Is it true she was pregnant by you, Chaz?" "Was that the reason for the violent beating?" They aggressively blocked Chaz and Kennedy from moving across the street.

Chaz was about to lose what little patience he had and was threatening to swing on anyone in his way when a black Escalade EXT pulled up along side of them. The rear passenger's-side door flew open. Yatta stuck her head out, "Come on, get in," she said, and slid over to make room for them.

Quickly, Kennedy hopped in first, then Chaz, who slammed the door and almost caught a reporter's face. The driver floored the gas, speeding away. "You aight?" Strick asked Kennedy from the front passenger seat.

"Yeah, I'm okay."

"Where do you want to go?"

"Home." She lay back on the seat, wanting it all to be over.

In a low pissed-off voice Yatta asked Kennedy, "Are you bugging the fuck out or what?"

Kennedy lifted her head, "What are you talking about, Yatta?"

"Don't play stupid," Yatta scolded her younger sister. "You know damn well what I'm talking about. That abortion you got."

Inhaling deeply, Kennedy shot Chaz a nasty look.

"Don't look at him; that's not who told me. Mommy told me."

"How could she tell you anything when she didn't know I was pregnant?"

"TaTa, with her big mouth, told her mother, who found it necessary to call down to Charlotte and tell Mommy and Big Ma."

"Oh the fuck. Well, I can't worry about who knows what right now. I'm dealing with too much other shit."

"Yes, you do need to be worried," Yatta snapped, "'cause

Big Ma down there in the hospital, and all she can do is worry about you."

Kennedy could feel her heart stop. "What happened?"

"She's stable. She had a mild heart attack last week."

"Last week!" Kennedy yelped. "And not one person thought to call me. I saw Aunt Karen today, and I know she knows."

"Big Ma didn't want anyone to tell you."

"Why?"

"You should know. The usual reason—she didn't want her little sweet Kennedy worrying, especially while she's going through so much," she mimicked.

Ignoring the blatant sarcasm from her sister, Kennedy asked, "Is she okay?"

"While I was down there the doctor said she recovered good, considering her age and heart condition."

"You went down there?" Kennedy shook her head, "Man, I can't believe you didn't tell me."

"I can't believe you aborted your baby."

"Fuck that abortion," Kennedy spazzed. "I'm sick of hearing about that damn abortion. It's over with, and I can't take it back. If you choose to keep talking about it, y'all might as well pull over and let me out, 'cause I'm done."

Quietly, Yatta peered at her baby sister for a few seconds. She knew Kennedy's world was spinning out of control. "I'ma let it go for now. But," Yatta warned, "we will talk later. Believe that."

Other than Strick's constant business calls, the truck was virtually silent for the remainder of the ride. When they arrived in front of Kennedy's building, she mumbled, "Thanks for the ride," climbed out, and exited the truck.

"Be easy, y'all," Chaz said, getting out on the opposite side. He followed Kennedy into the building. His plan had been to ride the elevator down to the garage and get one of his cars, but he changed his mind and asked Kennedy, "Is it aight if I come up?"

"I guess, your name is still on the mortgage," she replied, stepping onto the elevator.

It had been over four weeks since Chaz had been inside the lavish apartment. Once the door opened and he smelled the aroma of the baked apple candles that Kennedy burned daily, he realized how much he'd missed his home. That wasn't the only thing he missed. Although he was still very bitter about the abortion, he wanted to patch things up with Kennedy.

Kennedy dropped her things on the console table in the hall. She went into the kitchen, where she grabbed a bottle of water along with her favorite prescription sleeping pills, then headed for her bedroom.

"Ken," Chaz called out to her, "I came up 'cause I wanted to talk to you."

Kennedy inhaled deeply before turning around and going into the living room. She sat on the arm of the couch. "What's up?" she asked nonchalantly.

"I wanted to talk about where we stand with each other, since things have changed."

"Chaz, you just don't get it, do you?"

"Get what?" he questioned, puzzled.

"Nothing has changed. The only thing that happened today was Ria proving herself to be more psychotic than we thought; by taking lying to another level, this time about a pregnancy. That doesn't change the fact that you fucked her. It definitely does not change the fact that you hurt me in ways that you will never know. You betrayed me, Chaz. You've destroyed our boundaries."

"I'm sorry I hurt you, Kennedy, but it didn't happen the way you think."

"You don't know anything about the way I think! If you did, you'd know I don't give a fuck how it happened, or why it happened, and I'm beginning not to give a fuck about you."

Chaz knew by the iciness of her words that Kennedy had put the wall back around her heart—the wall that had taken him so long to penetrate. He knew that he could very well be on the verge of losing her, and that wasn't an option. Chaz walked over to her. "I know what I did was beyond foul." He cupped her face in his hands. "I'm so sorry for hurting you. That's something you never have to worry about again."

Kennedy stared downward quietly. She longed to believe him, but she couldn't trust his word, and she didn't know when she would be able to again.

"Look at me," he told her.

She raised her eyes to him.

"You know I love you. I want to come home so we can get through this." He leaned in to kiss her, and she turned her head.

Kennedy removed his hands from her face. Looking him directly in the eye, she spoke, "I love you, too. That will never change, but I can't let you back in. The best thing for us right now is to remain separated."

The next day Kennedy took the first flight to Charlotte. She didn't even bother to pack a bag. Upon landing, she rented a car and drove straight to Carolinas Medical Center, where she found out that Big Ma had been released earlier in the morning. Kennedy made her way over to Big Ma's, not far from the hospital.

Kennedy saw her mother, Kora, and her aunts Klarice and Janice on the porch drinking coffee. They all stared curiously at the unfamiliar car. When Kennedy got out, all were pleasantly surprised to see who it was. Kora came down from the porch, meeting her daughter on the walkway, "Hey, baby girl," she said gleefully.

"Un-uh, don't 'hey, baby girl' me."

"What's got your panties all twisted?"

"All of you people who didn't call me to tell me Big Ma had a heart attack."

"We only did what Big Ma asked. She felt like you was going through enough."

"Oh, so now all of sudden y'all wanna start listening to Big Ma," Kennedy snapped.

"Wait a minute, lil' girl." Kora waved her finger. "I'm still your mother, and I will still whip your big behind."

Kennedy rolled her eyes upward. "Okay, Ma, but you have to understand where I'm coming from. What if Big Ma's health had taken a turn for the worse and I hadn't gotten here in time to see her. I would have been so pissed."

Kora hugged Kennedy, "I do understand, and I'm happy that you here so we can talk. Because as soon as Big Ma got a little better, I had plans to come up to see about all this mess you got going on."

"I don't have no mess going on, Ma, despite what others may be saying. I got a few issues like just like everybody else that I'm dealing with fine all by myself." Kennedy greeted both her aunts with hugs and kisses then went in the house.

Like every home, Big Ma's house had its very own unique aroma. It was mix of collard greens, pound cake, and fresh flowers. Kennedy inhaled the lovely smell deeply, then rushed through the antiques-filled living room and into her grandmother's bedroom in the rear of the house. Big Ma was lying on her back sleeping peacefully. Kennedy thought she looked dead.

Standing over her beloved grandmother, Kennedy began to cry. She covered her mouth to keep her sobs from escaping. Big Ma was bigger than life in Kennedy's eyes. She could not imagine life without her.

"Get from over me, crying girl." Big Ma opened her eyes. "I ain't dead yet."

"Big Ma," Kennedy said, hugging her tightly. "How are you feeling?"

"I feel fine for an old woman. What are you doing here?"

"I came to see about you, lady."

"Well, there ain't much to see. There is nothing wrong with me but my heart, been beating for eighty-five years. It's bound to act up sometimes."

Kennedy took a seat on the edge of the bed. "You know I'm mad at you."

"For what?"

"Because you tried to keep your heart attack a secret from me."

"Girl, hush. I did what was best for you. I didn't want you getting all riled up. You got enough on your plate."

"Big Ma, my plate is just fine. I had some issues, but I've gotten past them."

Kennedy was Big Ma's favorite grandchild, which was no secret; she saw so much of herself in Kennedy. Big Ma placed a hand on Kennedy's knee. "You can't lie to me. I know that you're not all right. You went against what you believed and aborted your child. Baby, when I heard that, I was so hurt for you."

"I didn't have an abortion just to have it." Tears glazed Kennedy's eyes. "Chaz broke my heart."

"Yeah, I heard about that too, but it doesn't condone what you did. God had a plan for that child, and you ruined his plans." Big Ma coughed. "Hand me my water."

Kennedy picked up the glass from the nightstand and gave it to her.

Big Ma took a few sips, then continued. "Everybody round here talking about that stuff Kisa got going on, and you knee deep in the middle. All of you girls need to let them streets go. I'm telling you, I got a feeling that this is going to end bad this time. You girls are going to see death, prison, or both. Listen to what I'm saying, baby. You need to get with your husband, resolve this thing, and save your family."

"How can I go back to him when I can't forgive?"

"You still love him?"

"Yes, I love him . . . that's why it hurts so bad."

"Forgiveness is hard, especially when the person you love hurts you. The thing that you must keep in mind is that love is forgiveness."

Kennedy didn't doubt her grandmother's wisdom for one second, but she didn't know if she could follow the advice that Big Ma was handing down. The pain was just too great. "You know, Big Ma, the craziest thing is that she was never pregnant. She faked the whole thing, but I still can't get past the betrayal."

"I'm about to tell you something that I've never told any of my children. I expect you to treat this person the same and take what I tell you to the grave. Can you promise me that?"

"Yes," Kennedy responded, curious as to what she was about to be told.

"Your aunt Janice is not my biological child. But your grandfather, God rest his soul, *was* her biological father."

Kennedy gasped loudly and her mouth fell wide open. She was astounded, but so many things suddenly made sense. Now Kennedy understood why Janice was the odd child. All the children looked like a blend of Big Ma and their father, but Janice favored only him. Then there was her name: It started with a *J*, and the other girls' names started with a *K*. Kennedy always thought Big Ma couldn't come up with a *K* name for her. "So, so," Kennedy stuttered, "how did you end up raising her and keeping it a secret all these years?"

"Close my door."

Kennedy leaped up, shut the door, and rushed back to her grandmother's side. "Okay, finish."

"When Janice's real mother died, Janice was still a small baby. That's when I found out about her. Your grandfather could have let her go to the orphanage or a foster home, because the woman he'd had the affair with had no family. He made a courageous choice and faced me with the truth. I was hurt, Lord knows I was hurt, but I couldn't let that beautiful brown baby go to one of those god-awful places. So I took her in as my own and loved her as if I gave birth to her. It took a long time, but eventually I forgave your grandfather."

"How were you able to keep this from you own children?" Kennedy asked, baffled.

"At the time James Jr. was three, Karen was two, and

your mother was one. In their little minds it appeared that I had another baby. Your grandfather had a cousin that worked in vital records. We had him list me on the birth certificate as her mother."

"Wow," Kennedy said, amazed that a secret of such magnitude existed in her family.

"Now, I only shared that with you to show that you can get past the hurt, the pain, and be in love with your husband again."

Kennedy lowered her eyes, "Big Ma, I'm not as strong as you are."

"That's a lie," Big Ma countered. "You are just as strong if not stronger than I was at your age. Look at all of the obstacles that you've already overcome."

"We'll see, Big Ma," Kennedy sighed. "Enough about my never-ending issues. I came to take care of you for as long as you need me."

Giving Kennedy a stern look, Big Ma said, "I got plenty of people here to look after me. You know I love having you here, but two or three days is the longest that you need to stay. After that you need to get back to New York and work on your family."

*Chapter 17*

**B**utterflies danced around in Arnessa's stomach as she rode the elevator up to the eighth floor of Presbyterian Hospital in Charlotte, North Carolina. She couldn't understand why she was feeling so nervous about seeing Butta. Maybe her nervousness came from not knowing what to expect. When she got off the elevator, it wasn't hard to tell which room was Butta's; two private security guards dressed all in black flanked it.

Arnessa strolled down the hall with a large gift basket of Butta's favorite goodies in one hand and a large bouquet of get-well balloons in the other. When she got to the door, she opened it slightly and stuck her head in.

"Quit peeping," Butta said, "come on in."

Pushing the door wide open, she was amazed to see him sitting up in bed watching TV and eating applesauce. Although frail and gaunt, he looked nothing like the horrible images that had been dancing around in her head. His normally low-cut hair was now a plethora of sandy brown curls. "Butta!" Arnessa smiled brightly. She placed the basket in a chair, released the balloons, rushed over to his bed, and kissed him. Butta placed his arms around Arnessa and squeezed her tightly and returned her kiss. He inhaled her scent while running his fingers through her hair. She felt so good in his arms, he didn't want to let her go. "I'm so glad you came," Butta said into her ear.

"Did you think I wasn't?"

"I wasn't sure, since you were supposed to be here three days ago."

"And I would've been here, but of course I had to deal with some of Cenise's nonstop drama."

"Where is Cenise at, anyway?"

"At Lena's."

"Well, like I said, I'm glad you're here but . . ."

"But what?"

"What are you wearing?" he asked, frowning at the formfitting sky-blue Juicy jogging suit that she wore.

"What's wrong with this?" She gestured from her chest to her hips.

"It's nice and all." Butta smirked. "I was just hoping to see something short and sexy."

"And what could you do with something short or sexy with all those IV tubes stuck in you?"

"A whole lot." He winked.

Arnessa sat on the edge of the bed. She took Butta's hand. "I sure have missed you. I was so scared for you that night. I thought . . . I thought you were going to . . ." She stopped talking as tears filled her eyes.

Butta squeezed her hand, "It's okay, 'cause I didn't . . . I didn't die."

"Thank God." She smiled, wiping the tears from her face.

"I got to speak to Sincere for few minutes. I heard shit is real thick in the city."

"That's one way to describe it"—Arnessa sighed—"but insane is more like it."

Arnessa spent the next hour filling Butta in on all the events that had transpired since his shooting. He was angered but deeply saddened by what he heard. "That's too much shit poppin' off," Butta responded once she finished. "I don't want you to go back."

"I have to. I can't leave Kane and them to fight *my* battle."

"Trust me, they can handle it. Besides, I need you here with me."

"Butta, that's not fair to them at all. No one would be in this mess with Suef if it weren't for me."

"You're the reason I held on. I can't lose to this bullshit. Not now." He yawned, feeling the effects of his codeine drip. If anything were to happen to you, I would go straight seven. You're my heart. I love you."

"I love you too." She lifted his hand and kissed it. She noticed that he was struggling to keep his eyes open. "You need to get some rest now. Go ahead and sleep. I'll be here when you wake up, I promise."

"Promise me you'll be here every time I wake up."

"I promise."

\*      \*      \*

A week later the hospital released Butta. From that point on, Arnessa cared for him daily with a little assistance from Lena and Kisa's family. Arnessa rented a condo in the city's trendy South End section, and once she learned her way around, she did pretty much everything for him alone. Besides cooking, cleaning, and administering medication, she made sure that Butta got to his doctor's appointments, physical rehab, and therapy appointments. Arnessa was happy that she had chosen to adhere to Butta's wishes and remain in Charlotte.

At times, caring for Butta was strenuous, but there was nothing else Arnessa would have rather been doing. She was away from the drama in New York, and the bond between Butta and her became stronger. Their love flourished, growing to heights that neither ever perceived possible. Although an exciting time for their relationship, it quickly became bittersweet for Arnessa.

About her third week there, she received an unnerving call from Cenise's attorney, Mr. King. He called to inform her that he had reached an agreement with the solicitor's office. Cenise would do one year in prison, six months on house arrest, followed by two years of probation. It was a very generous sentence, considering her offense and the state in which it took place. The downside was that Cenise had less than a week to turn herself in. Arnessa was under the assumption that Cenise had at least another four months before she would have to go to prison.

*Why not me, God?* Arnessa thought, standing in the doorway of Cenise's bedroom and watching her blow-dry her hair. Inside, Arnessa was plagued with guilt and anger. She was so upset with herself for not protecting Cenise from the game and for the way she had treated Cenise in the previous months, Arnessa had been having a hard time eating and sleeping. On the other hand, Cenise was eating like a savage and sleeping like a baby. It was hard for Arnessa to understand.

Cenise caught a glimpse of Arnessa's reflection in the mirror. She shut the dryer off and turned around, "What's up, Ness? You need something?"

"No, I was just checking on you. I just wanted to make sure you were okay." Arnessa replied, wearing her worries on her face.

Cenise placed the dryer down on the dresser. She sat on the foot of the bed and motioned for Arnessa to have a seat by patting the space to her left. "I think it's time for us to talk," she said.

Arnessa obliged. Before she could get the first word out, her eyes were already tearing. "Neesie, I know that this last year has been real hard on you"—the tears began to trickle down her cheeks—"and, um, I haven't made it easy at all. I am so sorry for letting this happen to you."

Cenise blinked to ward off the tears that burned the back of her eyes. "No Ness, I would be wrong to let you take the blame for my situation. When all you ever did was try to keep me out of trouble. Too bad my hard head kept me from seeing that." She chuckled softly. "I guess hindsight is everything."

Arnessa's heart sank: Her baby sister finally got it, but she was hurt that it took going to prison for Cenise to come to this realization. "You know, if I could switch places with you I would go do your time."

"I know you would, but I'm okay with this. I'm ready to go in and get it over."

"How can you be so calm, knowing you're going to prison tomorrow?"

"Not knowing how much time I was going to get was the worst part. Now that I know, I'm okay. Plus Yatta's call the other day really helped too."

"Kennedy's sister?" Arnessa asked.

"Yeah."

"What did y'all talk about?"

"She told me what prison was like for her, what to expect, and how I should carry myself."

Arnessa rubbed the side of Cenise's face, "You have to be careful in there. I need you to come back to me . . . you're all I got."

"You've got Butta too."

"It's not the same, though. I mean, Butta and me, yes, we love each other, and we may be together for a long time, but you are my *blood*. Although you may have singlehandedly destroyed my nerves, you are the love of my life."

"I love you, Arnessa."

"I love you too. I promise, anything you need, you better call me. I don't care what it is." Arnessa pulled Cenise in, hugging her tight. "I promise you, I will be there for every visit. We're gonna get through this . . . together."

Sitting in a small coffee shop in New Haven, Connecticut, Kisa stared blankly out the window at the heavy falling snow. *Where the hell is Santangelo?* Kisa wondered, looking down at her stunning Audemars Piguet diamond watch. Every time she looked at it she thought of Sincere. It was the last gift she'd received from him. It had been almost three months since Sincere and Shawn went on the run. Kisa genuinely hoped that this talking to Santangelo would start the process of bringing them home. She had so much on her mind, particularly on this day, when her thoughts were with Cenise. Kisa felt so bad for her and hated the way that Cenise had been blindsided by the game, courtesy of a no-good nigga. Yes, she knew that Cenise had a strong tendency to be a know-it-all, but what teenage girl didn't? It seemed like Arnessa and Cenise had been dealt one bad hand after another. That's why Kisa was partial to them. Kisa promised herself that, once she made it through all the current havoc in her own life, she would continue to be a support system for them. Even more for Cenise once she got out of prison.

*Where the hell is Santangelo?*

Detective Santangelo was more than thirty minutes late. Meeting in Connecticut and driving an hour and a half out of the city during a blizzard was a precaution they had to take to ensure they would not be seen together. Kisa was ready to get back on the road before the weather got worse. Forecasters were calling for the biggest snowstorm to hit the Northeast in five years. Soon the roads would be covered in snow, making driving next to impossible. Like most northerners, Kisa could drive through snowy conditions, though she preferred not to.

"Would you like another macchiato?" The waitress asked Kisa.

"Yes please, and can I get an extra shot of espresso?"

"Let me get a cappuccino to go," Santangelo said, walking up behind the waitress and sitting across from Kisa.

"Anything else?"

"No, but you can make mine to go, too," Kisa replied, then turned her attention to Santangelo. "Where did you magically appear from?"

"The back office—my friend owns this place. That's why I chose it."

"You mean to tell me you've been back there the entire time I've been waiting?"

"Fuck no, you think I would make you wait?"

"Whatever, the money is in the envelope inside that *Daily News*." Kisa nodded toward the newspaper on the other side of the table.

Santangelo pulled a folded paper from his jacket pocket and slid it across the table. Kisa opened it. She studied the photocopy of the New York State driver's license. The young woman in the picture seemed vaguely familiar to her. "I swear I know her from somewhere."

"You probably know her from St. Luke's. She's a nurse."

Suddenly, it hit Kisa, and she remembered seeing the woman the night of the shooting talking to a detective at the hospital. Kisa folded the paper back and slipped it into her purse.

"How are Sin and Shawn?" Santangelo questioned, with a cunning smile.

"As if you care." Kisa rolled her eyes as she slipped on her whiskey-colored hooded swing mink.

"I do care."

"Yeah, about the money you can make off of them," she snapped. "Anyway, good looking out on this. I know you had to go through a lot to get it."

"Before you go," Santangelo paused while the waitress placed their drinks on the table. Kisa handed her thirty dollars.

"I'll be back with your change."

"I don't need any."

"Thanks," the waitress said. She walked away smiling, happy for the ten-dollar tip on such a slow day.

Once she was out of earshot, Santangelo resumed talking, "A lot of bodies are popping up—bodies that can be linked directly or indirectly to you or your people."

"And you're saying that to say what?"

"Bodies bring heat, and the last thing you need right now is Homicide sniffing around your door. A word to the wise: Be careful."

Kisa stood up, threw the oversized hood onto her head, and smiled at him. "Detective, I'm a big girl. I got this."

TaTa's short French-manicured nails tapped nervously against the table inside the cramped interrogation room. At times, she had to plant her feet firmly on the floor in order to keep her legs from shaking. TaTa could barely contain herself as she waited for the assistant district attorney to arrive. She had been anticipating this day for the last seven months. The day that her deal would be finalized and her obligation to New York's finest would finally be over. With the stroke of a pen, TaTa's career as a confidential informant would be over. Her sentence was reduced to probation. A sweet deal after setting up at least a dozen people. Today she would be able to move on with her life. She would receive probation for a hand-to-hand sale of fifteen ounces of coke to an undercover officer and move on with her life. Never mind the dozen or so people whom she set up to get such a sweet deal.

When TaTa heard someone about to enter, she sat up attentively and tucked the right side of her chin-length bob behind her ear. The door opened, and in walked Montera Robbins, the detective who had arrested TaTa. She was hard-nosed, with a chip on her shoulder and something to prove. The daughter of a crack addict, she knew firsthand the devastation of drugs. Montera's mother had overdosed and died the day before Montera's high school graduation. That's was all the fuel she needed to enroll in the police academy. In honor of her mother, Montera dedicated her career to locking up drug dealers. She vowed to lock up as many as she could, by whatever means necessary.

TaTa didn't recognize the red-haired lady who came into the room, but she knew she wasn't the ADA she had met months back. "Where is Miss Hanson?" she asked Detective Robbins.

"She won't be joining us today. This is Detective Sorcosky."

"Why didn't Miss Hanson come?"

"Well, she's not ready to sign off on your deal yet."

"What? Why not?" TaTa questioned furiously, tears filling her eyes. "I've done everything that was asked of me. I've set up close to thirteen dangerous people for you. Men and women who, if they had an inkling that I was an informant, would have me killed without a second thought."

"Calm down." Robbins pulled out a chair and sat next to TaTa. "We appreciate your hard work; we really do. It's just that Detective Sorcosky here needs a favor, and if you help us with this one last thing, the DA has to agreed to drop all charges against you. That means no suspended sentence, no probation."

"What's the big favor?" TaTa snarled.

Detective Sorcosky took a seat across the table. Without a word, she opened a manila folder and retrieved an eight-by-ten photograph, then placed it on the table facedown. She ran her fingers along the back of the picture, then locked eyes with TaTa and smiled. Rapidly, Sorcosky flipped the photo over and placed her left index finger on it.

TaTa's eyes became big as quarters. "Uh-uh, hell no."

TaTa shook her head while staring at the picture of Kisa, Eisani, and Kennedy eating at a downtown restaurant. "You're nuts if you think for one moment I'm giving you my sister and my cousins." She pushed the picture back at Sorcosky.

"Your sister doesn't really interest me. I want your cousins."

"First of all, they're not doing anything. Kisa has been running her spa. Anybody with access to the Internet or a TV knows who Kennedy is and that she's also married to one of the richest rappers."

"Blah blah blah. Save it for someone who doesn't know. The streets are talking, and they are saying Kisa is behind the recent infusion of quality coke into the city. We even know that you've been selling some of it. In light of your cooperation, we're willing to overlook your indiscretion."

"I'm not giving you my family," TaTa stated firmly.

"Oh, how cute," Sorcosky teased. "What is that, an ode to those little death-before-dishonor tattoos you girls sport on your arms?"

Ignoring Sorcosky, TaTa looked over at Robbins. "We had a deal. I upheld my part of that deal. I'm done. I'm not doing another thing, especially not snitching on my family."

Sorcosky slammed her fist on the table, forcing TaTa's attention back to her. "Listen, you little ungrateful bitch. You don't have an option. We own you! So what, you set up some dealers. You also sold nearly half a kilo to an undercover officer. You should be going to prison. Serve up what we want, or the deal's off the table. It's that simple." Sorcosky stood and left the room, slamming the door behind her.

Robbins stood up and placed a hand on TaTa's shoulder, "I know how hard this is for you. You don't have to make a decision right at this moment. You have until noon tomorrow to get back to me with your answer."

That night, wrapped in her favorite plush white terry-cloth robe, TaTa sat on a sand-colored chaise parked in front of a floor-to-ceiling-length window. All the lights were off in her Upper East Side loft. With a glass of vodka in hand, she watched as the snow continued to fall heavily upon the city. Looking out over the beautiful three feet of snow, the only thing on TaTa's mind was the dilemma she faced.

Why had she been so stupid to sell to an undercover? She had been thinking about that question for the past seven months. This was the loneliest time of her life, and she had no one to turn to. The people whom she was closest to would never understand or condone her cooperation with the police. TaTa eyed the bottle of prescription sleeping pills that sat on the end table next to her. She gave serious consideration to downing the entire thing. Guilty of loving herself excessively, neither suicide nor imprisonment was an option. Throughout the night TaTa pondered what she should do. If she were to set up Kisa and Kennedy, no one would ever know. TaTa was quite sure that she would be an anonymous informant, as she had been in all the other cases. She pretty much convinced herself that her cousins were stronger than she was and could handle prison time.

*I have to look out for number one first,* TaTa told herself as she dialed Detective Robbins's number around 8:30 AM. Her heart was beating fast as she waited for Robbins to pick up.

"Didn't expect to hear from you this early," Robbins said when she answered.

"I'm in," TaTa stated, then hung up. She sauntered into her bedroom, lay down, and slept as if she didn't have a care in the world.

"Where in the fuck have you been?" Sincere barked as soon as Kisa answered the phone.

"Snowed in, like the entire city," Kisa sighed, rolling her eyes.

"You must've had a nigga snowed in with you."

"What are you talking about?" she asked, annoyed.

"Why did you have the only phone I can call you on turned off all yesterday?"

"I broke the house charger, and this morning the snow was too high to go out. I had to wait until late this afternoon to replace it."

Things between Sincere and Kisa were so different now. He didn't know if he really believed that her answer was true. Since he had more pressing issues on his mind, he decided to let it go. "Did our friend get that information to you?"

"Yeah," Kisa replied. "I'm already checking for it. I should be able to get a face-to-face in the next few days."

Kisa's progress tracking the witness was excellent news to Sincere. He had the utmost faith in Kisa. There was no doubt in Sincere's mind that once Kisa got next to the witness, she would handle the situation. It seemed like an end to his days on the run was now in sight. "That's good . . . that's good. So other than that, how is everything else going?"

"Everything is everything. It's all flowing smoothly."

"What about you?"

"What about me?"

"How are you?"

"I'm straight, ready for this shit to be over so I can move on with my life."

Sincere knew that her comment was a shot at him; he dismissed it and kept right on talking. "Have you talked to the kids?"

"I talk to the kids every day," Kisa responded dryly. "They're fine."

"You sound like you still on that bullshit."

"Yep, I'm still on it," she snapped.

"Kisa, you are impossible. I can't believe you are still holding a grudge over a lie that a bitch told you two months ago. I'm on the run, and you acting straight foolish over nothing. I got enough shit on my shoulders. The last thing I need is you throwing me shade. This type of shit is getting old, and I'm getting tired."

"Nigga, I'm beyond tired of you of your shit, but for some reason you can't understand that. There will be no more playing me to left, then charming your way out with expensive gifts and a smile. We're done."

"I'm going to fall back," he said, still trying to dodge the inevitable argument. "This is an issue that can't be solved with you in one place and me in another. I know I made a promise to never cheat on you again, and I've kept that promise."

"Sincere, I want to believe you so bad, but I just can't. I refuse to let you continue to handle me this way," Kisa cried.

"Baby, please don't do this right now. I swear on the kids I didn't do nothing with that girl, or with anybody else." Sincere paused, having heard a knock on his door. "I'm on the phone. I'll be out in five minute, yo."

The door opened as if he had said come in, and a tall, svelte, scantily clad female waltzed in. "Come on, we've been waiting on you for like twenty minutes."

Sincere tried covering the mouthpiece, but Kisa heard the female's voice, and she was livid. "Who the fuck is that, Sincere?"

"That's Shawn's people."

"What-the-fuck-ever, yo. I'm done anyway." Kisa mashed the end button.

Irate, Sincere wasted no time turning his anger on the female. "Did I *tell* you to come in? Don't *ever* bring your dumb ass back to this room again! I don't care if God tell you. Tell Shawn I'm not going anywhere now, especially if your shit-for-brains ass is going. Get out my room and shut my damn door, you stupid bitch."

On the verge of tears, the girl did as he said, then took off running downstairs.

Sincere called Kisa more than five times before she answered. When she picked up, she straight spazzed. "Stop calling my phone, you ignorant bastard. I don't want to hear no lame excuses or weak, bullshit apologies."

"You need to calm down. That was Shawn's people you heard."

"Save it, Sincere 'cause. I'm not trying to hear it at all. Your bullshit never stops. It's just like your selfish ass to be on the run, partying, and fucking with bitches while I'm here, holding it down as usual. On everything I love, I promise you, the day that you get back, divorce papers will be waiting on you."

*Chapter 18*

E very February T.O.N.Y. Records hosted the Diamond and Fur Gala. All of the big hip-hop stars and street celebrities came out. It was their night to shine.

This year's gala would be the first one that Kennedy attended in more than three years. She was not in the mood to go, but Strick and her publicist insisted that she attend the gala as well as some other highly publicized events since she was trying to revamp her career. After a little arm twisting and cursing from Yatta, Kennedy decided to go. She knew that Yatta would be by Strick's side all night, so Kennedy enlisted her cousins to go with her.

Convincing Kisa to go was much easier than Kennedy anticipated. Of course, Kisa would do anything to support

Kennedy, but she had ulterior motives too. She knew that Suef would definitely be there. Kisa wanted to set a trap for him, and the gala would be the perfect place to lay the foundation. It would also be the perfect place to face her nemesis, since she knew she would be surrounded by Strick's security. In a way, Kisa hoped that Suef wouldn't attend so she could let her hair down, have drinks, and relax for at least a few hours.

Kisa's stress was becoming insurmountable. She missed her kids dearly, and her issues with Sincere were taking a toll on her. Finding Maria Espinoza was an even harder task than she had anticipated. An entire week had passed since she had gotten the information from Santangelo, and Kisa had yet to locate her.

On the evening of the event, Kennedy, Kisa, and Eisani rode together in a chauffeured Maybach. The three of them were a sparkling array of beauty, each draped in a luscious fur. Kennedy wore chinchilla, Kisa wore sable, and Eisani donned a mink. Their hands, wrists, and ears were laced in magnificent diamonds.

When they arrived on the red carpet, the cameras began flashing as soon as the car door opened. The paparazzi were going crazy. On the carpet, Kisa and Eisani attempted to stand to the side while Kennedy posed for pictures, but Kennedy wasn't having it. She pulled her cousins in for the photos. As they walked off the carpet, someone grabbed Kisa. When she looked up, she found herself in the arms of CoCo, the mega music mogul and the only other man she'd ever loved.

"I sure didn't expect to see you here," he whispered in her ear. "Damn, you looking good."

"Go ahead, CoCo, let go of me."

He pulled back a little, looking in Kisa's face, and asked, "Are you okay?"

"I'm good. I'm always good."

"I know that, but I've been hearing things."

"Come on, CoCo, you know better than anybody how the rumor mill churns out bullshit daily."

A model-type chick standing behind CoCo cleared her throat loudly to get his attention.

"Oh, my bad." He released Kisa and took the female by the hand. "Kisa, this is my friend Lydia."

"His girlfriend, Lydia," the female interjected with a roll of her neck."

"That's great," Kisa replied sarcastically, blowing the girl off. "It was nice to see you as always, CoCo." She turned and walked briskly to catch up with her cousins as they entered the party.

"What was that about?" Kennedy questioned with a raised brow.

"Absolutely nothing," Kisa replied, stepping through the door. "Wow, Strick spent a lot of money in here. This place looks crazy."

The venue had been an old thirty-thousand-square-foot warehouse. Now it was completely renovated and beautifully decorated. There was big stage set up in the front of the room. A huge dance floor and island bars filled the middle of the old warehouse. The luxurious VIP section was opposite the stage on a raised platform, where fifty circular tables sat topped in black tablecloths, burning candles, and white roses. Each ten-thousand-dollar table came with three bottles of champagne and three bottles of top-shelf liquor.

Kennedy's table was next to Strick's in the very center of the VIP section, giving Kisa a perfect view of everything. It wasn't exactly a perfect seat for Kennedy, since Chaz was partying at Strick's table. In fact, it was quite awkward for her. They had neither seen nor spoken to each other since the night he had bailed her out of jail two weeks earlier. Just by glancing at his wife, Chaz knew that his presence was making her uncomfortable. Therefore, to ease some of the tension, he went over to her table and sat next to her.

"How was your trip to Charlotte?" Chaz asked.

"How did you know I went to Charlotte?"

"Your aunt Karen told me."

"Oh. It was nice."

"How is Big Ma doing?"

"Much better than I expected." Kennedy smiled.

"It's been a long time since I've seen one of those on your face." Chaz pointed out.

"I haven't had a lot to smile about lately."

Chaz nodded his head. "I know I have a lot to do with that. I just wish you would give me a chance to make things right."

Kennedy took a deep breath. "I have been thinking about us a lot and how we could move forward . . . but I still need some time."

Chaz decided not too press the issue too much. He was happy that she was even a little receptive. He stood up and placed a hand on her bare back. "Aight, I'm going back over here. If you need anything, come get me."

"Okay."

TaTa, along with an unfamiliar friend, approached the table. "Hey, girls," she greeted.

"Hey, Ta," they greeted in unison.

TaTa went around the table hugging everyone. None of them could believe that she had actually shown up. "Kane, this is Anya," TaTa said, waving her friend over. "Anya, this is Kane."

Anya stuck her hand out to shake Kisa's, "It's nice to finally meet you. I've heard so much about you."

"Is that so?" Kisa questioned, wearing a phony smile as she eyed the woman suspiciously.

"Anya and I do a lot of business," Ta-Ta interjected nervously. "She's starting to place orders too large for me to fill, so I thought I'd introduce her to you."

TaTa's action astonished Kisa. Livid, she jumped up, grabbed TaTa by the arm, and dragged her off to the side. "What the fuck is wrong with you?" Kisa ripped. "Talking business in front of a stranger?"

"I know Anya well. She's bought like close to fifty bricks from me, and I've never had a problem."

"I don't care if she bought five hundred and wanted to move up to a thousand. She is your customer, *you* deal with her. Now get her the hell away from my table."

"Why?"

"'Cause I don't trust her, and neither should you," Kisa warned. "I mean, look at her in that old five-hundred-dollar fur, a Third Avenue dress, and those knock-off shoes. Can't you tell by now when someone is trying too hard? She looks out of place. Quite frankly, she looks like the police."

"Aight, Kane, I'll get her out of here. But I'm telling you, she is straight."

"Let her be straight around you and far away from me. Now beat it."

TaTa went back over to Anya. "Come on, girl. Let's go grab a couple of bottles."

"Can't the waitress get them for us?"

"Yeah, but I got a couple of people I need to go see."

"I can wait for you here," Anya said.

"You can't wait here, you're not welcome." She pulled Anya away. Once at the bottom of the stairs, TaTa turned to Anya, who was actually Detective Robbins. "I know my family! So the next time I tell you that something is not going to work, it would be wise to listen."

Back at the table, Kisa told Eisani, "I don't know what type of shit your sister is on, but I swear I'm this close to not fucking with her."

"What happened?" Eisani asked, confused

"She just tried to discuss business in front of that broad."

"No, she didn't!"

"Yes, she did, and when I checked her about it, she tells me the bitch buys mad bricks. That bum bitch look like she couldn't buy two ounces. I think the bitch could be the police."

"I'll talk to her about that dumb shit tomorrow." Eisani glanced to her left. She nudged Kisa under the table. "Here comes your boy."

Kisa looked up in time to see Suef walking through, his chin in the air as if he owned the world. He wore a long white mink with matching hat, a gray silk suit, and a plethora of long diamond chains. *He is the tackiest nigga I've ever seen*, Kisa thought. Suef and his crew of five men took a seat at a table diagonally across from Kisa. *Perfect.* She pulled out her phone and sent Mish a text that read: COME ON THROUGH.

When Kisa put her phone away, she looked up to find Suef staring directly at her. Smiling, she raised her champagne flute to him. He winked and blew a kiss at her.

Mish arrived moments later with her two deadly associates, Delinda and Felise. They walked through, driving
every man in sight wild. They were three exotic goddesses
dressed in barely there dresses and come-fuck-me stilettos.

Kisa watched Suef closely, reading his lips as Mish
passed his table.

"My God, I have to have to have her," he said, sending
one of his do boys after Mish.

Inside, Kisa was laughing at how easy he'd fallen for
the bait. Her joy was short-lived as a ghost from her past
sauntered by.

"Isn't that Rellie?" Eisani inquired.

"Yes, yes it is," answered Kisa, shocked to see her. She
was further surprised to witness Rellie kiss Suef, then sit
next to him, as if she were a queen taking a seat next to
her king. Suddenly, Kisa thought about the girl Sincere
had seen with Suef's men the night of the shooting. She
wondered if Rellie was the same girl. It made perfect sense
that Sincere did not recognize her. He had seen her only
twice, briefly. Though they shared a sister, Kisa never hung
around Rellie, whom she thought was one of the grimiest
females she'd ever come across.

Rellie looked over at Kisa, giving her a look that said,
*Yeah, bitch, it's me.* Her presence alone infuriated Kisa. At
this point, so many things were running through her head.
Kisa jumped up and shot over to Suef's table. Though her
blood was boiling, she coolly said, "My, my, my, Rellie. It
has been too long. Actually, it hasn't been long enough."

"I see you're still the same miserable bitch." Rellie replied.

Kisa laughed. "And I see you're still spreading your
legs to the highest bidder. Do you still clean out their safes
when you're done fucking them?"

*What in the hell does that mean,* Suef wondered, peering at Rellie to see her reaction.

Seething, Rellie calmly replied, "I don't have to steal, if that's what you are implying. My platinum pussy is the gift that keeps on giving."

Kisa turned her attention to Suef. "We clearly play for two different teams. However, there is nothing I hate more than a bitch that makes a lifelong career of setting up people who've hustled hard for their paper. All I'm saying is, you better keep this grimy bitch away from your cash and jewels."

Grazing Kisa's body with his eyes, Suef said, "You have some mighty big balls coming to my table. I've heard that about you, though. Guess that's why your man don't mind leaving you behind to fight his battles."

"When you have a thorough bitch, you can leave her to do anything."

Unable to suppress her rage for Kisa another second, Rellie blurted out, "How much of a thorough bitch do you have to be to kill your own sister?"

"Now I get it," Kisa said. "You think I killed *our* sister. Nah, she brought that on herself, probably by doing some of that grimy shit the two of you are notorious for."

"I know you killed Shea, you bitch!" Rellie yelled, flinging a full glass of champagne at Kisa.

Kisa turned quickly. The liquid hit her in the head and splashed all over the side of her dress. Kennedy and Eisani rushed over with two security guards in tow. Eisani was ready to go at Rellie and whoever else wanted it, but the guards stepped in between the girls and the table. "Is everything all right?" one of the guards asked Kisa.

"It's cool," Kisa assured him, wiping the side of her

neck with her hand. "I'll go back to my table. That should keep any trouble down." Before walking away she turned back to Rellie. "Since you're so sure that I killed Shea, you should've thought twice before crossing me."

"Is that a threat?" Rellie snarled.

"It is what it fucking is."

Kisa, Kennedy, and Eisani grabbed their things from the table and were escorted out by four guards. Suef sent two of his people to follow them, but the remaining guards would not allow them to leave until they'd received word that the girls were in their car and long gone.

On the ride home Eisani asked Kisa, "Do you think Rellie is a problem?"

"I sure do."

"How do you wanna handle her?"

"I don't know." Kisa shrugged.

"Do you think she's a bigger threat than Suef?" Kennedy asked.

Kisa thought before giving an answer. "No. I say that because Suef has the resources. Smash him, and all this nonsense stops. That makes him top priority." Kisa lit a cigarette. "And after he's eliminated, if she still wants to come for my throat, she can be eliminated too."

The next day in Virginia, Sicily was still reeling from the tongue-lashing she'd received from Sincere a few days earlier when she'd interrupted his call with Kisa. Scrolling through MediaTakeOut.com, Sicily saw the perfect opportunity to get back at him. Sitting slumped down on the couch, she looked over the top of her laptop screen at Sincere. He was sitting across the table playing a game of tunk with Shawn. "Um, Sincere," Sicily said, "isn't this your wife?"

"Where?"

"Right here." She spun the computer around and pointed at a picture of CoCo and Kisa hugging.

Sincere came over and snatched up the computer. The headline read: "Couple Alert!" His heart dropped as he viewed the multiple pictures of his wife hugging CoCo. Kisa appeared to be so happy in the pictures. Sincere read the caption beneath the photos:

> Music mogul CoCo and his former girlfriend Kane Montega are reportedly back together. They attended the Diamond and Fur Gala last night in Manhattan. According to court records, Kane is still married to reputed drug kingpin Sincere Montega. Here at MTO, we like these two together, but CoCo, you better watch your back! Because we hear Mr. Montega likes to get it poppin'.

Sincere slammed the laptop closed and threw it on the couch, narrowly missing Sicily. He pulled out his cell and walked away angrily. With a coy smile Sicily watched him walk all the way down the hall. When she turned around, Shawn was peering at her, shaking his head. "You one silly-ass broad."

"What?" She shrugged innocently.

"You was trying to be funny, but you probably done started some shit. When it blow up at you, that dumb-ass smile will be wiped off your face."

Sincere remained cooped up in the bedroom for the rest of the day, mainly because he didn't want to slap Sicily up-side the head. He left only to use the bathroom. *I should've killed that fuck boy years ago,* Sincere thought, pacing the floor. He couldn't get the image of CoCo hugging Kisa and the huge smile on her face out of his head. He tried unsuccessfully to reach Kisa by phone, which fueled his anger. It didn't help that the last time their marriage was in jeopardy he'd accused Kisa of cheating with CoCo, but never confirmed it. Truthfully, he didn't want to know. What he did know was that a pattern was emerging: Whenever Kisa thought that he was doing her wrong, she ran back to CoCo.

By the next morning, Sincere had still not talked to Kisa. All he could imagine was Kisa somewhere having sex with CoCo, or hurt, or dead. His thoughts were turning him into a madman. Then he made a decision. He called Shawn into his room and told him, "I want to leave for New York right before dark."

"Sin, I don't know about that," Shawn replied. "I know you're pissed, but you can take care of this once we're in the clear."

"This is not up for debate. Hell yeah, I'm pissed, but I also don't know if she is okay or not. So either get Sicily's dumb ass to drive me up there, or I will drive myself."

Shawn inhaled deeply, looking toward the sky. "You know I'm not going to let you get on the road by yourself. And I'm definitely not letting you go to the city without me," he said, even though he was 100 percent against the trip. "I'll go tell her to get ready." Shawn left the room, thinking, *I sure hope this goes smoothly, 'cause I'm not going back to prison for murder. Especially one I didn't commit.*

*Chapter 19*

"I think this chick done moved or something," Eisani remarked from the driver's seat of the Denali. Mish was in the passenger seat and Kisa in the rear. "I mean," Eisani continued, "we been checking for her for close to two weeks. No one stays away from home that long."

"E, I haven't been home in more than two months." Kisa peeped down at her watch, then across the street at the Douglas Projects, home to the witness, Maria Espinoza. "Give it another twenty minutes. If she doesn't show today, Mannie's sister lives in the building, and she knows who she is. I told her as soon as she sees her to call me."

Maria was a nurse at St. Luke's Hospital. Through her

contacts, Kisa had learned that Maria had transferred to the Beth-Israel branch of the hospital.

"I think we're going about this the wrong way," Mish offered.

"What do you suggest?" Kisa asked.

"I can go to the hospital, ask questions, and see what I can find out."

"Aight. Before you go, though, what's up with that Suef situation?"

"He invited me and the girls over for a private party around midnight with him and two of his boys."

"Where did he invite you to?"

"His condo."

"I know this nigga can't be that dumb!" Kisa commented.

"Shit," Mish said, getting out the truck. "He just like the rest of them niggas that smell pussy and lose their mind. Anyway, it can go down tonight, if that's what you want."

Kisa hopped out to get in the front. "That's exactly what I want. I don't want this thing prolonged more than it has to be."

"Aight, I will hit you in a little while." Mish got into her own car and drove away.

"E, I need to go to Essex House. It's on 58th between 6th and 7th."

"You meeting somebody?"

"Yeah, Alex. I gotta give her that money," Kisa nodded toward the small Louis Vuitton duffel bag in the back.

Eisani pulled the truck up behind Alex's chauffeured Bentley. Her driver, Puente, was standing outside the car smoking a cigarette. He saw Kisa and rushed over to open her door. "Hello, Señora Montega."

"Hello, Puente. How are you?"

"I'm good, and you?"

"Just fine. Did Alex go in already?"

"Yes."

"I have a bag in the back for her. Can I give it to you?"

"Sure, sure." Kisa went to reach for the back door, but Puente stopped her. "I get it, you go."

"Thank you." Kisa grabbed her YSL python bag and headed into the restaurant.

Kisa found Alexandria sitting at a table, engrossed in a conversation with two Colombian women. Kisa recognized one of them as Alexandria's deceased husband's sister.

When Alexandria saw Kisa approaching, she stood up to greet her with a hug. "Kisa, you remember my sister-in-law Delinda?"

"Yes, I do," Kisa said, reaching over to shake hands.

"This is Juana." Alex pointed to the other lady. "She is a very close friend of the family."

"Nice to meet you," Kisa said, greeting her with a hand-shake also.

"Likewise," Juana replied.

The server walked up and handed Kisa a menu. She looked at the plates of food already on the table; each looked like a work of art. Kisa returned the menu, "Just bring me a dry martini with five olives." She leaned over and whispered to Alexandria, "I gave the money to Puente already."

"That's fine. I asked you to meet me here because my people have thirty kilos of top-quality heroin coming in with the shipment today. Do you think your customers will be interested?"

"Honestly, I don't know," Kisa replied. "My people tend

to be a little funny about that boy. We all know how good the money is, but the time that comes with it is too crazy."

"I think once you hear the price," Delinda interjected with a slick smile, "you will not be able to resist."

Delinda's comment peaked Kisa's interest. "So what's the ticket?"

"If you take all thirty, you can get them for twenty-five K each," Delinda said. "I'm quite sure that you know the retail value is fifty apiece."

Kisa calculated the numbers in her mind. She already knew that she could sell them for less than the retail value and still make a substantial profit. "I do have two people who I believe would be very interested. If I can get them to want to buy them." Kisa turned to Alexandria. "I'll give you a call and you can send them over."

"That's sounds good," Alexandria replied. "Enough business. We have to finish our lunch, or we will be late for the matinee."

Right then Kisa received an urgent text from Eisani that read: WE HAVE TO GO ASAP.

*What now?* Kisa wondered as she took a few sips from her martini, then pulled out twenty dollars from her purse for her drink. "I hate to be rude, but something has come up."

Alexandria picked up the money and gave it back to Kisa. "Don't insult me like this."

"Whatever, Alex." Kisa smiled. "Good-bye, everyone." Kisa walked briskly out of the restaurant. "What happened?" Kisa asked Eisani as she climbed up into the truck. "Did Mish find the girl?"

"Yeah, she called and said she found out where that chick is staying, but that's not why I sent the text."

Kisa studied Eisani's face. She could tell that something

bad had happened. Bracing herself for the news, Kisa asked, "What is it, E?"

"Your old salon was shot up. Tyeis was hit twice in the leg, but she is going to be okay."

"Oh God!" Kisa exclaimed, covering her mouth.

"That's not all . . . they firebombed your spa too. Nobody over there got hurt, though."

All of the color drained from Kisa's face. Her head throbbed, and she became severely nauseated. She opened the truck's door, leaned over, and vomited.

Eisani grabbed some napkins from the glove box and a bottle of water from the backseat. "Here, Kane. Are you okay?"

"Yes," Kisa replied, taking the water and swishing it around in her mouth. She spit the water out, then cleaned her mouth with the napkins. "Let's go uptown."

"Where do you want to go—to the hospital to check on Tyeis?"

"No, we can't go to the hospital. You know Suef is behind this shit. They probably waiting for us to show up so they can shoot at us. I want to ride by the shop and spa."

Kisa's old salon, which was currently owned by Tyeis, had little damage besides the shattered glass front. Too bad the same couldn't be said for Kisa's spa. Due to the presence of the chemical products used at the spa, the flames had spread rapidly, causing severe damage to the spa and the adjoining businesses. Kisa was irate that her completely innocent younger cousin had gotten hurt. At the same time, she felt blessed that no one else had been seriously injured or killed.

Leaning her head against the cool passenger's-side glass, Kisa told Eisani, "We need to separate."

"Are you sure?"

"Yeah, 'cause the package is going to be arriving in the next hour or so. Kennedy is already waiting to bust it down. I need you to move everything while I get with Mish. Oh yeah. Do Boogie and Shake still sell h?"

"Yeah, why?"

"'Cause there will be thirty ki's in our package today. Let them know I'm letting them go for thirty-eight apiece. They have to get all of it, though, because h is too dangerous to sit on."

"Aight, I'll take care of that, but what are you going to do about Suef? Because that shit he just did is outrageous. So many innocent people could have died. I mean, what's next?"

"Nothing is next," Kisa responded coolly. "He'll be dead by morning."

Maria Espinoza no longer felt safe in her home. So when the offer came from a doctor to house-sit while he traveled in Africa for four months, she'd jumped on it. The opportunity couldn't have come at a better time. Her life was in turmoil, all because of a murder that she had nothing to do with.

After working fifteen hours straight, Maria couldn't wait to get to the comfortable confines of the doctor's home. She rushed off the crowded subway, up the stairs, and onto the sidewalk. It was a classic New York winter evening. The air was crisp, icy, and the breeze coming off the water made it feel colder. Maria wrapped her cashmere scarf tightly around the lower half of her face and her neck. She swiftly walked the five blocks to the building, her hands stuffed in her three-quarter-length goose-down parka. When she arrived at the apartment building, she dipped into the restaurant on the first floor to pick up a large serving of piping hot potato soup.

On the elevator ride up, the only thing on Maria's mind was devouring the soup. She opened the door, stepped inside, closed the door, and locked all four deadbolts. She flicked the light switch and almost jumped out of her skin. She dropped the soup, and it splashed all over her coat, pants, and the floor. She locked eyes with Kisa, who was sitting in a wing-back chair dressed in a black pantsuit and black Louboutin pumps. Instinctively, Maria turned to run out the door, but Mish, also in black, stepped in front of the door.

"Why me, God?" Maria sobbed, with tears tumbling from her eyes.

Kisa didn't have time for any theatrics. "Have a seat, Maria," she said calmly.

Cloaked in fear, Maria moved cautiously to the middle of the room and sat on the couch. Kisa just peered at Maria in complete silence for a while. Kisa studied the young, plain, but pretty woman.

Rocking back and forth and noticeably uneasy, Maria asked, "Are you going to kill me?"

"Why do you think that?" Kisa questioned.

"I don't know what to think anymore. I've never done anything to anybody. I go to Mass once a week. I take care of my grandmother, and suddenly my life is in danger."

"I didn't come here to hurt you. I came to talk." Kisa uncrossed her legs and leaned forward. "My name is Kisa Montega. I'm the wife of one of the two men you have falsely accused of murder, and I want to know why."

Staring down at the floor, Maria replied, "I can't."

"Why not?" Kisa demanded.

"Because, they will kill me."

"Who's going to kill you?"

"I don't know them," Maria whined. "That night that the man was killed outside the hospital, I was on my way back from my lunch break. I was minding my business when a woman walked up to me. She was so pretty and well dressed that I felt I had no reason to be afraid. That was until she pulled a gun on me and asked for my wallet." Maria stopped short, unsure if she should continue talking.

"And then what?" Kisa ordered.

"The lady took my ID and my Social Security card, looked at them, and then put it them her pocket. She told me she knew who I was, and where I lived." Maria took a deep breath. "The lady said that if I didn't tell the police that I saw who did it, I would be killed. I told her that I didn't see anything."

"Well, how did you identify my husband and his friend?"

"The lady had pictures of them with their names on the back. She said if the police asked me how I knew them, to say from uptown."

Disgusted, Kisa asked, "How come you never mentioned to the police that someone threatened you into lying?"

"The lady said that someone would be watching me. Her eyes were so cold . . . I knew she wouldn't hesitate to hurt me or worse." Maria wiped the tears and mucus from her face with the back of her hand. "On my way home from the precinct, after I gave my statement, I swear I thought about going back in the morning to tell the truth, but when I got home, the lady was sitting in the living room with my disabled grandmother drinking coffee. She had my poor grandmother under the impression that we were old friends. On her way out the door, she told me that I did a good job and that as long as I stuck to the script, no harm would come to my grandmother or me."

"What does this lady look like?" Kisa asked.

"Um, her skin is really light, and she has fire-red hair. She could be black, mixed, or Spanish."

*Fuckin' Rellie,* Kisa thought. "And you had no ties with her before that night?"

"No, none at all," Maria pleaded. "I truly believed that she or those scary guys that she got into the car with would kill me. You have to understand that I'm all my grandmother has. Between my student loans and her medical bills, we have nowhere to go and hide. I've been working mad overtime so she can stay in a nursing home until this thing blows over."

Kisa looked to Mish. "Do you believe her?"

Mish nodded yes, but only because during her search for Maria, she'd learned a lot about her. The people who knew Maria all described her as a good girl who was extremely green to the street life.

Maria breathed a sigh of relief. Kisa picked up her purse from the side of the chair. She pulled out five rubber-banded stacks of ten thousand dollars each. "This is fifty thousand dollars," she said, waving her hand over the money. "That's for starters. There is another hundred thousand where that came from after you clear this mess up."

Her eyes transfixed on the money, Maria asked, "What do you mean, clear it up?"

Kisa gave Maria a business card. "That attorney is waiting on your call. He can meet with you in the morning. You're going to tell him everything that you've told me. He's going to escort you to the precinct so you can retract your statement."

"B-but," Maria stuttered, "what about that lady? Who's going to protect me from her?"

"First, that lady's name is Sherelle Atkins, or Rellie, and I'll take care of her. Second, a hundred and fifty thousand is enough to relocate to another borough or another state, whichever you choose to do."

Swallowing her fear, Maria looked Kisa square in the eyes and asked. "How do I know you or your husband won't come back and kill me?"

"If I wanted you dead, you wouldn't be sitting here now." Kisa stated firmly. "Part of the reason that I believe you is the people that put you up to this play dirty. They don't care who gets hurt as long as they get their agenda across." Kisa stood to leave. "I pride myself on playing fair. So from this point on, everything is in your hands. I've given you the option to do the right thing and in the process make more money than I'm sure you have ever seen before. Now, if you choose not to do the right thing, I'll have to play it like you're down with Rellie and act accordingly. What are you going to do?"

Maria pulled her cell from her pocket. "I'll call the attorney now."

Having squared things away with Maria, Kisa rode home in silence. She worried about Mish's date with Suef. She didn't doubt Mish's abilities, but understood that there was a small margin for error. Kisa's ringing cell phone broke the stillness in the car. She checked the ID, then answered, "Yeah, Ta, what up?"

"What's good, cousin?"

"Everything is everything," Kisa responded dryly, still ticked off with TaTa about the stunt that she pulled at the gala.

"I need to get with you so I can get straight."

"You didn't get with Eisani?"

"Nah, I've been trying to call her all day," TaTa lied.

"I'm going to change my clothes, and then I can meet you at the uptown spot in one hour. Don't be late, Ta. I got some important shit going on, and if you not there, I'm not going to wait."

"I'll be there," TaTa assured her. She hung up the phone immediately before she cracked. TaTa looked back at Detective Robbins, who was standing behind her. "There, it's done. Are you happy now?"

"We sure are," Robbins said, smiling at Detective Sorcosky.

Sorcosky grinned wide. "Let's go get her."

On the way out the room, Robbins turned to TaTa and gave her a thumbs-up, "Great job! It has been so nice working with you."

TaTa stuck up her middle finger. "Fuck you, bitch."

Kisa pulled into the parking garage and parked in her assigned space. She opened the driver's door, extending her leg to keep it propped open. Reaching across the passenger seat, she gathered her things. As Kisa rose to get out the car, SMACK! She was stung by a hard, blinding slap across her face that knocked her back into the vehicle. Her purse flew into the rear of the car. *I've been caught slippin'*, Kisa thought frantically, trying to retrieve a gun from under the passenger's-side seat. The assailant tugged at her legs. Unable to reach the pistol, Kisa held on to the arm of the door and fought back by kicking. She was no match for her attacker. He jerked Kisa from the car with one hard yank. Kisa landed on the cement ass first, banging her head on the metal edge of the driver's-side floor.

The assailant grabbed her by the collar and pulled her to her feet. Kisa was shocked and relieved to see that it was Sincere. "You asshole," she yelled, mushing him upside his head. "What in the hell is wrong with you? I almost shot you, stupid." Kisa slammed her fist into his chest repeatedly. "You scared me."

Sincere grabbed her by the wrists, pinning her against the car with his weight. "You fucking that nigga again? Is that why you so ready to divorce me?"

"What are you talking about?" Kisa questioned, dumbfounded.

"I saw you with him, so don't lie!" Sincere shouted in her face. "Is that why you haven't answered any of my calls?"

"You are fuckin losing it, 'cause you didn't see me with nobody!"

"I saw the pictures of you on the Internet hugged up with CoCo at that party the other night."

Kisa racked her brain, trying to figure out what Sincere was talking about, and then she remembered all the cameras that had been flashing while she was talking to CoCo. "I wasn't with him, stupid! He was with his girlfriend, and I was there with Kennedy and E. We were only speaking on the way into the party. Not that I have to explain anything to you."

"You have to explain *everything* to me!" Sincere barked, squeezing her wrists tighter.

"No, the fuck I don't!"

"You talking real slick. The same way you was five years ago when you was fucking that nigga. Christen probably his son!"

Kisa snatched her right wrist out of his grasp and slapped him with all her strength. "How dare you! You know he's your son! He looks *exactly* like you."

"If you feed anybody long enough, they'll start to look like you."

"You are a heartless black bastard," she said, peering into his eyes. "Don't worry, though. DNA says that he is yours."

"So you snuck and had Christen tested? You must've thought there was a chance that he was CoCo's son."

"I did nothing of the sort. You must not remember the doctors had to test you before they allowed you to give him blood when he was really sick two years ago." Kisa yanked her other wrist free. "Sincere, you are so pathetic! You're the one always out doing wrong, but steady accusing me."

"Hey!" The building's security guard yelled, coming from across the garage, "Is everything okay over there, Mrs. Montega?"

"Yeah, Jim, everything is fine," Kisa said, smoothing her disheveled hair and forcing a smile. "This is my husband. We were just playing around."

"Oh, sorry for disturbing. You have a good night." The guard turned and headed back to his office.

Kisa shoved Sincere away and retrieved her purse from the back of the car. "I suggest you come on upstairs in case someone else called the police. You know they're still looking for you." Leading the way, Kisa placed a call to Eisani.

"What up, Kane?" Eisani answered.

"What you doing, E?"

"I just got through putting some money up."

"Were you able to get rid of that new thing that came through?"

"I sure was. Boogie and Shake jumped all over that deal."

"That's good. How much of that other thing we got left?" Kisa asked.

"Um, like three or four."

"That's it?" Kisa questioned.

"Yeah, ole boy from upstate damn near wiped us out by himself."

"Aight. Well, I need you to meet your sister at the spot in about forty-five minutes and give her whatever is left. I was going to meet her, but something came up," Kisa said, cutting her eyes at Sincere.

"Is everything okay?"

"Yeah, I'm straight."

"I'm not far from the spot, so I'll head there now and take care of TaTa."

"Good looking out, E. Call me when you're done. I want you to go with me whenever I get the word from Mish."

Shawn decided that he'd visit his mom and kids at night when he could slip in and out unnoticed more easily. It was just his luck that his money-hungry babies' mom, Marquetta, saw him entering his mother's building. She had a long-standing chip on her shoulder. She felt that Shawn should be sharing his money with her, although Shawn's mother was the legal guardian to his kids. Seeing him with Sicily sent her into a jealous rage. So she picked up the phone to call Crime Stoppers about the ten-thousand-dollar reward on Shawn's head.

An hour later Shawn decided to leave. He had an eerie feeling as he stepped down off the building's stoop. Looking around, he summed it up to a case of nerves as he climbed into the passenger side of Sicily's silver Tahoe. They pulled onto 8th Avenue from 141st Street. Police cars came from every direction and surrounded the truck. The officers jumped out with their guns drawn.

Beads of perspiration spontaneously popped up on Shawn's entire body. "What in the fuck is this?" he wondered aloud.

"Oh Jesus," Sicily panicked loudly. "Oh God, Shawn, what do you want me to do?"

"I want you to shut up so I can think!" His heart was beating so fast he thought that it would burst through his chest. All he could envision was the inside of his last prison cell. *I can't go back to that place,* he thought.

A voice came over a loudspeaker. "Step out of the vehicle with your hands in the air."

"I should've stayed my black ass in Virginia," Shawn muttered, pulling a gun from the passenger's-side door pocket.

Sicily's eyes widened. "What are you going to do with that, Shawn?" she asked, afraid that he was about to use her as a hostage.

"Not going back to prison for a murder that I didn't commit."

"Shawn, please let me get out," she cried.

"Go on! Get out now. I'm not holding you."

"Then what are you planning to do with that gun?"

"Don't worry about it. Just get far away from the truck. Listen, I need you to tell my mother and my kids that I love them. Make sure when you talk to Sincere that you tell him I said 'Death before dishonor.'"

Sicily extended her hand to Shawn. "Please put the gun down and get out with me. There are too many jakes out here. You cannot win a shootout with them."

Shawn pointed the gun at Sicily. "Get out," he ordered.

Shaking, Sicily slowly opened the door, making sure that her hands were visible as she emerged from the truck. As soon as her feet touched the pavement, the cops ordered her to the ground. Remembering what Shawn had said, she moved away from the truck, then dropped to her knees.

Shawn placed the muzzle of the gun on his right temple. He closed his eyes, "God, please forgive me," he whispered, then pulled the trigger, blowing his brains out the left side of his skull.

# Chapter 20

L ook, I said that I was sorry," Sincere roared, tired of the tongue-lashing that he was receiving from Kisa.

"I don't give a damn about that weak-ass apology." Kisa came out of the bathroom wrapped in a towel. "You slapped the shit out of me and snatched me from my car. I thought I was being kidnapped, and look at my face. It's starting to bruise."

"You should've answered your phone," he quipped, "instead of running around with CoCo."

"You are the fuckin' biggest idiot I know." Kisa scowled. "I wasn't out with nobody. My day has been too fucked up to try to keep track of three different phones. Dumb-ass Suef had the spa firebombed, and Tyeis's shop was sprayed with bullets. By the way, she took two in the leg, if you care to know." Kisa pulled on a pair of jeans. "I haven't even had time to wrap my mind around any of that because I've been too busy tracking down the witness in your case and dealing with her."

"You found her?"

"Yes, I found her, and if you bothered to ask me about that, instead of some dumb-ass pictures on the Internet, you would know."

"And," Sincere asked, anxious for the details.

"And what?"

"What did she have to say?"

Kisa ran down everything that had happened when she'd met with Maria a few hours earlier. When she finished, Sincere asked, "How sure are you that she's going to retract her statement?"

"I'm ninety-nine-point-five percent sure that she's going to do it. This was a fucked-up situation for her too, and my hundred and fifty K incentive for her to tell the truth was a lot better than what Rellie and Suef offered."

"I hope so," Sincere said, doubtful.

"At this point, all you have to do is wait until the morning." Kisa dashed into the bathroom to answer her ringing cell. She saw that it was TaTa and answered, "Yo, Ta, I couldn't make it, but—"

"Kane, I'm so sorry," TaTa cried. "They made me set you up. I didn't want to do it, I swear. You've got to get out of the spot right now."

"Ta, what in the hell have you done? What are you talking about? Because I'm not at the spot, your sister is, and if anything happens to E, I'm going to stomp a hole in your weirdo ass."

"Eisani's there?" TaTa gasped loudly. "Oh no."

"You better tell me what's going on right now. Did you let Suef use you?"

TaTa hung up with no response.

Hysterically, Kisa dialed Eisani's number.

Sincere stood in the bathroom doorway, "What's going on?"

"Fuck if I know," Kisa snapped. "That was TaTa talking all crazy."

"What did she say?"

"Something about she didn't mean to set me up. I gotta tell E to get out of there." Kisa could not reach Eisani. She tried repeatedly to call, but her phone was not even ringing, just going straight to voicemail. "I'm going over there." Kisa put on her coat and stepped into a pair of flat rider boots.

"I'm going with you," Sincere said, following her.

"You can't go with me. You're not even supposed to be in the city. You need to lay low until after Maria changes her statement and gets those charges up off you."

"I'm not letting you go alone. That crazy call could be a part of the setup."

"Fine," Kisa replied, with no time to argue. "It's your decision, not mine." She opened the door to find Arnessa standing there. "What are you doing here?"

"Nice to see you too," Arnessa responded. "I'm here because of what Suef did."

"You came because he firebombed the spa?"

"No, I don't know anything about that. Didn't you hear what happened to Tasha?"

"No."

"Suef's goons beat her, raped her, and left her for dead in

her house last night. Her kids found her unconscious when they got up this morning."

"E, wake up," Kennedy tapped her sleeping cousin's shoulder.

Eisani lifted her head from the armrest of the couch. "I didn't even know I dozed off. I'm tired as I don't know what. If TaTa don't get here in the next fifteen minutes, I'm out."

"I have to leave now," Kennedy said, buttoning her coat. "I'm going to meet Chaz for drinks so we can talk."

"That's good, cousin." Eisani sat up. "I hope y'all put all that drama behind y'all and work everything out."

"We shall see." Kennedy sighed. "By the way, I stretched two of those bricks out so TaTa could have six."

"That was nice of you, 'cause I wouldn't have done it. If her lazy ass would've gotten with me earlier, she could have gotten more than those six."

"You know how your sister is." Kennedy opened the door. "I'm gone, I'll call you later." She made her way down the three flights of stairs and out the door. Once out on the stoop, she rummaged through her bag for her car keys. Then she heard a unique but familiar sound—the soft pitter-pats of multiple police officers running in unison. Kennedy looked to her left but didn't see anything. She turned to her right and saw twelve narcotics tactical squad officers coming toward her with their weapons out.

The first ten officers ran straight past Kennedy into the building. The last two aimed their weapons at her and ordered her to the ground. Kennedy obeyed. They snatched her purse, patted her down, and cuffed her. One of the officers pulled her to her feet, escorted her to an unmarked car, and placed her in the backseat.

Ten minutes later Eisani was brought out in cuffs. They placed her in the same car as Kennedy. The two cousins glanced at each other and simply shook their heads. They knew better than to say a word and give the police the satisfaction of taping their conversation. In silence, Kennedy and Eisani watched as the police carted boxes of evidence out of the building. Suddenly, Kennedy's door was flung open. Detective Robbins stuck her head in and looked at each of their faces. Both Kennedy and Eisani instantly recognized her as TaTa's guest at the gala. Eisani shook her head, thinking, *Kisa was right about that bitch.*

"Damn it." Robbins slammed her hand on the top of the car, "Montega isn't in here, but I think we got someone you would like to see."

Detective Sorcosky leaned into the car. When she laid eyes on Kennedy, she grinned like a Cheshire cat. "Well, well, well, look who we have here," she taunted. "Sanchez, didn't I tell you I would get you one day?"

Kennedy smirked. "You don't got me now, you foolish-ass detective, and you'll never get me because you want me too bad."

"What do you see?" Sincere asked from his slumped-down position in the backseat as they rode past the barricaded block.

"A whole lot of police," Kisa replied, worried that she didn't see any EMT or fire trucks, leading her to think that Eisani might be dead.

Arnessa opened the door. "I'll go see what's up," she said.

Kisa grabbed her by the arm, "You can't go down there!"

"Kane, I'm not crazy. I ain't going down there." She got

out of the car and walked up to the first junkie she saw. "Aye ma, I need a favor."

"I don't do no favors for free," the junkie replied.

"Trust me, I already know," Arnessa replied, holding up a crisp fifty-dollar bill in the air. "Go down the block, find out what happened, and when you come back, this is yours."

"I don't have to go down there. I already know what happened," the woman cackled. "The pigs busted two girls in 216 with mad bricks of that powder. Shit, I wish they woulda let me get some to cook up. I'd be smoking all night. Can I still get that fifty, baby girl?"

Arnessa gave her the money and jogged back to the car. She jumped in, telling Kisa, "Pull off now!"

Kisa sped away. "What did you find out?"

"The jakes ran up in the spot. They got Eisani and Mish."

"Mish wasn't there."

"They must have Kennedy, then, because that crack-head said they got two girls."

Kisa called Kennedy's phone.

It rang a few times then an unfamiliar voice answered. "Hello?"

"Who is this?" Kisa asked.

"This is Detective Sorcosky. Is that you, Mrs. Montega?" Kisa ended the call. "Shit, they got Kennedy too." Kisa was angry, hurt, and frustrated. "I swear to God," she said aloud, "between Shea and TaTa, I've learned that family will fuck you first!"

"Who was that with you at the party if you don't have a woman?" Mish questioned Suef while sipping champagne in the sunken Jacuzzi in the great room of his skyline condominium.

"That was my companion. We're not serious, though, not like how you and I could be." He was under the impression that Mish was a Brazilian model named Aryanna. Suef didn't have a clue that he was spending time with his younger cousin's murderer. Mish's deadly associates, Delinda and Felise, were also in the Jacuzzi with Suef's top lieutenants Trenton and Abdul.

"Where is your companion tonight?" Mish inquired of Suef.

He looked at her strangely, feeling like she was being a bit nosy. "Why are you so interested in her?"

"I'm not interested in her at all. I just happened to notice her things laying around. I just want to be sure that she's not going to bust up in here with a bunch of drama," Mish replied, rocking Suef's suspicions to rest.

"Oh nah. Nah, baby, I sent her out of town to the spa for a few days to relax so I could relax with you." He nibbled on her neck.

This was one job that Mish couldn't wait to end. Suef's touch made her skin crawl, and his corny game made her sick to her stomach. Pretending to enjoy his sloppy tongue going across her neck, Mish said, "Let's go to your room so we can have some privacy."

"Beautiful, you must have read my mind." He tripped over his own feet rushing to get out of the hot tub.

*What a buster.* Mish smirked to herself, gliding out sexily.

"We're taking it on back," Suef announced. "Do not bother me unless a nigga is about to die or the jakes kick in the door." Mish followed him into the master suite. "Ah man, I forgot to get a fresh bottle," he said, turning to leave.

Mish stepped in front of him. "Go ahead and lay down. I can get it. Where's it at?"

"The bottles are in the refrigerator in the bottom drawer."

In the kitchen, Mish got a bottle out, popped the cork, and poured some in a champagne glass. She glanced around, then pulled a tiny vial out that she had hidden between her cheek and her gum. It contained a strong dose of GSB. Mish emptied all of it into the bottle. She winked at Delinda and Felise on her way back to the bedroom, signaling them to speed things up. If the plan was to go off without a hitch, it was crucial that they complete their task first.

When Mish reentered the room, Suef was sitting in the middle of the bed nude. She shut the door, locking it behind her. "Here you go, sweetie." Mish handed him the GSB-laced bottle.

Suef took two big gulps of the champagne, then extended it back to Mish.

"I have a glass already," she said, standing next to the bed.

"Come lay down, what you waiting for?" He took another big gulp from the bottle.

"I want to freshen up right quick." She stepped into the master bathroom and closed the door. Mish cut the faucet on and sat on the toilet, hoping that the GSB would quickly take effect. After what she felt was a sufficient amount of time, Mish left the bathroom.

Suef's body was paralyzed, and though his mouth and eyes were open, he was unable to speak.

"No need to fight it," Mish said to him. "Just relax."

She put on her clothes and checked the living room, happy to see that it was empty. She allowed ten minutes to pass, then went to check on the girls. In the first room, she found Delinda standing over Trenton. He was laid out on the floor with his throat slit from ear to ear.

Hearing a struggle in the next room, Mish and Delinda rushed over to see what was going on. Abdul held his bloody neck with one hand while choking Felise against the wall with the other. Mish picked up a metal floor lamp and hit him on the head. He fell backward, releasing Felise. She landed on the floor next to him, coughing and gasping for air.

Delinda, after spotting Felise's blade on the foot of the bed, grabbed it, lodged it deep into Abdul's neck, and dragged it across.

Mish helped Felise off the ground and asked, "What in hell happened?"

"His neck was too fat. I must've only cut skin."

"Well, I got him," Delinda bragged. "That means you owe me part of your money."

Suef began to come to in the wee hours of the morning. He had a pounding headache. The first time that he cracked his eyes, everything was blurry. He felt his hands bound together and duct tape on his mouth. Suef squeezed then opened his eyes again. As his vision became clearer, he saw Kisa standing in front of him, smiling.

"Did you sleep well?" she asked.

Suef grunted at her.

"I can't hear you." Kisa put her hand behind her ear. "What was that? Oh, my husband left me behind to take care of business, and I'm doing a wonderful job."

Suef started grunting again.

Kisa snatched the duct tape from his mouth.

"Ow," he squealed. "You fuckin' bitch. Untie me now."

"That's not going to happen."

"Bitch, when this is over, I'm going to come after you with everything I got."

"And what do you have? I sure hope you're not talking about them." She pointed to the lifeless bodies of Trenton and Abdul, which lay on the floor side by side.

Suef saw his two friends with the huge gashes in their necks; vomit rushed from the pit of his stomach and flew out his mouth, narrowly missing Kisa. It rapidly became clear to him that he might be in the last moments of his life.

"Nigga, I know your tough ass didn't just earl. Not the big man that had me shot at while I was with my kids. Not the tough guy that sent an innocent young girl to jail. You need to man up, nigga."

Water crept into Suef's eyes, but he refused to let one tear drop. "What is it you want, money?"

"Fuck no," Kisa shot back. "I don't want anything . . . on second thought, I do want Rellie."

"I don't know where she is."

"You must have selective memory, 'cause that's not what you told my homegirl." Kisa nodded at Mish.

Suef looked over and saw the girl he knew as Aryanna, "You low-down bitch," he snarled. "You set me up."

"No need to insult her," Kisa said. "She was only doing her job. You don't have to tell me where Rellie is. She'll play herself, as she always does. That's when I'll catch her. Before I leave there is someone else that wants to have a word with you."

Arnessa entered the room and stood directly in front of him. She didn't talk, just simply stared. The hate that Arnessa carried for him was radiating from her. Suef knew that he was going to die regardless of what he did. He pulled as much saliva as he could from the back of his throat and spit right in the center of Arnessa's face.

Snickering, Arnessa wiped the spit from her face with her sleeve, then struck him hard with the back of her closed fist. "That's for my sister." Suef's lip split open. Arnessa struck him once more even harder. "And that's for Butta."

Suef licked the blood from his lip, tasted it, and smiled. "Fuck your sister and that faggot-ass nigga."

Undetected, Mish crept up behind him.

"No, Suef, fuck you." Arnessa smirked sinisterly. "Die slow."

Mish clutched his head, pressed the sharp blade firmly into the left side of his neck, and sliced it all the way around. Arnessa felt great satisfaction from watching his death, knowing that his reign of terror against her family and friends was finally over.

*Chapter 21*

A lthough it had been a long exhausting night, Kisa and Arnessa were front and center the next morning for Kennedy and Eisani's arraignment.

Following his lawyer's advice, Sincere did not attend, even though Maria held up her end up of the deal with Kisa. His lawyer thought it was best for Sincere to remain low until the police formally dropped the charges. Sincere didn't mind, though. He wanted to be alone for a while to mourn Shawn's death. He was plagued with guilt since it had been his idea to come back to New York before they'd been cleared.

Around noon, bailiffs led Kennedy and Eisani into the courtroom. Neither showed any emotion. The state charged them both with possession with intent to distribute six kilograms of cocaine. Kennedy's attorney argued that the charges against Kennedy needed to be dropped immediately, since the police did not catch her inside the building, let alone inside the actual apartment with the drugs. She said that the police had no proof of whether Kennedy was coming or going. Amid protest from the prosecutor, the judge agreed and tossed out the case against Kennedy.

Eisani entered a plea of not guilty to the charges. The prosecutor requested that the judge deny her bail because Eisani had access to large amounts of untraceable money, making her a high flight risk. This time the judge sided with the prosecutor, remanding Eisani over until trial.

Kennedy, happy to be free, could have cared less about who sent the police or why. She expected to see Kisa and Arnessa when the processing was completed and she could leave jail. Instead, she was pleasantly surprised to see Chaz.

"We'v got to stop meeting like this," he told her.

"If you weren't picking me up from jail, we might not ever get to see each other," Kennedy joked. She threw her arms around him, hugging him tight. "I'm so glad you're here."

Chaz was taken aback by Kennedy's affection. He hesitated a little then returned her warm embrace. "I will always be here." He kissed her cheek, "I love you, Kennedy."

"I love you too."

"Let's go home and have that talk we were supposed to have before you got locked up."

"Okay, but I have to pick up Jordan from Auntie Karen's."

"He's already at the house. My mom is there watching him."

"Kennedy Sanchez-Harris," a female voice called out.

Kennedy turned to see a slim white female in business attire coming toward her. "Yes," Kennedy answered.

"This is for you." She handed Kennedy an envelope. "You've been served," she said politely, then walked away.

Kennedy opened the envelope and read the contents. "This muthafucka can't be serious," she yelped.

"What's wrong?" Chaz asked.

"It's from Brian. He's suing me for custody of Jordan."

He took the paper, skimmed it, and ripped it up. "Don't worry about this. I'll take care of it."

Chaz dropped Kennedy off at home off then set off on a mission to find Brian. It didn't take long, since Chaz knew that Brian had a strong gambling habit. They'd run into each other at several illegal gambling spots throughout the city. Chaz knew which place Brian favored, so he went there first. He saw Brian's car parked right outside the building. Instead of going in and causing a big scene, Chaz parked across the street. He waited patiently for Brian to come out.

A few hours later Brian walked out in a bit of a pissy mood, having lost a lot of money on the card table. Chaz got out the car. Crossing the street, he yelled, "Aye, my man, I need to holla at you."

"Oh shit," Brian chuckled. "Did wifey send you to get tough with me?"

"My wife didn't send me nowhere. I came to tell you that you need to dead that custody bullshit right now."

"Who gon' make me?"

"I don't believe you want to go there, my dude," Chaz shot back.

"Man, please." Brian waved his hand at Chaz, dismissing him. "You think I'm frightened by a lil' fuck-ass rapper?"

"Muthafucka, you better check my résumé."

"I already did, and if I must say, I'm highly unimpressed."

"Foolish niggas never are," Chaz responded. "I don't have time to trade lines with you. Just drop the case 'cause you can't win. You already know my paper is long. I got the best lawyers that money can buy. If you choose to pursue this, we'll win, and there will be consequences. The same goes for if you keep toying with my son's feelings."

"Jordan is my blood—that makes him my son!" Brian shouted.

"Nigga, please, you don't deserve the right to claim him ever. Like I said, my man, end it now, or I might just put in a call to your connect that you're getting all that good raw from. After all, he is my man." Chaz smirked. "He tells me that you been getting sloppy with the money lately, trickin' on bitches and gambling too much. Says he's looking for a reason to cut you off before you fuck up some real paper, and if I just say the word, you dead on any work. Because of my résumé that you're so unimpressed by, I can call in favors like that."

Brian stood quiet, clenching his jaw. It was true that he'd been having disputes with his connect about money coming up short. The last thing he needed was to lose his connect altogether. Nevertheless, he didn't take Chaz's threat idly. "I'll let it go for now, and not because of that little dust you kicking up. I don't have time to raise a rug rat right now anyway. The only reason I filed those papers was to let Kennedy know that she don't run shit but her mouth."

"You telling me that you were willing to drag Jordan through some dumb shit just to prove a point to Kennedy?" Chaz shook his head. "Man, you are sadder than I thought."

Kennedy was on the couch drinking wine from a big goblet when Chaz returned. Her eyes were red and puffy from nonstop crying. She stood up, "What happened?"

"I talked to that ignorant-ass nigga." Chaz tossed his coat on the couch. "We came to an understanding. He's going to drop it."

"Did you hit him?"

"No, but I wanted to. I just threatened his pockets, the only thing that silly, greedy-ass niggas like him understands."

"Thank you," Kennedy said, tears filling her eyes. She dropped her head, sobbing heavily.

Chaz cupped her face in his hands. "Stop crying, I'll never let that nigga take Jordan away from you."

"It's not that."

"Well, what's bothering you?"

"I have to go to Charlotte . . . Big Ma died today."

# Chapter 22

Rellie decided to return from her spa vacation early because she was bored as hell and she hadn't spoken with Suef in more than twenty-four hours. When he'd sent her on a surprise trip to a luxury resort in Connecticut she felt like he was trying to get rid of her so he could be with someone else. Rellie arrived at the condo in the middle of the night, hoping to catch Suef up to no good so she could spaz on him. She unlocked the door gently and eased in quietly.

Inside, the condo was pitch-black and freezing. Rellie dropped her bags, closed the door, and fumbled for the lights. The one that she cut on barely lit the entry. Her heels clicking against the hardwood floors echoed loudly in the eerie stillness as she rushed to turn on more lights and some heat. As Rellie crossed the dark living room, she tripped, fell, and landed on top of Suef's stiff, cold body. She jumped up screaming, stumbled to the floor again, and crawled away backward.

Suef's nude body was positioned between Trenton's and Abdul's naked corpses. Rellie covered her own mouth to mask the loud sobs. She pulled it together as best she could and crawled over to Suef's body. Resting her head on his chest, Rellie cried even harder. He was the only man that she ever cared about, and now he was gone. "Why, God?" she whined. "Why are you punishing me?" Rellie looked up at Suef's face. She noticed something sticking out of his mouth. She reached up and pulled out a magenta thong. Her grief quickly turned to rage. With the thong in hand, she knew that Kisa was behind this.

"How could you be so stupid?" She slammed her fist against his abdomen. "You let her catch you slippin' with some pussy. If you were not dead, I'd kill you." She kissed Suef's face. "Don't worry, baby, I'm going to finish what you started."

Looking at the other bodies, Rellie thought, *I gotta get out of here.* She went into the laundry room, dampened a towel with bleach, returned to Suef's body, and wiped it down to remove any traces of her DNA. She then hurried from room to room packing everything that she owned. Though Rellie was distraught, she had the presence of mind to grab Suef's jewelry collection and all the cash out of the safe.

Rellie hauled everything down to her car in four trips. Before departing, she wiped down all the hard surfaces and doorknobs. On her way out, she blew a kiss at Suef's lifeless body. "I love you, baby. I promise you on my life . . . I will get her."

Eisani entered the visitation room of the Rose M. Singer Center in a bland gray prison jumper. Her long hair was in a ponytail sitting atop of her head. Heartbroken by Eisani's imprisonment, Kisa began to cry as her cousin approached. They exchanged a brief, firm hug, then sat down.

"How are you holding up, E?"

"I'm okay. I'm adjusting. That's crazy about Shawn. What was he thinking?"

"I don't know," Kisa replied. "Guess he thought things were not going to work in his favor. That girl that was with him said he kept saying he couldn't go back to prison."

"That's so sad, though. I hate that for his mother. Did everything work out the way you wanted?" Eisani inquired.

"Yeah, it all worked out, with the exception of you being in here."

Eisani shrugged, "It is what it is."

"It can't be this," Kisa replied, big tears sliding down her cheeks. "What did your attorney say?"

"She said that the police thought you were going to be at the spot. They want you bad. The D.A. already came through here trying to offer me a deal to snitch on you."

"What did they offer?"

Eisani looked at Kisa as if she had two heads. "The conversation didn't even get that far. You of all people should know I'm no snitch, and that's what they want me to do to get a deal. I'll just take my chances at trial."

"E, take what they offer you. I don't care. I can't let you take the rap alone. It wouldn't be fair."

"Kane, you are talking crazy. You got kids! Christen and

Kai need you out there. I caught the case, I respect the game, and I follow the rules."

"But, Eisani, I can't stand by—"

"Yes, you can and you will. The only thing you can do for me is promise to take care of my mother."

"You know I'm going to do that!"

Leaning in, Eisani said in a low voice, "I also need you to keep Mish off TaTa."

"That's out of my hands."

"No, it isn't. She'll listen to you," Eisani insisted.

"Not on this one. Are you forgetting how much your sister knows? People are not going to sit back and wait for her to dime them out too. Word on the street, Ta been setting up niggas for months. Do you expect me to protect her from them too?"

"I expect you to do me the one favor that I asked for while I do this bid. It would crush my mother to have one daughter in prison and the other in the grave. As much as I hate my sister right now, I have to think of my mother first."

Kisa folded her arms firmly across her chest, "Eisani, you yourself just said seconds ago that you know the rules and you respect them. They don't change according to the person. We both know snitches get found in ditches. I didn't make the rule, and I can't adjust it to suit TaTa."

"You are a piece of work," Eisani hissed.

"I might be, and if your sister had her way, this piece of work would be sitting in your chair wearing that uniform, and you expect me to keep someone off of her."

"I wish you would've never moved back to New York," Eisani spouted coldly. "Then maybe I wouldn't be sitting here."

"No!" Kisa twisted her neck. "If your weak-ass sister had been twenty-one about her shit, you wouldn't be sitting there."

"You know, cousin, you don't ever have to worry about where I sit anymore." Eisani stood up. "As a matter of fact, don't bother visiting or writing. Just enjoy your life." Eisani walked away and never looked back.

# Chapter 23

Big Ma's funeral was standing room only. Nearly a thousand people came out to pay their respects. The family planned the service according to Big Ma's final wishes—no sad music, no sad eulogy, no drawn-out service.

Kennedy held up much better than many expected. She didn't cry much. She had the comfort of knowing that Big Ma was no longer suffering. Having Chaz by her side helped too.

After the burial, Kennedy's massive family gathered at Big Ma's house. Kennedy hung around briefly, but she wasn't in the mood for a huge crowd. She had her own small separate repast at the home that she and Chaz still owned in Charlotte. Yatta, Strick, Kisa, Sincere, Butta, and Arnessa, and all of their kids were the only guests. They had a great time well into the night.

Kisa and Sincere were the first to leave. They wanted privacy, so they checked into the Ritz Carlton in downtown Charlotte because they had allowed several family members who were in town for the funeral to stay at their home. They also had a 7:00 AM flight back to New York for Shawn's funeral Mass the next day.

"I'm starving," Kisa said, entering the hotel suite. "We were talking so much I barely ate my food."

"I'm still hungry too," Sincere replied. "Do you wanna order some room service?"

"Yeah," Kisa told him as she slipped out of her black suit.

Looking over the menu, Sincere said, "I'm getting the stuffed chicken."

"Do they have salmon?" Kisa asked.

"Um, yeah."

"I want salmon and a salad with balsamic vinaigrette dressing."

While placing the order, Sincere watched his wife as she moved around the room in a sexy black slip. *She's crazy if she think I'm ever letting her go.* He smiled to himself. Once done ordering the food, Sincere walked up behind Kisa. She was bent over her duffel bag getting her toiletries out for the shower. Sincere wrapped his arms around her waist. Pressing his body firmly against hers, he said, "Tell me you love me."

"You know I love you."

"I'm not sure, since you haven't told me once since we made up." He spun her around so she faced him.

"You know how I am once my guard goes up. I mean, I wanna hug on you, kiss you, and tell you how happy I am that you're home. My heart says to do all that, but my brain says to be cautious, because I can't allow you to keep hurting me over and over."

"I thought we were through this already."

"We came to an agreement to stay together, but it's going to take a lot of work."

"I love you, Kisa. You and the kids are the only things that matter. I'm willing to work hard to keep our family together."

Kisa was worn down emotionally. The only thing that could help her get through this difficult period was the love and friendship of her husband. She decided to put her problems on hold. "I love you so much, Sincere, and no matter what happens, that will never change. Those issues that I would like to air out can wait. Going to bury Shawn tomorrow, I know, is hard enough for you. I don't want to bring you down with all this heavy stuff tonight. I just want to be here for you."

"You're always here for me. You always put everybody you love first. So whatever issues you want to air out, we can talk about them right now."

"I just want us to enjoy each other's company." She smiled. "Something we haven't done in a long time."

Sincere kissed her passionately, "I love you, wife."

"I love you, husband."

"Go ahead and get in the shower." He smacked Kisa on the ass. "I'll wait for the food."

"Okay," Kisa replied, and headed into the bathroom.

Sincere undressed down to his underclothes and slipped on a pair of basketball shorts. He sat on the foot of the bed and flipped through the channels until he landed on ESPN. Just as he got comfortable, there was a knock at the door. *That must be the food,* he thought, hopping up. Sincere looked out the peephole and saw a female room-service attendant. Her jet-black bob covered the side of her face. Sincere opened the door and held it open for her.

The room service attendant pulled the dining cart inside the room. Just as she was about to pass Sincere, she pressed a taser gun against his neck. He dropped to the floor, never knowing what hit him.

Kisa stepped out of the shower and called out to her husband, "Sincere, did the food come yet?"

There was no answer.

Kisa assumed that he had dozed off or stepped out to get ice. She hurriedly slipped into a pair of white terry-cloth pajama pants and exited the bathroom, pulling a thin white tank top over her head. She rounded the corner to the sight of Sincere unconscious on the floor. Kisa rushed to his side. "Sin, what happened?" She jerked his body. "Baby, wake up," Kisa said, checking his neck for a pulse. Feeling the rhythm of his heart, Kisa spun around on her knees to see if her phone was nearby. She looked up to find Rellie smiling sinisterly.

Rellie advanced on Kisa quickly, kicking her hard in the side and knocking her onto Sincere. "Bet you didn't think you would see me again." She kicked her again in the same spot.

Kisa clutched her waist, grimacing in pain. Rellie pulled Kisa up by her hair and flung her across the room. Kisa hit her head on the table. A bit dazed, she managed to stand up. Rellie came at her swinging, and Kisa didn't duck quickly enough. Rellie landed a mean right hook. Kisa fell back onto the table. Standing over Kisa, Rellie began beating her in the face with closed fists. Rellie wrapped both of her hands around Kisa's neck. Squeezing tightly, she banged Kisa's head over and over.

Seconds away from blacking out, Kisa reached behind her, grabbed a metal dish cover, and slammed it into Rellie's head twice. Rellie stumbled backward. Kisa leaped to her feet, continuing to slam the metal cover against Rellie's head until she fell against the wall. Rellie slid down to the floor. Kisa gripped the metal cover in both hands, raised it over her head, and hit Rellie in the face, knocking her out. Kisa continued to pummel her with the cover, although Rellie was clearly unconscious.

Kisa was so transfixed in the beating that she did not hear hotel security banging on the door. Eventually, they let themselves in. The police were with them. The police pulled Kisa away from Rellie and placed her in cuffs.

An ambulance rushed Sincere and Rellie to the hospital. Investigators tried to interrogate Kisa at the police station to sort out what had happened. Of course, she refused to talk to them without an attorney present, so they placed her under arrest for assault. Five hours later, the detectives informed Kisa that Rellie had died. They charged Kisa with second-degree murder.

# One Year Later

Kisa sat nestled between four of Charlotte's top at-
torneys at the defense table in a hushed courtroom. For two long weeks, she'd been fighting
voluntary manslaughter charges. Now the jury was back
with a verdict.

The D.A. had amended the charges from second-degree
murder to manslaughter for Rellie's death. Due to the special circumstances, they could've let her off on self-defense,
but they didn't because they felt that Kisa could have shown
restraint and that she was largely unwilling to cooperate
with their investigation.

"Would the defendant please rise," the judge said.

Kisa stood up, dressed in a charcoal pantsuit and with

big soft curls framing her face. She glanced over her shoulder and nodded to her family members who filled the rows behind the defense table.

"Have you reached a verdict?" the judge asked the jury forewoman.

"Yes," the forewoman replied.

"Go ahead with your verdict."

Inhaling deeply, Kisa closed her eyes.

"We, the jury, find the defendant not guilty."

# *Epilogue*

I mmediately after the trial, Kisa and Sincere took a much-needed two-week vacation to Turks and Caicos. They were accompanied by Butta, Arnessa, Kennedy, and Chaz. The trip was a well-deserved, relaxing getaway for the three couples after a tumultuous two years.

No longer wanting to die on the streets of Harlem, Butta settled down with Arnessa in Charlotte. Though he and Arnessa had no immediate plans to marry, both knew that they never wanted to part.

Cenise finished her prison sentence. She was allowed by the state of South Carolina to serve out her house arrest at Butta and Arnessa's home across state lines in Charlotte. Over the course of her time on the inside, Cenise had matured and her bond with Arnessa had flourished. Now that they were in the same house again, they were tighter than ever.

Kennedy and Chaz managed to wade through their problems and work out their marriage. They still had their share of ups and downs as in any relationship, but overall they were happy. Kennedy recorded one more CD, then decided to leave the music industry behind, choosing to devote her time to writing books and doing charity work. She rotated between their homes in Charlotte and New York.

Upon returning to her home in Charlotte, Kisa came across a letter from Eisani. She was shocked. It had been more than a year since they'd argued in the visitation room. At first Kisa was anxious to open the letter, but then she became a little apprehensive, fearing that Eisani was still angry. She knew that there was a good chance Eisani was writing to blame her for TaTa's murder. Seven months earlier, TaTa had been found in a vacant lot in the Bronx badly beaten and with a bullet in her head.

After fretting for a little while, Kisa locked herself in the bathroom and began to read.

Dear Kane,

What up Cousin? I know its been awhile, but I wanted to drop you a few lines. First let me say congratulations on beating trial. That was a real good look for you. I guess you know by now that I copped a plea for a five year sentence thanks to Mazzetti. He still works miracles. I'm good though. The first year flew by, hopefully the next four will too. Anyway let me get to my real reason for writing.

I'm sorry for the things I said and the way that I acted the last time that we saw each other. I miss you and needless to say I still love you. I can still see the hurt expression on your face when I spazzed on you. It breaks my heart every time I think about it. I'm so sorry. I swear.

At the time I was frustrated, angry, and bitter. I had no right to expect you to look out for TaTa. She signed her own death certificate the day that she became an informant. Isn't it funny how we used to run around saying that the game chose us, when in reality we're the ones that chose this game. Even though we knew the extreme lows, we loved playing for the highs, such as the cash, cars, and clothes. A few days ago I heard that Jay-Z song "Allure" and thought of us. Especially when he says, "But the Allure of the game, keeps calling your name."

That one line was so powerful, because every since the first run we ever made we have been addicted to this life. Hopefully my time in here will rehabilitate me. I'm not going to bore you with this jail talk because you and I have heard it all before. We both know more than likely I'll step out of here four years from now and step right back into the game.

I hope you can find enough forgiveness in your heart for me to write back. I know a visit would be too much to ask for considering how things ended between us. Anyway, kiss the kids for me and tell everyone that I said hello.

Love always, Eisani

P.S. Thanks for looking out for my mom, paying my attorney, and putting all that cash on my books. I know that you wanted me to believe it was all Kennedy, but I know that it was you too.

\*     \*     \*

Elated that Eisani had reached out to her, Kisa wiped tears of joy from her face. She folded the letter, placed it in her pocket, and rushed to her study to write back. Sitting at her desk Kisa pulled out her stationery and pen, but then quickly put them away. There was so much Kisa wanted to say that a letter just would not suffice. She cut on her computer, logged on to US Airways' website, and booked a flight to New York for that upcoming Friday. Staring at her flight itinerary on the screen, Kisa smiled. *I'm on my way, cousin.*

*Acknowledgments*

First, I would like to thank God, my heavenly father, for every blessing and most of all the blood of Jesus. A special thanks to my wonderful editor, Malaika Adero, for bearing with me through all of my life issues that often interfered with the completion of this book. Thanks to Judith Curr, Todd Hunter, and the staff at Atria. Thanks to my family and (true) friends who have supported me. Carlos, over the years, many things have changed but the love hasn't, and it never will. My Kaden and Madison, there is nothing on earth that makes my heart smile the way that you two do. To my loyal readers, thank you so much for being patient with me. I hope that this book was worth the wait. Thanks to all the book clubs across the nation, bookstores, street vendors, and all the media outlets that have shown me love.

God Bless, Danielle Santiago

# AUDITION AND OTHER STORIES